Ever

A Dark Faerie Tale #1

Ever

Shade

A Dark Faerie Tale #1

Alexia Purdy

Ever Shade

A Dark Faerie Tale #1

http://alexiaepurdy.blogspot.com

This is a work of fiction. All characters and events portrayed in this novel are fictitious and are products of the author's imagination and any resemblance to actual events, or locales or persons, living or dead, are entirely coincidental.

Edited by Kendra Gaither
Cover Design by Alexia Purdy
Photography used with permission and licenses
© DepositPhoto.com

ISBN-13: 978-1483959276
ISBN-10: 1483959279

Evangeline (A Dark Faerie Tale #0.5)

Published by
Lyrical Lit. Publishing

Cover Design by Alexia Purdy
Cover Photos: © elisanth ~ canstockphoto.com
© enrico01~ canstockphoto.com

Acknowledgements

I want to thank, first and foremost, my husband Joshua Purdy, whom without your love and strength; this could not have come to be. To my family, who are always by my side through all things. Thank you to all my co-workers who read my stories and believed in me no matter what. I want to thank Scott Prussing for all your help. My writing family Linna Drehmel, Jenna Kay, Kyani Swanigan and Madison Daniel - you guys are amazing and some of the most talented people I have ever met. You keep me in awe. With all of you, I've been able to make the dream a reality.

This book is dedicated to my grandmother Edisa Salas. I love and miss you every day. ~Alexia

Prologue

ONE LONG PAUSE and the man pondered the choice he just made. The faery exile, Verenis, watched the woman and her new husband as they laughed and chatted away inside their house. Her long, honey-brown hair shone in shimmering waves down her back and swung around as her husband twirled her about the kitchen, dancing to the music from the radio, which sat on the windowsill. Verenis didn't acknowledge the pangs of jealousy that swirled in his stomach; he'd made his decision, and now had to let it play out. She'd be safer this way.

The child would grow without knowing him, without knowing her powerful potential. He would not be there to teach her the ways of their magic and life. It had to be this way. He could not change it, no matter how much he longed to. For the safety of the child and the love of his life, he erased the woman's memory of him forever. He watched them as the happiness spread across their faces. He handpicked the man for her, made sure he would be a great father, love the child as his own, and love the woman more than life itself.

The faery closed his eyes, feeling the breezes of the cool winds graze his face. He never wished to leave her like this but longed to hold her and be the one to swing her around in a flowing dance. The tragedy of it all caused a fierce ache in his heart and arrested his breath in his throat. Glancing back to her one more time, he turned away and ran with the wind toward the embrace of the forest.

Chapter One

"YOU DIDN'T REALLY mean that, did you?" Shade said as she observed her friend Brisa, whose face reddened with frustration.

"Rachel had it coming. She's the one who started it!"

Shade looked at her friend's ruined shirt, streaked with the remains of a red strawberry smoothie. The substance was sticking to her, and it felt cold. Her top was no longer the vibrant yellow it'd once been.

"She's a dumb idiot anyway," Brisa muttered. "She shouldn't be calling you those names. I only stated that she was a 'dumb as a wall, self-deluded bitch' in self-defense. I said it for you. Besides, it's only the truth."

Brisa frowned and gave up rubbing at the stain with a washcloth and soap. She pulled the shirt over her head and let it slip to the ground. Glaring at her locker, she realized her only other shirt was her gym T-shirt. *It figures there's nothing else to wear.* She sighed. "She shouldn't have thrown her smoothie at me. The next time I see her, she's going to pay," Brisa hissed

3

and looked at Shade. "You're not a freak. Don't ever believe anything she says. She's wrong!"

Shade peered at her friend. Brisa rarely got along with anyone. Not a day went by that she wasn't in the principal's office, cleaning chalkboards, wiping down desks, or doing some other tedious job. Many times, she'd received these punishments for whatever trouble she'd gotten into, instead of hanging out with Shade.

Still, Shade had known Brisa since they were toddlers and would stand by her through anything. She was the only one who knew about Shade's strange abilities–hearing voices in her head. Brisa was the only one Shade trusted.

"It's all right, Brisa. I guess I would think I was a freak, too," Shade gave her friend a shrug. "Besides, it's my fault for blurting out what they told me about Rachel. Who would have known she was cheating on the final if I hadn't said anything? She needs to wise up. Well, at least you didn't smash her nose in. You only need one more fight to get that suspension they've threatened you with already. Your mom would hang you!"

Brisa grinned with a slight shudder at the thought of her mother. Brisa's face was smooth and olive-toned with bright blue eyes. Her dark brown hair flowed lazily in waves to her mid back. She wasn't gorgeous, but she wasn't bad looking either. She rarely had makeup on and preferred to wear her hair in a low ponytail instead of letting it flow freely around her shoulders. She was as much of a tomboy as a girl could be–completely opposite of her friend's more girly disposition. Shade's dark, brown hair was similar but longer than her friend's, and her complexion was creamier. Otherwise, they looked a lot like sisters.

"Like I need help in that department," Brisa groaned as she pulled her hair out from the collar of her gym shirt and smoothed the wrinkles down. Brisa and her mother rarely got along. She tended to spend more time at Shade's house than at her own.

Shade pulled out her cell phone to peek at the time. It was getting late, and their afternoon class was starting in two minutes. Dropping the phone back into her bag, she scooped it up before shoving away her own long, brown locks. She tapped her friend's shoulder, urging her to hurry. "Gotta go. Do you want to be late? Ms. Temor is going to lock us out! Chop, chop!" Shade turned and sprinted toward the entrance to the locker room and shoved the heavy metal doors out of her way.

"Wait up!" Brisa called as she stuffed her ruined shirt into her backpack. She stumbled behind Shade and cleared the doors just before they slammed shut.

***

SHADE SIGHED. SHE swung her legs down from the stone ledge she'd propped herself on by the main entrance of the school. *Might as well start walking*, she thought. Her mom had forgotten to pick her up *again*, and it was a long walk home. Her backpack was heavy but not as much as some days when her homework was piled high. Luckily, today was a light homework day.

The warm air rippled along Shade's face. The final bell had rung ages ago, yet here she was, still waiting, *again*. This had been happening too often lately. Brisa rode the Portland, Oregon city bus home and was long gone. Shade wished she'd hopped onto that bus with her friend. *Mom has too much on her plate*, Shade thought. Her full-time job, two sons and Shade's younger sister, kept her busy. Shade, being the oldest, was on her own.

The streets were quiet as she walked home. A slight breeze swept up some litter and floated it past her. She was feeling good, especially compared to how she'd felt a couple of weeks ago when she caught pneumonia. The illness caused Shade to miss a lot of school, and her grades had taken a beating. She'd been feeling pretty out of it for the past month. Now, she wasn't so sure she'd be able to get caught up enough to raise some of her D's to B's, much less A's again. One class was still an F.

Squeezing her eyes together, she gritted her teeth and tried to not imagine having to endure getting an F for the first time in her life. She'd graduate either way, but the drop in GPA was not going to go over well with her. Shade sighed and looked ahead, hoping her luck would get better soon.

The bright sun was glaring down, and it reflected off the white concrete sidewalk like a floodlight, blinding her. Shade's little brother, James, had smashed her last pair of sunglasses just two days before while playing one of his infinitely, highly imaginative games. She wished she'd replaced them already.

Shade passed the main streets of the city and continued walking down the sidewalk, skipping over cracks on the aged concrete. The roads turned into longer stretches of periodic houses and empty lots as the worn brick buildings of the city's center faded behind her.

"Only a whole mile or so to go," Shade mumbled to herself. Both her feet ached a little. She was thankful she'd worn tennis shoes today instead of her usual thin flats. Still, she wasn't used to walking so much since it was only her third day back to school. Feeling one of her shoelaces loosen as it began to whip her calf and flop around, she stopped walking and bent down to retie it firmly.

Hesitating, she glanced up and scanned the street and the warehouses surrounding her. The cool autumn breeze whirled around her, causing the fallen leaves to float in the wind and slung dust into the air. She squeezed her eyes shut and let the dust and debris blow past her before getting back up.

Holding her breath, she could've sworn she'd heard something. *Is it footsteps?* It sounded like someone scurrying about, or running, but also trying to be quiet about it. Shade peered around her, surveying the area. Whatever it was, it seemed to have come from an abandoned warehouse to her right. She studied the dilapidated brick structure, the only tall building for miles, and it gave her the creeps. She listened hard for anything to betray itself but heard nothing. The windows were mostly boarded-up, and weeds littered the ground all around it.

Go inside, now.

Shade paled. She hadn't heard the voices sound so desperate in quite a while, and this wasn't good. It wasn't her inner voice or her conscience. It was very different, like someone else whispering into her ears, but she was the only one who had ever heard them. Shade never could explain it to anyone, mostly because it would've just sounded so crazy.

They were an entity who spoke inside her head and asked her to do their bidding. Shade never understood the reasons why. The voices would become clearer and stronger when they wanted her to do something specific. It wasn't ever anything absolutely insane, like killing someone. That comforted her, but nevertheless, she cringed at the sound of their voices tingling in her ears. No one knew of this ailment except Brisa.

Shade shuddered as she thought about telling someone else about them. No one would understand or even look at her like an ordinary person again if she told anyone. She'd become another institutionalized, psychotic, hormonal teenager.

They'd think I was another paranoid schizophrenic teenager if I told anyone, she thought. *Can't go to a loony house where they'd pump me up with drugs until I'm comatose. I can't.*

Hurry, said the voices.

Hurry to what? Shade inquired silently. *There's nothing here!*

Quick, they told her with urgency.

Shade pressed her lips together. She *had* to obey. The voices wouldn't leave her alone if she defied them, and she couldn't handle that. She'd tried to ignore what they'd wanted her to do once before, and there'd been dire consequences. Three nights of relentless chatter inside her head was enough to drive anyone to a nuthouse. She couldn't go through that again.

Okay, already!

She bent over and slipped through a hole in the fence that was nearest to her. The building looked even scarier up close. The wind howled around her, whipping her long, brown hair up and caused it to smack her face. It was as if it was taunting her decision to inspect the building. The front door was boarded up with thick bolts and two by fours. Apparently, no one was meant to enter this place.

There's no way in. Where do I get in?

The basement, the voices said together.

Shade gulped. It would be dark in the basement, and whatever was in there would not be welcoming her. She didn't even have a flashlight. Nothing good would come of this at all. Even so, she walked around the building toward the rear, searching for any openings.

There it was; a small, dusty and rusted window near the ground. As she knelt down, the rocks crunched under her feet and dug into her knees. She lowered herself so that she was level with the window and frowned. The dust and moist earth stuck to her jeans and fingers.

Ewww, I hate getting filthy!

The window was tiny and probably just big enough for a small person to fit through. Shade groaned. *Just like me.* She cringed at the thought of crawling through it. It would be a tight fit, but she thought she could probably make it. She pushed on the windowpane, but nothing happened. It'd been years since anyone has moved this frame, and now it was stuck.

Maybe I should give a good hard push....

Shade scooted onto her bottom and got closer to the window, pressing her feet against it. She gave it a good shove and heard a loud screech as the metal frame screamed in protest, opening to the world. The dust billowed around her in a swirling cloud, causing her to go into a coughing fit.

She dusted her clothes off as she muttered to herself. There was no doubt that she'd need another shower tonight. She peeked inside, but it was a deep void of darkness. *Oh boy, this is gonna suck,* she thought. Shimmying through the frame, she heaved herself into the darkness below.

Shade crashed onto the floor, tumbling to a stop. *Ouch! That's definitely going to leave a bruise,* she thought. Shade rubbed the sore spots and scanned the room for signs of movement. There was nothing but dust and darkness to greet her. Standing, she dusted her jeans off again.

There was a dim light coming from the now busted window, but her eyes had begun to adjust to the darkness of the room. The small room was empty, except for a worktable at one end of the basement and the parts of an old bicycle at the other end. There were also a few pieces of junk strewn across the floor. Even in poor light, she could see there was a staircase in the middle of the room. She walked to it and grabbed the thin metal banister. She started up slowly but froze, hearing a sound that made her stomach tighten.

Footsteps were fluttering above her, but they quickly faded. It seemed like they'd stopped to listen for something or someone. Maybe they heard her. She didn't move for what felt like a millennium, her heart pumping quickly and loudly in her ears. She stood still, holding her breath and fearing discovery.

The time ticked on, but Shade didn't hear any more noises and decided to ascend the stairs slowly to the door at the top. Her hand gripped the old brass knob, and she paused. As she gulped back her fear, she listened for anything that might be waiting for her beyond the door. *Pray, just pray that no one is waiting on the other side.*

Shade turned the knob as quietly as she could, but the slow creaking moan of the door echoed in the silence. The wind was still howling outside the basement window, shaking it in its frame until the vibration loosened it, and it slammed closed. Her stomach tightened at the sudden noise. *Claustrophobia must feel like this*, she thought.

Shade opened the door and looked around the gloomy building. Light streamed in through the boarded-up windows as she peered into the long hallway that was just beyond the door. The place was vibrating from the forces outside. Everything creaked and sighed like a ship tossed about in an angry sea. Shade wished more than anything to be home, snuggled in her room, safe. She stepped out into the hall and closed the basement door behind her as quietly as she could.

Now what? Which way do I go? She hated having to listen to the voices for an answer. At least she knew if she had to ask them anything, they'd answer her without fail. She just hoped it wasn't the answer she didn't want to hear.

Upstairs, follow the stairs to your right. Take them now, the voices commanded in unison.

Shade turned toward her right, seeing that the hallway ended by a small banister near the wall. She could see another window frame at the end of it, and light spilled through the streaked glass, illuminating the bottom of the staircase. Dust particles swam and danced all around in the rays.

Here we go, thought Shade. *Please don't let there be a crazy person up there!* She swiftly walked to the stairs and looked up, hearing nothing but the wind making the walls moan. Moving slowly over the loose floorboards, whose creaking was driving her mad with fear, she reached the landing just as she heard a crash. Her eyes widened, and she fought the urge to fly right back down the stairs.

Something big is up there! It's moving, too! I don't want to meet that! She couldn't move from her spot, so she listened again, but nothing else banged around upstairs. Shade craned her neck so she could hear better. *It must have stopped.* After taking a breath, she continued up the stairs.

"Don't ever ask me to do this again," she muttered under her breath as she reached the landing and peered down to her left. There was another hall, and it opened into a big room, which must have been the warehouse's office area. There were cubicles and papers were strewn about on the desks, and old chairs laid turned over as if someone had thrown them across the room. *Um, not pretty.* She looked around. Whatever had been up here might still be lurking and hiding from her. It wouldn't be too hard with all the furniture upturned and scattered throughout the room.

Shade didn't have to wait too long before she was diving for cover. A bolt of lightning shot across the room and smashed into one of the bookshelves lining the walls. She ducked under a desk, which was still standing upright and tried to take cover from the flying debris.

What was that? She tried to pace her rapid breathing, for she felt like she had a heart attack. What if she died and no one could ever find her? Her remains would be here in this desolate place for years *if* ever discovered.

Shut up, she told herself, shooing the morbid thoughts away. *Now, voices, come on. Why am I here, to get killed? You better tell me soon, 'cause I'm about to hightail it out of here!*

Shade peeked above the desk to look around the room. A sonic boom knocked her onto her back, causing more debris to fly past her. The sound had come from a different direction than the lightning. *Is there more than one person here? What the hell?* She stayed down and prayed they wouldn't notice her in the mess.

"You can't hurt me, Jack. I know all your tricks, and they're pointless against my magic. You can't best me with your powers. Mine will always endure against you," a woman cackled with a spine-tingling voice. She sounded like the Wicked Witch of the West.

"Give it up, Evie. You don't have it in you. We're banging our heads against the walls. I can have reinforcements

arrive in a heartbeat. Give it up before I'm forced to make you."
It was a man's voice, and it echoed with strength in the large
room.

Ok, this is getting complicated, thought Shade. *I hope they
don't know I'm here.*

"Not so fast, *Jack*. And the name is Vange now." She
spoke his name as though she was speaking of poison. "You've
trespassed on my domain. I didn't know you liked hanging out
with ordinary folk now. You might frighten one of them as you
speak. You should return to the forest and mountains you claim
as your great domain. The cities are mine." Another boom and
crash shook the room.

Shade held her breath. *Well, now I know she knows I'm here.
Now he does, too! Great!*

"The mortal is of no concern to me. You should stop right
now before I hurt you. The Queen wants you alive, but I'm sure
if you're wounded, she'll understand it's a matter of life and
death. Or, you could just give me the talisman back, and we'll
call it even." Jack sent another lightning rod, or what looked like
a lightning rod, toward the left corner of the room and jumped
from his spot. Shade peered over at him as he ran forward and
ducked behind a large wooden beam. He glanced at her for a
moment, narrowing his gaze as he watched her. Now he knew
just where she was.

What now? Shade turned and looked down the hall to the
flight of stairs. *If only I can get to the stairs and get the hell out of
Dodge.* She glanced back at the scene before her. Jack hunched
down behind the desks and stealthily crept toward the woman.
He paused periodically to listen and search for her. The woman
was hiding quite well behind an office divider if she was still
there.

Don't run, the voices said.

What am I supposed to do, die? Shade's heart raced, and
sweat beaded on her forehead and neck. She gulped and felt

lightheaded as her chest burned from hyperventilation. What could she do? They would see her if she bolted. She hung her head down, wishing to be small and invisible. She heard Jack curse as another crash shattered a window on the north end of the building. Shade jerked her head up in time to see Vange flash a smile at Jack.

"I'm truly sorry, Jack, but this isn't your day. *My* Queen will love this little artifact. Its powers will indeed add to our array of weapons against your precious Queen." The woman then sprinted toward the shattered remains of the windowpane and jumped, no, *flew* out the window and disappeared.

"We will finish this some other time, Vange." Jack stood at the windowsill and stared into the light of the day. The cool autumn breeze wafted in and stirred up the stale air inside. He shook his head while he groaned and cursed under his breath.

Shade stood and peered at Jack; he had yet to turn toward her. She decided to sneak away discretely when he suddenly caught her by the shoulder. She screamed and quickly spun around, forced to face him. His eyes pierced hers as his hands gripped her upper arms. "Let me go!" she yelled as she wriggled around in his grip.

"Oh, quit it. Who are you? Why are you here?" Jack questioned as he stared at her with searing eyes. He squeezed her arms just enough to make her cry out.

"I don't know! I don't know! Let me go!"

He sighed and released her as she pulled away, sending her crashing to the floor.

"Ow!" Shade grabbed her elbow, now streaked with blood.

"You said 'let me go.'" Jack turned and picked up some of his weapons from the floor. He took hold of the sheath hanging on his belt, putting his knife away before he began dusting off his clothes. He wore a tight black shirt with a leather belt tightened around his waist with multiple items strung onto it, including a sword.

His face was strong and well defined, portraying a radiance of youth. He appeared to be about twenty-five but didn't have a hint of stubble, making him not quite look like a teenager. Jack's dark, black, wavy hair was long, grazing his neck, and his bangs covered some of his tanned face. His eyes had an ancient wisdom about them, making it obvious that he had seen too much for one lifetime.

He's not bad looking though. Shade stood up and brushed off her clothes as well. She peered up at him, wondering if she should try to run.

"Who are you? Who was...*what* was...that woman?" Shade's voice shook as she spoke. "And how do you throw lightning like that? How can she fly?" Shade couldn't hold back the torrent of questions.

He stared at her quietly. It seemed as if he were trying to decide whether or not to answer. His piercing gray eyes examined her, making Shade flush as she stuttered. "Don't worry," he said. "I'm not going to hurt you if that's what you're thinking." If he'd been a teenager, he would've rolled his eyes, Shade thought. "I'm Jack, by the way. I have the power to throw lightning because it's part of what I am." He grinned, watching her face drop in disbelief. "She can't really fly. It's more like floating gracefully."

What the...?

"Okay then..." she chuckled nervously, more scared than ever. "How'd she make the room explode in a sonic boom? What do you mean, you're made of lightning? That's insane." Shade shook her head and squeezed her eyes closed before blinking nervously. This strange, young man just stared at her, a wry smile upturning the corners of his mouth. He seemed amused by her rant.

"That was Evangeline. Vange is what everyone calls her now though I used to call her Evie." He paused, looking lost in thought. "But, that was a long time ago. She's an elemental fire

14

witch, but not just any old witch. She's a hybrid offspring of a witch and a faery. She's a skilled fighter, and she has taken something from my Queen. I was sent to get it back." Jack started to walk toward the staircase, leaving Shade stunned with her mouth hanging open in silence.

Okay, that was unexpected. She watched him begin down the stairs. *Now what?* What was the purpose of her being here? Why did she have to witness all that? *Hello, voices?*

Why, oh why, do I listen to the stupid voices? Why can't they leave me alone? All they have ever done for me is get me into a lot of trouble.

"Wait! Why was I brought here? Stop! Don't walk away from me...I need answers here!" Shade scrambled after the strange man, nearly tripping down the stairs. "The voices told me to come here, and I want to know why. What am I supposed to see or do here? Stop already!" she cried out again.

Jack was already at the front door. He studied the nailed in boards and began tearing them down. *How did he get in?* His muscles rippled as he held one plank and pulled. It crashed to the floor as he went for another one. She grabbed his arm to get his attention, but he spun around, grabbed her wrist instead, and squeezed it tight. Shade whimpered, surprised by the pain.

"Don't touch me, I might inadvertently electrocute you."

Her eyes widened as she stared at his hand, which was tightening on her wrist. He let her go and sighed, his lips tightened with discontent.

"I don't know why you're here. You say you hear voices? Only oracles can hear voices. Strange," he said, more to himself than to her. "Anyway, I'm made of lightning and blue fire. I guess I have to show you because if you happen to touch me when I am not properly shielded with this glamour, I can hurt you, and it could be fatal." Jack stared at her with some concern in his eyes. He stepped back from her and seemed to shake a bit, as though dusting himself off. The air around him liquefied as his glamour melted away, and the brightness of his skin

15

illuminated the dark hallway.

Shade gasped. He still looked like Jack, but his skin glowed with a blue aura. Blue fire flickered all over him. Electricity crackled along his entire body, yet he didn't burn. His eyes blinked at her, smiling at the awe pasted on her face.

No way!

"You see, I'm made of electricity, like lightning, and white-hot blue fire. One touch and I can zap you to heaven." He closed his eyes as the air, like liquid, poured over him. His glamour reappeared on him, like a drizzle of honey. Jack opened his eyes and studied the shocked expression on her face.

Shade could hardly stand. She was confused, stunned, and in sheer disbelief. "How do you do that? What the… no… can't…how?" She leaned on the wall, her legs feeling dangerously limp.

Jack straightened up and narrowed his eyes at her. The air was still shimmering around him. He seemed to pull it in tighter around him, solidifying whatever it was that formed his glamour. The glow was all but gone. His skin lay smooth, tanned and flawless.

Turning, he pulled the rest of the boards off the door and swung it open. It screeched on its hinges, letting the fading light illuminate the doorway. He stepped out onto the steps and turned to look at Shade. "I suggest that you come with me. I don't know why your voices led you here, but the Oracle where I live might be able to help you. You would have to follow me right now though. What do you say? Maybe she has the answers you seek." He watched her slowly step outside.

Shade breathed in the fresh autumn air and felt more grounded. Gazing up at him, she nodded. It seemed like the only solution to her predicament. *Might as well.*

Jack had begun walking and stopped before he reached the sidewalk. He waited for Shade with a look of concern. "You can't tell anyone what you see or where we go. No one.

Understand?"

She took in the seriousness of his face. "Of course," she answered hesitantly.

He nodded, made his way onto the sidewalk, and then headed off toward the forest.

Chapter Two

THEY WALKED FOR so long, it seemed like an eternity before they reached the edge of the woods at the city's end. Entering the quiet forest made Shade more aware of how alone she suddenly felt. Should she trust this stranger? Where were they going? She peeked over her shoulder as the city faded behind them, engulfed by the shrubs and trees as they progressed deeper into the woods.

She shivered as the breeze caressed her skin. The forest came alive with animal calls. Leaves rustled and branches swayed violently above them. The day was vanishing, the sunset swirling in colors of tangerine orange, pink, and a smear of blue.

Shade suddenly felt panicked, realizing she didn't have a flashlight and that night was quickly approaching. "Um, Jack?" Her voice seemed loud in the open air, but he kept going.

"Yes, what's up?" Jack pushed branches aside and avoided tripping on the thick, gnarled roots crawling across the forest floor.

"It'll be dark soon. Are we close yet? I don't have a flashlight. Do you? Maybe I should come back during the day tomorrow?" She ducked under a low branch as the forest around them thickened, swallowing them in its embrace.

"We're quite near. Don't worry. The dusk is nothing to fear. Just don't go near any little faeries you might see. They like to enthrall you, suck you into their charms, and they won't release you. They enjoy torturing mortals."

Her eyes widened as she dug her heels into the dirt. "What? Did you say 'faeries'? Are you kidding me? You don't really believe in them, do you? They aren't really real...." Shade's voice trailed off as she examined her surroundings more carefully.

What the heck is he talking about?

He chuckled. "I'm not joking. They really do exist. What do you think *I* am? The fey—faeries—like me come in many sizes. We live in this world, parallel to yours, hidden in plain sight. We're magical beings, but most are bound to stay within the boundaries of the land of Faerie," he offered but found her face still full of confusion. "Don't worry. I won't trick you or charm you like the tiny demi-fey do. The farther you go into these woods, the more and more you'll see." Jack grunted as he pulled away some overgrown branches that stood in their way.

"It's a whole new world out here, with things you could never imagine. This is our territory, away from the iron cities." He continued to wrestle with an unrelenting vine, turning red and impatient with the vegetation. Was it fighting with him? Shade thought it odd that it appeared almost alive, trying to ensnare him. "Faeries can't stand iron, you know. It's our kryptonite." He pulled his sword by the hilt tied to his back and began hacking at the thick vegetation that surrounded them.

Shade crept forward, more wary and spooked than before. *Faeries aren't that bad. I guess things could be worse. Could be tigers and lions and bears, oh my!* She hurried to keep up with Jack, pulling her sweater tighter around herself. The sun had gone down, and the heat receded with it. "Jack?"

"Yes?" A slight impatience now tainted his voice.

"It sounded like Vange knows you... intimately. Do you know her well?" Shade fumbled over a root sticking up from the dirt.

Jack pressed his lips together as his pace hesitated for a moment. He furrowed his brow as she waited.

"I did know her... intimately, I mean. That's all changed now. We *were*, well, lovers. Engaged once." He swung his sword harder, making the branches fly easily out of their way. "I loved her very much. Then the Unseelie Court started raging war against the Seelie Courts of Faeries, especially the one I reside at. She changed then, switched sides, started using dark magic. I'm not sure what made her choose to change, but she up and left one day and never returned. She became one of the evil Queen Aveta's top lieutenants.

"She's been stealing magical artifacts from our clan. They're probably trying to beef up their armory of weapons and magic against us." Jack stopped, breathing in slowly as the memories washed over him, morphing his face into a still mask.

"So you were in love, and she just left? Just like that?"

"Yes. It was a long time ago, and I'd rather not talk about it anymore."

Shade frowned, scanning the darkening woods. Jack seemed pleasant enough, and she didn't want to get on his last nerve, especially not when the woods appeared to be dangerously alive.

Jack came to a sudden stop in front of an enormous oak tree. It looked ancient like it had lived longer than anything else in the world. He kneeled down, put away his sword, and pulled out a flask, taking a swig.

While Shade looked around and up into the tree, something swatted her calf, making her jump. She scrambled around to get a better look at the forest floor. Fluttering near her was what appeared to be a small fly. Its wings batted like a hummingbird's, and a snarled smile emerged from its lips.

Lips? Flies don't have lips.

She narrowed her eyes at the creature. It had a soft golden glow to its skin and looked like a tiny elf with white cottony hair and long pointy fingers. It also had a malicious smile painted across its face. "Um, hi, how are you? I'm…." Shade didn't get a chance to finish her words before the wind flew out of her as her arm was jerked back.

"Stop!" Jack snapped, still holding onto her wrist. "Don't speak to them! The demi-fey aren't very merciful or nice. They like to play games and mind tricks, which can kill you. There's almost no way to snap out of their enchantments. They can make you dance until your feet are bloody stumps! Weren't you listening? And, never eat or take anything they give you! You understand? You will belong to them forever!" Jack let go of her arm and angrily turned back to the tree. Shade rubbed her arm, pushing her steamy anger away.

"*Endora, philis montie!*" He touched one of the tree knots, causing the earth to quiver and move near the roots. They vibrated alive, snaked and moved as they parted, like tentacles. An opening with stone steps revealed itself at the base of the tree. Eventually, the rumbling ceased, and the ground remained open.

Shade had to close her mouth, which was hanging open like a flycatcher. She'd never seen anything like this in her life.

"Follow me and stay close. Humans are not usually welcomed here." Jack stepped down into the darkness, holding onto the small roots sticking out of the crumbly walls as parts of a banister. Shade followed reluctantly, but silently wished she'd never gotten out of bed that morning. As she descended deeper into the void, the grass and trees disappeared from sight.

When they had almost reached the bottom of the

staircase, a loud rumble shook the ground, sending dirt trickling down. Her arms instinctively flew up over her head, waiting for a cave-in that never did come. She looked up when the noise died away. The hole in the forest floor had closed above them.

Shade now stood in what appeared to be a hallway made of dirt with smooth stones all around them. Roots dangled from above, and the only light came from lamps hanging on the walls. One by one, each magically flared up. The lights gave off an eerie flickering glow of dim light.

Jack dusted his shoulders and shook off the dirt. He started walking down the hall. Shade had no choice but to follow while attempting to breathe in and out slowly and deeply, easing her anxiety. The floor was flagstone, nestled into the moist, soft dirt. It was cool in the dark tunnel, but it wasn't uncomfortable; there was no trace of wind to chill her.

There were many tunnels branching off from the main one. Shade stayed close to Jack, afraid to lose him in a dizzying maze. Dangling roots gripped her hair, like fingers catching her long strands and pulling hard as if they were alive. She used one hand to cover her head to keep it from catching the snarled roots. Her other hand was stretched out to help her balance against the cold, smooth dirt walls. She hoped they would soon get to wherever it was they were going.

There was a soft glowing light up ahead, growing brighter as they inched closer to it. She could hear voices echoing in waves down the hall. The hall abruptly ended and opened into a large, round room. Shade realized the sounds were coming from the many bodies fluttering around in the room. Most looked human from what she saw, but others were unlike anything she'd ever seen. Their faces glared at her, an intruder from the world above. Somehow, she had a feeling that they didn't see too many strangers down there.

Shade felt naked under the scrutiny of the dozens of eyes which were scanning her as though she were a freak. She stumbled behind Jack, who seemed oblivious to the commotion around them. He finally stopped when a giant troll stepped in front of them, blocking the path.

"Out of the way, Renny. I must see Ilarial immediately," Jack yelled up to the gruesome beast. "I have some strange news about Vange for her, and I brought someone who needs to see her." The troll narrowed his vision and casted his glowing, yellow eyes over Shade. She felt herself shrinking under his glare; he was monstrous, and one of the scariest things she'd ever seen.

"Can't do that, Jack. No strangers allowed without prior approval. You know that. We have to be sure she isn't a spy. The forest is crawling with them. They could only be so lucky to have you waltz one right into the center of our residence. I have to tie her up now." The troll pushed past Jack and reached for her. His large hands were hideous and reminded her of moldy green cheese. They looked burly, and if he got a hold of her, she didn't know how she would break free, even if she tried.

"Jack?" She stepped back as he came closer. "I'm not a spy! Don't touch me! *Jack?*" She peered around at him as the troll's fingers grabbed her arm and squeezed, digging hard into her flesh. The next second, the troll was on the floor, staring at the ceiling and blinking in disbelief. Jack had his sword at the troll's throat and his foot pressed down onto his massive chest.

"I told you, Renny, we must see the Oracle Ilarial. I vouch for this girl. She's no spy. Now stay out of my way, or the next time, this blade will slice your throat all the way through."

Jack pushed off and looked at Shade. She trembled as she let out the breath that caught in her chest. He motioned for her to follow him and sheathed his sword. She nodded and stepped past the troll, who glared at her with his burning yellow eyes. Turning away, she scurried behind Jack as he continued walking down another corridor off the main room. She didn't let her gaze deviate from the place until it was out of sight.

Shivering, she hugged her arms around herself, even though the room wasn't cold. She was afraid, more than she was willing to admit.

"I apologize for the security around here. We've had a lot of break-ins, and Queen Zinara is not pleased. You must understand, if I suspected you were a spy, you wouldn't be standing here with me at all."

Shade nodded, feeling most unwelcomed.

"Ah, here we are!" Jack stopped at the end of the hall and tapped on a wooden door. It had deep woodland carvings that curved and twisted throughout the ancient wood, smoothed over by time and use.

"Come," a woman's voice commanded. Shade hoped she'd be friendlier than the bunch they'd already encountered.

Jack heaved the door open and let Shade go in first, closing it softly behind them. She studied the room as it glittered in the dim candlelight shining from the center of a round wooden table near the floor. There were also several large pillows tossed about the room for seating.

From behind the table, a platinum-haired woman stared at her. She smiled and lifted her arms, motioning for them to sit. Her gown flowed around her like liquid ice, white and sheer. Her hair glistened in the light, and her eyes were like gray shining pearls. The oracle's eyes brought out the smoothness of her face. Her dark pink lips smiled, and nothing about her seemed old. She looked like an angel without wings, ethereal. Shade tried not to stare, hoping she hadn't been rude. She settled onto a large blue pillow.

Shade let her eyes wander over the small space, noticing several objects on the table before them. There were stones of different colors and markings scattered in the wood. Placed among the stones were some small, bleached animal bones.

"Please, take my hand." Reaching out from her long, white robe, Ilarial brought her slender pale hand toward Shade. Shade took the hand, finding it soft and surprisingly warm.

"Um, hello, I'm Shade. Jack brought me here because I...."

"I know who you are and why you're here, Shade," Ilarial interrupted. "I've been waiting for you a long time. I was hoping that you might run into someone like Jack a little sooner, but this will do. I'm Ilarial, Lady Oracle of the faery tribe of Guildrin." Her smile made Shade feel warm and suddenly very calm. The woman was full of magic, and it radiated toward her like a warm fire on an icy night.

"I know you're confused, but I've known of your existence for some time. You say you can hear what you call 'voices' in your head from time to time?" the Oracle asked kindly.

Shade nodded. She was in awe of Ilarial but couldn't shake the strangeness of the room's atmosphere. Was she under a spell? Being in Ilarial's presence was like being drugged or sedated. It filled her with a sweet and fuzzy feeling.

Ilarial smiled sincerely, and crow's feet appeared around her eyes, revealing wisdom and age. Even so, Shade found it impossible to tell just how old she was. Her long hair draped around her shoulders and down her back like a thick, rippled curtain, shining in the dim candlelight.

"The voices in your head are spirit guides. They're your ancestors trying to help you on your way. It's difficult to tune into them because you're not trained, but they mean only to help you. You must not fear them, but let them fill you with their power and knowledge. After all, they've led you to find us. You must know now that you're not all human. You're one of us, part faery, and part human. This is why you can sense magic around you, and it has called you here."

Shade concentrated on Ilarial's words, unconvinced. *What the heck? Impossible.* Shade shook her head. "No. My parents aren't faeries. My mother is not magical. She's a modern soccer mom with four kids to feed, and a single mom at that!

My father's dead. He died two years ago, and there's no way he was a faery!"

Shade was growing agitated. Her father a faery? No, it couldn't be. He'd been so normal. She could still remember his calm voice reading to her at night before bed and the wrinkles that hugged his eyes when he smiled. Faeries aren't parents. They don't die in car accidents like her father had. None of this made any sense.

"I know this may sound impossible," Ilarial offered softly. "I knew that it would be difficult for you to accept. You're the oldest in your family, right?" Shade nodded. "Your mother loved a faery once. He charmed her into loving him instantly. She had no choice, really, but that's how she became pregnant with you. Of course, this faery placed a spell on the man that you call your father almost as soon as he knew there would be a child. He wanted to make sure you'd be taken care of, provided for." She paused, letting the information sink in.

"Your adoptive father fell in love with your mother, married her right away, and then you were born. Both were none the wiser." Ilarial stopped, watching Shade's reaction.

"My dad was not my real father?" Shade's voice quivered at the thought. "How would you even know that? Who was this 'faery' then? Did he tell you himself? What if you're lying?" Shade suddenly stood up and looked down at Ilarial, her heart beating hard within her chest. Her breath caught in her throat, causing it to feel tight.

Jack was suddenly standing behind her, where he took hold of her shoulders and pressed down softly. "Shade, please, sit down. You must listen to her. She knows more than you think."

Shade took a breath, eyeing Ilarial with suspicion. Sighing, she decided she didn't have much of a choice. She sank down into the sea of pillows once more, shaking and unsure.

Ilarial was still. She wasn't angry as Shade expected but smiling. The same warm feeling flooded over Shade once more, calming her.

"You must know, faeries can't lie, unless of course they're not full faery, like you. We can enchant, stretch the truth or work a way around it, but never straight out lie. I do hope you believe me. I mean you no harm, child. I only wish to find the truth for you." Ilarial nodded and looked down on the table before them. She picked up the stones and warmed them in her hands. She then dropped them on the table and watched them roll to their places.

"These stones are quite powerful. They're mined from the heart of the earth, deep within crevices never seen by man. They're called seeing stones, and the runes on them foretell futures or sing of the past. For you, I see a great journey you must undertake, a misshapen love with a broken heart, confusion…." She pointed to each stone; first a blue stone, then a pink-red one, and then blackened quartz. The last three were turquoise, purple, and yellow, and they were wedged in a group together. She paused before them, turning her head slightly as if waiting for them to speak. "Ah, yes, a most extraordinary task has fallen to you where your true self shall be revealed."

Shade stared at Ilarial. Nothing made sense to her — absolutely nothing. The stones glistened and vibrated on the table, almost glowing. Shade felt the power radiating from them like a nauseating heat, making her slightly dizzy. "What does that all mean?"

"It means that you've come here in a time of war within our kind. Our Queen wants a force assembled to retrieve the Santiran Water magic. This power comes from a pool of water, where all elements and creatures are derived. It holds life and death and summons the powers of the earth. It helps keep the balance between good and evil in our land, and evil will wither against it.

"It is said that only the one who belongs to both man and

faery can hold this liquid and return it to the great city of Aturine here in Guildrin, where the Queen resides. Only then will we be safe from the Unseelie attacks." She paused, studying Shade's face. "The stones tell me that someone must be you, Shade."

Shade tried to close her mouth as if the words would taste bad if they reached her lips. Why was she so special? She was just a senior in high school, and she wasn't even sure if she was going to college. Most days, she couldn't even decide what to eat for lunch. "No way. Sorry, but you've got the wrong girl. This is nuts. I need to go. It's getting late." She chuckled nervously, shaking her head. She turned to look at Jack as she stood up. A frown played about the corners of his mouth.

"Has the Queen called assembly yet?" he asked Ilarial.

"She's doing so as we speak. I let her know that Shade would be here today. We must go now and listen. Such a historical event is not to be missed. Shade, we must take you there now," the Oracle beckoned.

Shade was sure she should've never gotten out of bed that morning.

Chapter Three

ILARIAL'S MOVEMENTS WERE light and airy, almost as though she were floating. She waved at Shade to follow as Jack opened the wooden door to the hallway. Shade was in too much shock to object, so she followed them both down the tunnels, returning to the main room, where Renny had attempted to arrest her. She stood wide-eyed at the scene. The room swelled up with more people, or faeries, or whatever the heck everyone was down there.

Ilarial pushed through the crowd, or rather it seemed to part just for her until they reached a large platform. Here stood several guards and another woman in a great, long, red velvet gown. A tall crystal tiara flashing with diamonds and blood-red rubies rose from her long black hair. She watched them as they approached the raised platform, passing her eyes from Ilarial to Shade. Gleaming green irises bore into Shade, like fire burning in pale skin. This woman wasn't to be trifled with. The air of command and power swirled around her like a cloud. Shade suddenly felt quite tiny.

31

"Most Seelie queens have light, fair hair," Ilarial whispered to her. "But Zinara was born with the dark hair of an Unseelie queen and the legendary Ancients. Nonetheless, she won the Seelie crown and paid for it dearly with flesh and blood. She deserves loyalty, more than any queen ever has." Shade listened to Ilarial's short history lesson as she watched the room turn to give the Queen its full attention.

Ilarial bowed to the queen deeply and kissed her hand. "Your majesty, I present to you Shade, a halfling who has joined us today. I have read the stones, and she's the one I've been telling you about. She has finally returned to us and is the one I've foreseen for this journey. The magic of Faerie has finally brought her back to us."

The Queen listened intently, letting her eyes drift over her. Shade felt homesick already. The pressure of all the things they told her bore down like a suffocating pressure that swallowed her up. She was sinking into the depths of a deep dark well, without any hope to escape. She studied the crowd and desperately wanted to fade into it, to run down the tunnels and out of the forest as fast as she could.

"A pleasure to finally meet you, Shade," Queen Zinara said as she fixed her gaze on her and offered her hand.

Unsure of what to do, she copied Ilarial's gestures and kissed the Queen's hand. She noted Ilarial's approval and returned her eyes to the stunning Queen as she let go. The Queen turned back to the crowd, and the room fell silent.

"I find it difficult to address you today. The evil that surrounds us has threatened our peaceful lives many times as of late. My heart breaks with the death that seeps into our precious earth. I've been forced to ask of you the most dangerous of requests." The Queen's pensive pause made a ripple of curious whispers ignite. "We must obtain the magic of the Santiran Fountains once more. Our ancestors used this when the earth was once out of balance and evil lurked around every corner.

We've attempted to fight the Unseelie court but have failed to hold them back, with terrible losses. I fear our only chance against their vast army is this magic, and we must undertake a perilous journey to obtain it."

She paused, sighing and seemingly upset by what she was saying. "Unfortunately, I cannot go myself because being near the fountain would prove fatal for me. The magic of the Santiran Fountains can only be bequeathed unto a halfling, one of both worlds, human, and faery. To my great joy, we have finally found her, on this night of all nights. I'm most pleased to introduce Shade." Her hand outstretched toward Shade, and the crowd cheered thunderously.

Shade was sweating with anxiety. How much longer could she stand here? She felt lightheaded, and the room was growing dim.

"She will take this journey for it is her destiny. She needs an entourage to escort her and help get her there safely. I must ask for volunteers for this most dangerous task. Can anyone selflessly swear loyalty and guide Shade, our only hope?"

Silence engulfed the room. After a moment, soft whispers echoed throughout the great chamber as everyone shuffled and shifted about. The excitement was electric, and it reminded her of Jack's unglamoured figure, crackling, and static.

Speaking of Jack, where did he go? Shade thought.

Shade caught sight of him as he stepped before the Queen. "I'll go. I found her, and she's my responsibility." Jack bowed to the Queen and then stepped back. Zinara nodded and smiled at him, approval evident in her eyes.

Others stepped out from the crowd, one after the other. The fey each introduced themselves as they bowed before the Queen, and she quickly approved of all of the volunteers.

"Now, only magic can fight magic. I also need one brave volunteer who is proficient in sorcery to join the others. Is there anyone of such skill that would accept such a feat?" The room was once again quiet. Shade was definitely feeling lightheaded now. Her stomach lurched, and soon the room began to spin. Ilarial stepped over to her and placed her hand on Shade's arm. Ilarial seemed to sense Shade needed some aid and steadied her with one hand while her other hand retrieved a small stone from her gown.

"Shade, suck on this stone. It'll make you feel better." She reached over and placed it into Shade's mouth. Shade did as told and let the flavor coat her tongue. It tasted sweet, like honey. The spinning ceased, and her stomach calmed instantly.

Wow.

"I, Braelynn, will take this task at hand," a young woman's voice echoed through the crowd. She stepped forward, causing the throng of people around her to part. She wore a light brown dress, and honey-colored hair draped about her shoulders. Her bright hazel eyes glowed with fire and ice, and freckles splashed across her nose and cheeks. Her eyes burned with fire and appeared as hard as stones.

"Dear Braelynn, yes, I would be honored if you would accompany Shade on this quest. I've heard how quickly you've moved from apprentice to great sorceress. I'm pleased that you have passed your trials with exceptional grace." Zinara nodded in approval and turned to face Ilarial and Shade. "Dearest Shade, I am indebted to you now. Please, get some rest and some food. You will need it, as tomorrow the quest begins." Without any further instructions for Shade, she bowed and turned to leave the great room, moving to the right as she walked down the corridor.

Now what? Shade felt panic rise in her throat. How could she get out of this? What would her mother say? *Mom! She must be so worried.* Shade turned and searched for Ilarial and Jack, who were both softly discussing something. It all felt so surreal.

Ilarial motioned for Shade to follow as they left the platform. "I know this is very overwhelming for you. I can't make you feel more at ease, but I do hope that I can answer any questions you have. First, of course, we must eat. It is late, and the journey will be long and tedious. We should join your entourage and get to know them. They will be vital to your safety."

"My safety?" Shade widened her eyes but followed along.

Ilarial ushered Shade down another corridor that opened into yet another large area, where many people were already sitting at wooden tables. They were eating a variety of vegetables, fruits, bread, and meats. Shade's stomach grumbled with desire. She'd already forgotten how sick she'd felt not a moment ago. All she could think about was food.

She followed Ilarial to one of the great banquet tables. It looked extravagant and overfilled. Ilarial pulled a plate from a stack and handed it to Shade. Her new entourage of friends were following closely behind, piling berries, meats, and vegetables high on their plates.

When Shade was done filling her plate to the brim and accepted a drink from a friendly lady, who was handing out stone cups of fruit juice. Shade followed the group to an area far to the left of the banquet hall. They all sat down and began gorging themselves as though they hadn't eaten in ages. Shade joined in and inhaled most her food as she glanced at everyone, evaluating them with an inquisitive eye and noting how different they all were.

She had already forgotten most of their names. It'd been too stressful to concentrate during the assembly, and being hungry hadn't helped. She listened to all of them chatting. Murmurs of conversations and laughs rang through her ears and filled the great hall.

One of the warriors caught her eye. Long, honey-brown hair laid across his eyes before he swept the strands from his face, catching her staring. He smiled genuinely and started laughing at whatever joke Jack was telling him. Lean muscles rippled under his snug shirt and form-fitting armor made of flexible leather. A sword lay strapped to his back, reflecting the torchlight of the room. He seemed younger than Jack did but older than Shade. She watched him talk while he chewed his food, which seemed to add to his charm. He stopped eating once he noticed her watching him, and she flicked her gaze away, back toward her plate. Her cheeks flushed, and she swiftly lowered her head to take another bite of food. Chancing another look, she caught him winking at her.

"Ilarial?" Shade spoke softly to the Oracle beside her, avoiding the man's stare.

"Yes, Shade?"

"I was just wondering, does everyone here have secret powers like Jack? He showed me what he looks like under the glamour. I was wondering if everyone here wears glamour too." Shade glanced at the group once more as she spoke. They were still engaged in their conversations.

Ilarial paused thoughtfully and glanced at the crew. She seemed to hesitate but not for long. Her small mouth slowly chewed her last bite of food, and she fixed her gleaming gray eyes upon Shade. A warm smile slowly spread across her face, and she now appeared less hesitant.

"Shade, I'm surprised that Jack has already let you know what he is. He's usually wary of strangers. Some refuse to use any kind glamour and do not venture into the human world, such as Renny. I believe you've met him. He's one of the guards of this underground city. He never leaves. He thinks humans are inferior and powerless.

"But, you've also seen Jack and how he mixes among mortals easily when he's glamoured. He's so easy to get along with too. You'll often find him on errands in the human world since he can remain within the iron of the cities for much longer periods of time. We do try to keep any incidents to a minimum, and Jack has a stellar track record. I, on the other hand, don't get out much, and I'm most sensitive to iron sickness if I tread through the cities for too long. Though, it's quite common in faeries." She then turned her eyes toward everyone else at the table. Some were partially listening, and some had yet to notice their conversation.

"You need to understand what and who everyone is, Shade. These are your guardians, and you must have complete trust in them, even if that means their identities must be revealed to you. Let's see," Ilarial waved her hand toward Braelynn, seated on the other side of her. "You already know that Braelynn is a great sorceress. She needs no glamour because all witches and warlocks look quite human. Then, there's Than. He glamours his pointy nose and pointy ears to blend with humans of the Orient. He's a skilled hunter and warrior, excellent with knives and has lived here in Aturine all his life."

As she said this, Than gave them a curt nod, melting his glamour away with a quiver. Shade held in her breath in surprise and stared at a more beautiful version of Than. He now had pointy ears, larger eyes, and a thinner nose. He looked the same, but all his features were more exaggerated.

The Oracle continued in one fluent breath. "Sary is a warrior princess." A fiery redhead waved at them with a sweet smile. "She's human but immortal. She's also set to be the queen of the immortal Vyn people of the south when her mother passes the crown to her. It's a lesser kingdom, but powerful. They're very strong, and most are rather efficient archers though Sary prefers to work in the medical arts." The princess nodded toward Shade and then continued to eat.

"Stephen is a full faery." A tattooed man grinned at her, his smile reaching up to his eyes, which twinkled in the torchlight. "He glamours himself to look less startling. His marks and vibrant skin would be unnatural to humans. He's an expert at tracking and can find almost anything and anyone, anywhere." She smiled at Stephen, who also bowed his head while melting his glamour away.

This Stephen was stunning; he would definitely stand out in a crowd. He kept his brown hair shoulder length, but his strong, beautiful eyes glowed grayish white, and sharp, swirling Celtic tattoos framed one side of his face in brilliant blue, quivering under his skin. He had a scar, probably earned in battle, which ran down the other side of his neck. It reminded her that she hoped she wouldn't have to engage in any type of fighting on the upcoming journey.

"And then, there's Rylan. He's quite extraordinary," Ilarial continued. "He's part Teleen, like Jack, but he has a skill for shape-shifting since he's part changeling too, and can become anyone you can think of. There are not too many of his kind left. We don't know what else his heritage holds. He came to us as a young child, lost in the forest, but he's loyal and handy in a pinch."

"Who's Rylan, Ilarial? I don't remember him being introduced." Shade's eyes landed on the handsome man sitting next to Jack, whom she'd stared at earlier, and who was now studying her right back intensely. She couldn't recall his name. His brilliant green eyes flashed a honey-brown color as they gleamed at her. This man winked at her across the table earlier. Meeting his eyes again, Shade felt her cheeks flush once more.

"People call me Soap, M'lady," he said. "But, my real name is Rylan. Nasty little nickname I caught when they first found me, dirty and lost." His chuckle sent a shiver through her, like someone tickling her with a feather. She let her eyes wander back to him as he continued. "Not a flattering story." His face grew serious. "But, I'm thankful for Ilarial and my Queen's most gracious hospitality ever since. It would be an honor to defend you on this quest, Shade."

He bowed his head as her name rolled off his tongue, making her heart flip. His presence was intoxicating. He didn't seem to drop any glamour at all. She ripped her gaze away from his, certain her face was an unfavorable shade of scarlet red.

Traitorous blushing cheeks! Shade kept wondering if he had any glamour on, but it didn't seem like it.

"And, last but not least, Ewan," Ilarial said, waving her hand at the husky quiet man who sat at the other end of the table. He happened to be sitting next to Sary. Ewan was a large man with big hands and burly hair all over. His squared jaw was busy chomping hard on each bite of food. His thick, black hair was slicked back and fell just past his shoulders. He was gigantic and didn't seem like someone you would want to fight with in a bar. "He's part giant, part human, and very strong. He'd be the one you would want next to you in a fight, and he's been almost everywhere. Ewan will be your guide to the land of the Santirans. I believe he's the only one who has even been there."

The husky man gave a slight nod to Shade and continued shoveling food into his mouth. He polished off two plates already. He wasn't bad looking, Shade thought, just rough around the edges and enormous.

Shade sipped her juice, realizing how exhausted she was. She wished to see her family. What would they be doing? And Brisa—what would she think when Shade didn't show up at school in the morning? She slipped her cell phone out of her pocket and looked at the time. It was eleven pm, and there were ten missed calls from her mother and three from Brisa. She began dialing her mother's cell when Ilarial placed her hand on the phone and shook her head.

"No calls will work from here, Shade. We're too far underground. I know you fear for your mother, but I'll take care of it. She will be okay, and I can weave a spell to help her believe you will not be gone long. I can make her think you have been at a friend's house, perhaps? And the rest of your family too. They won't notice you're gone. There will be no pain for them, I promise. Time works differently here in the faerie lands than it does in the mundane human world. You will not be missed. I say that in a good way, though."

Shade swallowed hard with a nod. She obviously had to trust these people and saw no other way but to do what they asked of her. "Ilarial, about the voices in my head... what do I do with them? Can I make them go away or learn to control them? I feel like banging my head against the wall sometimes when they won't stop. They make me go where they want, and if I don't listen to them, they become intolerable. They're the ones who led me to Jack and then to you and this strange world. I can't live like that." Tears prickled at her eyes as she swallowed the growing lump in her throat. "It's distracting. I feel like a slave to it, and I'm powerless to ignore them. What if they drive me insane?"

Ilarial nodded, thinking hard about Shade's words. She seemed to come to a decision and smiled back at her. "Follow me. You will sleep in my quarters tonight. I will give you a potion that will help you control the voices. It will aid in blocking them out when you want to, and it will also help you listen to them when you're ready. Having more control over the voices will help you develop your own powers. You'll be able to decide your own fate while you're still so young and untrained. If you practice, in time, you can learn to use them for your own benefits. This is a difficult task, but I will help you. Will you agree to this?" Shade nodded and felt a weight lift off her shoulders. Finally, someone could help her, after all these years. She just prayed that it would work.

Ilarial guided her back through the branches of tunnels that led to her own chambers. She made up a bed in the second room and then motioned for Shade enter. She handed her a bottle filled with silvery liquid.

"Take this, Shade. It will last until you return here, probably a couple weeks. It will help you remain calm, too. Don't worry. I'm not drugging you. It's just a pleasant side effect of the potion, and it will quiet the voices in your head," she reassured her. "I'll be in the other room if you need anything at all."

She gave a warm smile, and Shade felt the familiar calm flood her insides. She nodded and poured the liquid down her throat. It was sweet but left a metallic aftertaste. Licking her lips, her eyes followed Ilarial as she exited the room. Shade pulled the thick soft blankets over her body and squeezed her pillow under her head. Closing her eyes, she drifted off to sleep in the soothing silence.

Chapter Four

SHADE STIRRED AWAKE while it was still dark. The door was open, and there was only a sliver of light shining around the corner from the adjacent room. A queasy feeling overwhelmed her, and for a moment, it felt like she had temporary amnesia. Sitting up, she dangled her legs over the side of the bed. She was beginning to wake up a bit more and remembered why she wasn't home. As she looked around at her surroundings, the events of the previous day rushed back to her.

Her cell phone was still working, and she grabbed it from atop her backpack on the floor beside the bed. Flipping it open, the bright screen hurt her eyes, and she squinted at the little digital clock. 5:15am. No wonder she felt tired. She was not used to waking up so early and had always been a late bird, rarely making it to school with more than a minute to spare.

Shade slipped to the edge of the bed until both her feet touched the cool stone floor. Bending down, she felt around in the dark for her socks and shoes. She wondered what she'd take for clothes on this journey. *I can't very well ask to stop by home to pick up some stuff. Well, maybe.* Perhaps her mother would be gone most of the day. Shade would have to ask Ilarial if it were possible, or she'd be faced with an endless stench from not changing her clothes.

She slipped on her shoes and stood up, shaking her head and stretching her sore limbs. *Nope, definitely must get some stuff from home.* She walked into the main room of Ilarial's chamber, where she'd first met the great oracle.

She was unsure of the coming events of the day, but she had her backpack, and she decided to examine her 'supplies'. *I doubt there's anything useful in here for a perilous journey.* Shade sighed. She unzipped the bag and observed the contents: her schoolbooks, some snacks, her mp3 player, a dozen pens, pencils, erasers, a stapler, and a tube of lip balm. Other than her books and snacks, there was her notebook full of poems and stories she wrote when bored.

Emergency preparedness at its best.

Shade shook her head disapprovingly. She had to stop by her house, dump her textbooks and fill her bag with badly needed essentials. Running her hand through her matted hair, it caught in the frizzy knots from sleeping on it. She groaned. It was a frazzled mess. Hearing a swish behind her, she whirled around to see Ilarial standing at the doorway of the suite.

"I tried to be quiet. I did not want to scare you. Here, take these clothes. I know you need things from your house. I have already cast a spell on your mother. She will leave at seven am to run errands and shop with your siblings. She's just fine and very happy. I will make sure of it." She handed Shade a pile of light but luxuriously soft tunics and trousers. The material was smooth and felt like pajamas. Ilarial gave her a belt and leather strings to tie the tunics with. She also furnished some hard-soled leather shoes, which were also soft but surprisingly sturdy.

"Soap can take you to your house. He's on his way. Do come back by ten am, as that is when they will be about ready to leave. Can I see your backpack?" She held her hand out for the pack. "I can help lighten the load with a shrinking spell. Anything you place in your bag will shrink hundreds of times its normal size and return to normal when you take it back out. Whatever you want, just summon it, and it will come straight to you. You can bring anything you wish." Shade nodded in awe as she handed the pack to Ilarial. Ilarial whispered the spell softly and ran her hand over the bag, closing her eyes. When she was through, she returned it to Shade.

"There, see? It's as light as a feather."

Shade held the pack, and it felt very light, as though it was empty. She opened it, reached inside for one of her textbooks, and it appeared in her hand immediately though she couldn't see anything inside the now darkened interior. "Wow! That's amazing! I can put whatever I want, right? Does it have a weight limit? That's just way cool!" Shade felt her excitement fluttering through her now, and her fatigue evaporated.

Ilarial laughed, "Yes, dear Shade, anything you can think of. A most useful spell, don't you think? You could move your whole house in one trip."

Ilarial smiled warmly. It was that same smile that felt like cozy hot chocolate melting the cold of winter away. She motioned for Shade to follow her into another bedroom. This one belonged to Ilarial and was centered in the middle of the house. It was layered with thick, clean but colorful blankets, and there were also a number of pillows. On the far side of the room was a rack filled with weapons. Silver knives, sharp stone arrows, and wooden-tipped ones filled the corner. There were also hatchets, axes, throwing stars, and daggers overflowing the rack.

"Please, choose some weapons. I find that if a weapon calls to you, it's meant to be yours alone. Feel them sing to you, Shade. Touch the metal and the wood, and tell me what you

45

feel. Please, take the ones that you like." She motioned to the weapons as Shade gaped at them from the doorway. As Shade stepped closer and reached out to touch them, her fingers landed on an ornamental dagger. There were gems on the hilt, and they were glistening in the candlelight along with the blade of the dagger. The blue and blood-red jewels brightened as Shade's fingers brushed the handle.

Shade stepped back with excitement in her eyes. "Wow, they feel like they're buzzing under my skin! Is it magic?" She reached out and touched some of the throwing stars, which hummed equally as loud as the dagger. They were glowing with an eerie blue and green hue around the steel. She could feel the power radiating through the dagger as it made her heart race and her fingers tingle.

"Go ahead, Shade, take some and place them in your pack. You may need them sooner than you think. Your aim will be true. Your strength will increase a hundredfold with them. Just use them wisely and never in haste."

Shade frowned at the ominous statement. She didn't want to *need* to use any kind of weapons. Who would? Even so, she placed several stars, daggers, and a sword in her pack. All were small enough for her thin hands but big enough to do some kind of damage, if only she knew how to use them. She looked at Ilarial, pausing with slight fear rising to her throat.

"What if I don't come back? What exactly are we going to go through that I'd need such an entourage and magical weapons? It's freaking me out a bit. I'm just a regular girl. I'm really not the outdoorsy type. I don't see why it has to be me." Shade felt a tightening in her throat as panic set in, and it became hard to breathe. Pressing her lips tight into a flat line, she took a moment to gather her thoughts before she frowned and continued. "You need a half-blood, I know, but why me? I can't be the only one on earth. Please don't be offended, but I really don't want to go!" Tears welled in her eyes, and she did her best to keep them from spilling onto her cheek'

"Shade, I am truly sorry that you feel th'
it's very overwhelming and confusing. I have f(
and only you, can do this and come back aliv'
you this, but there have been others brought to me
they were not suited for this, even though they tried."
paused, sighing deeply and stroking Shade's hair. "Don't
underestimate yourself. You are strong and carry powers you
have barely begun to explore. The warriors will help you and
teach you how to use your magic and strength. Let them in.
Heed what they say and show you. You are in the best hands
now. I know you will come to know that this is not a curse but a
blessing."

Someone cleared their throat, and both Shade and Ilarial
turned around. Rylan bowed his head as he entered, ready to
take Shade into the unknown. "Soap at your service, Shade.
Hello, Ilarial. It's time to for us to leave." He straightened and
waited quietly.

Shade swallowed her tears and sighed. There was no
turning back now. She gave him a weak grin and swung her
pack over her shoulder. Running her fingers through her rat's
nest of hair, she suddenly wished she'd brought her brush with
her, especially with Soap's twinkling gaze lingering. She
straightened up and followed Soap out the door as Ilarial
waved a farewell.

The walk down the corridor seemed endless. Neither of
them spoke, but they moved briskly on the stone floors. They
soon passed the great hall, now abandoned and silent. Soap was
in the lead as they continued on to the roots of the tree where
the entrance lay. Soap paused and called out the same words
Jack had spoken to open the stairway.

"Endora, philis montie!"

The roots shook, and dirt sprayed down onto them,
making Shade swat to keep it off her clothes. The grand stone
staircase emerged from the earth walls and came together in a

ive spiral. Light streamed in through the opening, and the
ne steps sparkled in the sunlight.

"Wow!" Shade stepped forward in awe. It was unlike
anything she'd ever seen before, brilliant and beautiful.

Soap grinned at her comment. "It is said the steps were
made out of crushed diamonds and stone more than a
millennium ago. Nothing else can compare to such a fantastic
entrance. Our kingdom boasts the most incredible underground
palace this side of the country."

He took the steps two at a time and moved so swiftly that
he looked as if he was floating like a feather. It appeared as
though he was evaporating through the ceiling as he climbed
the stairs. Shade struggled to keep up but finally cleared the
opening. The morning air was thick with mist; all the leaves and
flowers were wet with dew, glistening like rainbows. The air
was fresh and clean out in the thick forest. She watched the
gravel and rock swallow the staircase until there was nothing
left on the forest floor but dirt and plants. *It must be hidden by
magic,* she thought, turning to see Soap waiting patiently.

He picked a brilliant purple flower from a bush and
smiled. "Here is a real beauty, so rare to find in the mornings.
These mostly bloom at night." He reached over to hand her the
flower, bowing slightly. "A beauty for a beauty." His long
brown hair swept forward and swayed in the breeze, as the
gold highlights shone in the sun and made his hair a brilliant
honey brown, lush and loose.

Shade smiled, blushing pink, and taking the flower, she
sniffed its wild aroma. "It smells fabulous! I've never smelled
anything like it." She looked up at the young man, her eyes
widening. She felt different like a calm ocean had swept her
away, and she was now floating gently. Her vision swayed for a
moment as she shook it off, thinking it was just fatigue. These
feelings were new to her, and she didn't know what to do with
them.

Alexia Purdy

"Night-wind Tigerlily. It has a calming, sleepy effect but only when you smell it. It goes away almost immediately, but it helps calm the nerves and is good to have on hand if you suffer from insomnia. Stuffing a few of these petals in your pillow keeps you almost sedated. That's not an effect you want to have right now, but it will relax you." He winked and turned, his long hair swaying in the breeze. He walked through the shrubs, moving gingerly and skillfully, as only a trained soldier could. Shade followed him almost as if she was in a trance. This world was incredible so far. She hoped that whatever was out there would be just as thrilling and not terrifying.

They walked swiftly, dodging bushes and ducking under branches. The woods was brimming with life. Birds chirped and squirrels raced by, hurrying up the trees. The deer glanced at them as they walked past, and insects buzzed by, intent on unknown errands. Shade could actually feel the life around her, and it was like warm sunshine spilling onto her like never before. *Why did the world seem so different this morning?* She didn't think anything had changed all that much. Maybe this was how the land of Faerie was all the time. It was a wonder she hadn't stumbled upon it before.

Maybe it's because I avoid the outdoors like a plague.

She observed Soap. He was graceful, dodging things quickly and maneuvering around like a nimble dancer. His body seemed to float around obstacles and trees, like the rustling of a flowing stream of air. She wondered again if he was wearing glamour at all. "Soap?"

"Yes, m'Lady," he said as he looked over his shoulder at her while winking one of his gleaming green eyes.

"I was just wondering why you didn't remove any glamour before. Do you wear one like Jack? Ilarial said you were part Teleen like him. Wouldn't you have to wear glamour to not electrocute things?" She pushed a branch and let it snap back with a crack while she fired her questions at him.

Soap slowed and came to a stop, turned toward her, and

49

stared intently. "Shade, I'm part Teleen, like Jack is. I'm also a shape shifter. I don't need glamour to look human. This *is* me as I am. I can shift and look full Teleen, like Jack, if I wish, or I could change into a bird, lion, wolf, another person or faery, anything, even...." He paused. He'd been moving closer while he spoke and now stood almost touching her. He bent down slightly so that if either one of them stepped forward, they would bump faces. "I could even change myself to look like other people, other men or women, anyone you could think of or want me to be."

She could feel his warmth radiating across the air and over her skin. It was hot and rippling. Her breath caught in her throat with him so near. He smiled. "Do you want to see?" His eyes widened with a sense of mischief dancing around in them.

She nodded, hoping she wouldn't regret that decision. In a flash, the lines around him blurred like a steamy window. Now, before her stood a pale young man with jet-black, spiky hair and fair skin. Gleaming blue eyes shone back at her. His build was similar to Soap's but slightly shorter and thinner, yet still taller than she was. Their eyes were almost level, and he stepped even closer, one hand reaching up and stroking her face. Shade felt her heart thud in her chest.

"I could look like anyone you can dream of, anyone you could ever want me to be." His lips were mere centimeters from hers, arresting her breath with their proximity. He reached up to run his fingers down the curve of her cheek, making her step back as a surge of energy prickled along the line of his touch. It was enthralling and made her woozy. *What's going on here?*

Soap lowered his hand, still not changing back. He was radiant and glowed slightly, but it wavered. "I can use enchantments on anyone, so they'll forget who they are or even what they're doing. You stepped away. Why is that?" He contemplated his words as he stared intently at her. "I don't seem to have absolute power over you, Shade. That's very strange… unusual." He continued to look at her, frowning at his thoughts, looking slightly unnerved. A moment later, curiosity gleamed in his eyes.

"Could you change back, Soap? You're scaring me." She stepped back, her eyes wide open. "What did you do to me exactly?"

Soap smiled and just as quickly blurred right back into his usual self. His long brown hair and green-gemmed eyes glinted at her. "Pardon, M'lady. I meant no harm. I won't do that again, but you can see that my magic could be quite useful. Most fey and human alike can't resist my charm, but you, on the other hand…." He tilted his head, confused. "It barely touched you. It's as if you're immune to it or something. Amazing. Oh well, can't have everything, right?" He turned away and continued as if nothing had happened. Shade took a deep breath and followed. She felt slightly enraged by his admission that he'd tried to use magic on her. He never asked her if it was okay or not. Biting her tongue, she followed silently.

The forest seemed to stretch out for miles. Twigs and leaves crunched under their feet, snapping and crackling as they walked. The noise seemed louder in the vastness of the woods and quiet of the morning. Shade kept her eyes on the forest floor, but she glanced up every so often to watch Soap's long brown hair swinging in the cool breeze. He tied it back with a leather string matching the color of his hair. She wondered who he was and why he was coming on this journey with her. She supposed it might be for her protection, but she was nothing to him. Why risk himself for her?

Her mind continued to race with questions. Why had he been alone as a child in this desolate forest? *He could've been killed, eaten alive by an animal.* She looked at the thick shrubbery around her and shivered at the thought.

Finally, they reached the forest's edge and could hear traffic in the distance. For a brief moment, Shade had almost forgotten about the reality of her world. She'd been so mesmerized by Soap's magic, charms, and of Faerie itself. The road was not far from the woods, and soon they were walking in the direction of her house. Shade wondered if her mother had already left. She secretly wished she would run into her anyway, just to say hello, and maybe she could get a warm hug and kiss goodbye. The little things she would miss overwhelmed her. What if she didn't come back? When they reached her house, they stopped and examined the exterior.

The worn-down exterior consisted of bricks and old siding that happened to be partially dry-rotted. The house was old but comfortable, the rust-red exterior bricks rough with age. Weeds clung to the base of the house. Toys and balls were carelessly tossed across the yard. She smiled. Her little brothers and sister were loved dearly, but they were also spoiled rotten.

Their mother worked hard, especially now that she was a single mom. Somehow, there was never a lack of love to go around. Sometimes she did get a little absent-minded, with so much going on between all of them, but forgetfulness was forgivable. It made Shade's heart twist with a hollow pain to think of her small, tight-knit family.

She was sure her mother was gone. The beat-up minivan was not parked in the driveway, and there were no crazy little kid screams filling the house, like usual. The place seemed eerily silent. Shade shook away her disappointment and started for the door, with Soap following closely behind.

Shade jingled her keys out of her pocket and turned the knob. No one came running to greet her when she swung open the door. The house was still and vacant. The usual noises echoing through the rooms flitted through her mind. She sighed and headed in, closing the door behind them. She turned toward Soap and nodded. "If it's ok, I'll gather my stuff. See if you can find any canned, non-perishable food we can take. And I'd like to take a quick shower," she added.

He gave her a deep nod and smiled that iridescent smile

of his. Gleaming white teeth flashed at her for a second.

Shade smiled back nervously, turned, and raced up the stairs. Her room looked pretty much the same. Because she was the oldest, she and her little sister didn't share a room. It was nice that her mother had agreed with her that she needed her own space. Her mom always asked a lot of her during the day, and it was nice to have some privacy at night. Of course, that meant Anna, her little sister, had her own room, too–lucky by default.

Shade smiled, taking in the loveliness of the room. The quilt on her bed had pink and red patches in it. The walls of her room were a light shade of rose. There were also items in various shades of pink and purple scattered throughout the room. She loved to decorate and had tons of girlie stuff all around. She'd obtained most of her things from thrift stores, people at church, or friends who'd given them to her. Everything was a treasure to her.

She opened her drawers, began rummaging through the clothes, and stuffed some into her backpack. She riffled through her closet, found a pair of hiking shoes, and grabbed them. After Shade had finished throwing some towels, a pillow and a few blankets into the backpack, she noticed a picture frame on her nightstand. All of her family was in the photo. It was taken at the park on a sunny spring day, and their faces were gleaming with laughter and flashing.

Shade picked up the little frame, feeling her eyes burn with tears. How she missed them already, and it was just yesterday that she'd last seen them. Her father was in the picture as well, her human father. She held back a sob and stuffed the picture into the pack. Reaching over to hook up her cell phone for a quick charge while she finished packing, she began getting things ready for the day ahead. She pulled a clean outfit out of her closet and laid it on her bed. Peering into her dresser mirror, she studied her hair, which was lying in tangled waves, glistening in the morning sun that streamed in from the windows.

What a disheveled mess! She sighed and looked around once more. *Now for that shower!*

She finished quickly, tossing her toothbrush, toothpaste, body wash, and sponge into a Ziploc bag to stuff into her backpack. She ran her brush through the tangles of hair and groaned at the knots. She finally got them out, and the brush went into her bag, too. She loved Ilarial's spell. There was no need to worry about packing light with that! She pulled her hair back into a ponytail since it was still sopping wet from the shower.

All set except for the water and food downstairs. She listened for a moment for Soap, but he was terribly silent for cleaning out the cupboards. She shrugged, left the bathroom, and went down the stairs.

Soap was standing by the kitchen window, which looked out at both the side yard and the front yard. He didn't seem to notice her coming in. She paused and watched him. He seemed so serene. She wondered just how old he really was and how easily he could pass for a senior in high school; well, maybe not. She smiled at the thought of Soap in gym shorts and shirt, not really a fitting look for him.

He was staring at her when she came out of her thoughts. "What are you smiling at? Do I have breakfast stuck to my face?" He blinked at her, baffled and furrowing his eyebrows.

Shade laughed and shook her head. "No, silly, I was just thinking about how you would totally not fit in at school. You don't really look like a human teenager. How old are you anyway?" She glanced down at the pile of cans and water bottles stacked neatly on the floor in the middle of the kitchen. She bent down and began shoving them into her pack.

"I'm about twenty in human years, no difference in fey years, actually. That's if you go from me being six years old when I was found. Anyway, that was what they guessed me to be. Who knows? I don't remember anything before that." He bent down to help her with the food. His long ponytail hung over his face as he kneeled over the pile.

"Wow, so you could be older or younger, huh?" He nodded, not looking up. They finished and stood. "Can you think of anything else?"

"I found flashlights for you. I don't need them, but you might." He tossed some at her. She caught them just in time and frowned at him.

"What do you mean, you don't need them? Do you see in the dark?" She pushed them into the pack.

Soap laughed. He had a contagious warm laugh that made her want to smile.

"No, we have witch light. We can all conjure it up if needed. I don't even need witch light. Being part Teleen I just let some of my element of lightning glow out of me. I can see just fine with that." His handsome smile flashed back at her again.

Shade stared hard at the floor, frowning. "I don't have any powers."

Soap chuckled, finding her confusion amusing. "All faeries have powers, even half-bloods like you. Don't underestimate yourself ever, Shade. It could be your undoing." He looked at her thoughtfully, his eyes flashing to light amber, like honey.

She could've sworn that he'd had green eyes before. They seemed to change into different colors every time she looked at him. It was intriguing. Shade gulped and nodded. What could she say to that? There wasn't anything, so she just quietly agreed.

After they had left, Shade locked the front door, stopping as she stared at its worn paint. She had a gut feeling she might not see it, or the rest of the house, again. It felt like butterflies knotted her stomach. She thought more now than ever about how much she would miss her family. She never got to say goodbye. Her hand reluctantly fell to her side from the doorknob as she turned toward the street. *Nothing like saying goodbye without a goodbye.*

They walked silently in the direction of the forest, passing all the houses and buildings she knew. The day was brilliant and warm with a slight breeze. Some kids were playing in their front yards, hollering and screaming as they ran around. Shade's ponytail tossed about her face with each small gust of wind.

She watched Soap walking ahead of her. His sword was still strapped to his back, and his long, golden-brown hair was swaying in the wind. She stopped, realizing how different they must look to everyone on the road. Most people didn't walk down the street in tunics or have swords strapped to their backs. "Um, Soap?"

He turned, stopping to look at her, and noticed the horror on her face. He quickly darted his eyes around and looked for any signs of danger.

She jogged until she caught up beside him. "Don't we look unusual walking around in the streets dressed like Robin Hood and not wearing modern-day clothes? And your sword, why hasn't it freaked out everyone passing us or driving by?" She watched him grin and relax. That smile was getting to be unnerving.

"We're glamoured, Shade. I've extended glamour over both of us to appear like we're just two teenagers walking along in grunge clothing. Besides Jack, I'm the only one who ventures out into the cities and gets to mingle with humans. The iron doesn't even faze us at all."

Shade listened closely, slowly beginning to understand this phenomenon.

He turned back and began walking again. "I kind of like wandering around the city, sometimes. It's soothing to me, and I like to watch people or just blend in sometimes. We must hurry, though. It's already getting to be late morning, and the plan was to leave around ten a.m. I think we might be late."

He began walking again at a brisk pace. Shade sighed, shook her head, and scrambled after him.

Chapter Five

THE ENTOURAGE FILLED the entranceway, with all their things spread out in massive mounds. It was almost time to leave the faeries' dwelling. Everyone was stuffing bags or strapping last-minute weapons onto their bodies. Braelynn looked up from the many small bags of herbs and ground stones she and Sary prepped, slowly arranging them in a medicine bag. The low hum of voices stopped as Shade and Soap approached the group. Sary and Stephen turned toward them and stopped sharpening their knives. Jack stood erect, ready to go. He gave them both a curt nod. No one seemed to know what to say to them.

"Guess your ears were burning, Shade, Soap. We were waiting for you," Ewan said. "Here are your sleeping tent packs, and they're all ready to go. Ilarial will be up in a moment. I'm sure she already knows you're here." Ewan's deep voice boomed like a drum, seeming to come from deep within him, like a belly laugh echoing in a large room. He walked up to them, smiling. His husky shoulders were wide, but he was not by any means fat. Shade smiled at him. He was big-boned and looked like a fluffy teddy bear.

"Thanks, Ewan," Soap answered. He was quieter now, within the group. Soap didn't seem to volunteer much information about anything, now that she thought about it unless she pried it out of him. There would be plenty of time to ask him more about faeries and himself during the journey.

"Hello," Ilarial came to stand by them, looking brilliant. "I'm happy to send you off with news of great weather to come, at least in the beginning. I sense good fortune for the start of your journey. I trust everyone is ready. Ewan will be your guide to the land of the Santirans. Your journey will be perilous, fraught with danger and a challenge to your endurance. Not many have ever traveled so far from the Guildrin mound. My heart and spirit are with you, Shade." Ilarial motioned to her to come closer.

"Shade, you're incredibly unselfish to aid us in our fight. Your entourage will take good care of you. They'll teach you the ways of our magic. You may seem fragile and harmless, but the potential to be great lies within you. Now, I send you off, my friends. Good journey!" Ilarial smiled and wrapped her arm around Shade's shoulders. Shade felt instantly alert and happy. Ilarial sure had a way of comforting others. She was like walking Xanax, Shade thought.

Ewan turned toward the group. Everyone was stuffing the last of their items away into their charmed packs, and, like Shade's, they appeared to hold many things. He cleared his throat and held his arms out above his head.

"Alright everybody, listen up, for this will not be repeated. I'll be guiding you on the path to the Santiran lands. Our stop today will be the Teleen caverns. Please stay with the group at all times. We start north until almost dusk. The Teleen are private people, and Jack has assured us of their complete cooperation. They will host us for the night. I remind everyone to keep their hands to themselves for, like Jack, they can electrocute with one touch, so be wary.

"Second, if we are separated for any reason at all, follow the North Star to the great hills of wildflowers. From there, you will find the great gate to the caverns on the northwest end of the valley. Please let them know who you are, and you will have safe passage. They have our names from Ilarial already. Good journey, everyone." He nodded, bent to grab his own pack, and slung it onto his back. He waved for everyone to follow.

Shade quickly shoved the sleeping roll into her backpack and zipped it up. She watched everyone filing in behind Ewan and cut into the line to join him, right ahead of Soap. She glanced at him as she turned her head slightly, absorbing his relaxed, smiling eyes. There was so much behind those eyes that Shade wondered about. She wasn't sure his overly happy exterior matched the soul within.

The forest floor crunched under their feet as they walked at a slow and steady pace. Some of the group was shifting into pairs while others chose to remain in single file. She looked over her shoulder to find Soap and, for a moment, couldn't see him. He had somehow snuck up and was walking beside her. He glanced over at her. Smiling, he lifted his eyebrows with a questioning look.

"What's wrong, dear Shade? You looked mighty concerned." He was now shoulder to shoulder with her.

She gave him another quick look before darting her eyes back to the trail. Often, she had to check for fallen tree branches, tangled vines, and roots that impeded their pathway. *No wonder we're moving so slowly.* "Um, nothing. Just nervous, I guess. Isn't there a better way to travel than on foot? How far away are the Santiran Lands? I hope it's not that far. I hate hiking…Hey, why are you laughing?" Shade pressed her lips together, feeling the blood rushing to her cheeks.

Soap was chuckling. "Sorry, you just crack me up. My

dear Shade, I meant no disrespect. You're a breath of fresh air. I guess it can be enlightening, chatting about our peculiar lives. To answer your questions, yes, there *are* better ways to get around than on foot. We have to leave the Guildrin forest, for it's forbidden to fly or travel any other way near the kingdom. Once we leave the trees behind us, we can fly, run fast, or travel by horse if available. We won't have horses because there are none so close to an iron city. We can't run because you wouldn't be able to keep up, and we can't fly because some of us can't fly at all. That leaves one option: walking." He kept his eyes on the path, swinging his short sword in front of him to slice off a branch that swung back toward them.

"What about using a car? Or even an airplane? Why not go that way?" She felt utterly confused and not one bit satisfied with his answers. She was starting to wonder what was so great about being a faery if you couldn't do regular things like drive, or ride in an airplane.

"No way would any faery ride in one those things. They reek of iron! Like I've told you, iron is deadly to faeries. If faeries stay around iron for long periods of time, they become seriously ill." He snickered as he beat back another branch and walked along. He seemed amused and maybe a little frustrated that he had to explain the iron sickness again.

"But, you and Jack can tolerate it," Shade replied. "Is it just you and him then? Plus, it doesn't bother me at all either. Why? I'm part faery, supposedly. Is it because I'm part human?" She dodged a large leafy bush that was in her way just before it slammed into her chest.

"Yes, I suppose it's because you're part human though not all halflings are so lucky. Because you're half human, you get the best of both worlds. It's the human part of you which allows you to escape from the dangers of iron sickness, and you can hide in the iron cities without any problems."

"What else are the faeries vulnerable to?"

He furrowed his brows and seemed to pause for a second to ponder her question. His contorted features made her smile, realizing she'd never get over how amazingly handsome he was. She wondered if he had a girlfriend in this fairytale life of his. It made her glad he didn't need glamour, even though none of them wore it at the moment, besides Jack. They were staying in the Guildrin forest until they reached the valley of the Teleen so no human interactions would be part of the trip. It made her wonder how big the forest really was. She had so many questions, she just didn't know where to start.

"Well, if you think about faery stories, they can be quite useful in helping you defend yourself against the fey. Cold iron is toxic, as you know. People can fend the fey off by reversing their clothes. That works mainly against the most sinister creatures of Faerie. We also have an ointment of truth that humans can use to have 'true sight' unless a faery allows them to see past our glamours or tricks. Fire keeps most wild fey away. I guess they don't like the burning carbon. I'm not sure, though. Not much of it bothers me, but anything not related to nature is pretty much an anti-faery charm.

"I would always keep some sort of a memory charm on you to remember your way home. Those are impervious to spells any faery might throw at you to make you forget who you are and enslave you."

"You don't sound like a friendly bunch." Shade snickered. "Honestly, I can't see you guys being that bad." She waved toward the other warriors and shook her head. "I just don't get it."

Soap laughed a deep, taunting laugh that made Shade glare at him. She hated being laughed at. Shaking her head, she continued on, ignoring his snarks. The other warriors were already a good deal ahead of them.

They remained in silence for a long time after that. No one spoke. Everyone silently hiked along, slicing down branches. Only the crunch of dead leaves and twigs filled the afternoon air. The birds twittered above, sometimes flying in groups with their wings flapping loudly. It wasn't easy moving fast in the forest. Roots and uneven ground were plentiful, threatening every footstep with a fall, or worse, broken bones if one was not careful. *This situation is just a twisted ankle waiting to happen.* Shade gritted her teeth, concentrating on the loose rocks and roots that lay haphazardly across their path.

They finally came upon a clearing in the forest. The warriors paused, watching Jack and Ewan for a signal. Jack scouted the clearing's edge and looked for any kind of movement. The rest of the group was hunched and hiding behind trees and bushes, waiting for the all clear. Shade perched herself behind a large redwood tree. The bark was rough and crumbled under her fingers. It felt warm under her touch like there was life pulsating inside the massive trunk. She wondered why she could now feel the life all around her. Did it have to do with this forest being fey territory? She wondered if there was something new happening within her, or if they were all being affected by an unknown force.

She suddenly realized it'd been quite some time since she'd heard the voices in her head. She felt relieved, but it also felt like something was missing. Maybe she'd try what Ilarial had mentioned. Since she'd taken the medicine Ilarial had given her to control the voices, it was easier to think. She thought now she'd try to speak to them with specific requests, and then listen for a particular answer. Ilarial had said this exercise would help her get to know the voices, and hopefully she'd learn to use her spirit guides to her own advantage.

Are we safe? Shade waited, quieting her mind and listening for the response.

Yes, they said as one.

She jumped. The answer came like a voice on the breeze, or like someone whispering into her ear. She spun around, but saw no one, and glanced over to Soap, who was behind another tree to her left. He placed a finger to his lips, signaling for silence, and turned back toward the front of the group.

Wow, a one-word answer. It was enough to make her freak out. *Ok, well that was a good little exercise.* She watched Ewan give them an 'all clear' signal. Standing up, she shuffled back into line behind the warriors. Elated, she felt a renewed sense of peace inside.

The sun felt warm on her back as they worked their way across the field. They made sure to avoid the center of the clearing, choosing to avoid being too exposed. They were near the edge, and even though it would take longer to get through, it felt safer knowing cover was nearby. Shade inhaled the fresh air of the countryside. Flowers, pine trees, and deadened mulch were on the ground and mixed with dirt, but perfumed the air.

The forest was surreal compared to her usual reality of constant smog, exhaust, honking cars, and the smell of iron in the city. Out here, none of that seemed to exist, and she let herself enjoy the beautiful afternoon. Dragonflies and Ladybugs buzzed around her and disappeared into the forest. She wondered if they were close to a body of water with so many dragonflies about. She was surprised not to see any more of the tiny winged fey she'd encountered with Jack. There was no one else around.

Where is everyone? Are there more fey out here? Shade wondered.

Yes, they're watching, wondering who you are. Wondering why so many are treading the trails with you.

She smiled. The voice was gentle and did not scare her as the voices had before. It seemed like a light caress, a lover's promise in a whisper. She knew then that it would never be like before. Ilarial used the medicine to channel the guides, to help Shade better understand them. The voices wouldn't be an overbearing force on her ever again. She had to remember to thank Ilarial profusely for this gift.

Do you have a name? Is there more than one of you?

Yes, the voices answered. *There are three of us that remain with you. Each of us will answer you in a particular situation. We each are helpful in certain things. I am Duende. The others are Astrid and Elaby. We are your spirit guides. There were more, but Ilarial has forced them away, for they're too much for you to handle. We're entrusted with your wellbeing, Shade. Ask us what you will, and we will always answer.*

Shade shivered, despite the heat of the sun. Their whispers were like the gentle chill of winter. The feeling prickled her skin and was full of magic. She wondered if she'd ever get used to these changes.

The group re-entered the forest on the other side of the clearing. The cool cover of the forest canopy felt colder than it had before. Shade noticed how much darker it seemed on this end. It seemed quieter too; only a breeze rustling through the leaves broke up the silence. Even the forest floor was more barren, with packed, dark dirt and occasional twigs littered about.

This was not the same territory. Shade wondered if this was the start of Teleen territory or maybe even something else.

"Keep together, everyone. We're near the borders of the Teleen's property. It's guarded well by the dead, along with soldiers that were banished fey, and ghosts alike. Welcome to the Haunted Forest." Ewan snickered, apparently thinking that everyone enjoyed his humor. No one was laughing. Shade hurried up to him as the group tightened. She was curious about the place and figured he would be the one to ask about the name of it.

"Ewan!" She slowed her breathing as she neared him. He was a lot farther ahead of the group than she'd thought. She hunched over, holding her knees as her breath returned to her.

Ewan paused and looked at Shade. Even without the sun breaking through the canopy, the irises of his eyes shone like small flashlights glinting back at her. He was big. He had to be at least six-eleven. He hovered over her like he was one of the trees himself. His broad shoulders were wide, and strong muscular arms followed. He looked like a tall, husky human male with dark stubble almost long enough for a beard shadowing his jawline. A long, black as night ponytail was tied near the base of his neckline. He had a rounded nose and full pink lips. Although his height and bulk made him scary, he wasn't that bad looking. Ewan never bothered with any glamour.

"Well, little one, what heeds you?" Smiling brought out deep wrinkles around his eyes and laugh lines that creased at his mouth. This man had a smile that showed he enjoyed living and had experienced many wondrous things. He started walking again when she'd caught up, moving together in stride.

"I was just wondering why they call this the Haunted Forest. What do you mean it has ghosts? Will we see any? Will they hurt anyone?" She fired her questions at him all at once.

Ewan's deep booming laugh echoed around them. The forest made no reply. "Slow down, miss. Wouldn't want to wake the dead, would we? Nothing to fear now. Yes, there are ghosts and spirits aplenty here, hence the name, but since we will leave this forest for the Great Teleen caves before nightfall, we will mostly miss them. They can harm you, but only if you let your fear overwhelm your mind. They'll sense that and focus on you, so just ignore them. Show no fear and stay calm. They will pretty much leave you alone." He grinned down at her.

Shade liked him instantly. He was like a large teddy bear. At least he was nice. He made her feel warm and safe. "Do we have a long way to go to the caves?"

"I'd say two to three hours' journey. We will hit the hills first and then the incline to the mountains of the Teleen. They live in massive caves that run for miles underground. You'll be most impressed." Ewan's face stilled. He glanced at her, and his eyes intensified. "Miss Shade, may I ask a question?" He continued the trek forward, glancing frequently to assess each step.

"Yes, of course, Ewan, feel free."

"Are you all right with this, being the chosen one and all? Do you want to turn back yet?"

Shade's eyes widened as she stared at him. She *was* scared. She didn't want to go, but how could she say no? Her voice failed to answer.

"I thought so." Ewan nodded, keeping in step with her and dodging the massive tree trunks in their path. It was much easier to walk on the packed earth. It was dark, rich in color and remained smooth over the small hills of the forest floor. The previous shrubs and plants they cut down had been such a bother. The trees seemed to grow larger here, too and were flat out gigantic.

"Ewan, I can't say no. Something just tells me I should be here. I don't even know how to explain it. It's as if I'm being pulled involuntarily along for a ride I didn't sign up for. I can't unwrap myself from it. Besides, maybe I might find out who my real father is and more about myself, too. I do want to learn about my faery powers if I have any. That would be pretty cool. I have so many questions about things now and no answers yet, and I guess this is the best way to find out." She stared at the ground. She felt weary already, and they hadn't even gone very far.

"Understandable." He winked and continued.

Shade stopped in her tracks. The hair on her neck stood on end, and a sense of being watched crept up her spine. Her eyes widened as they darted, glancing around them.

"What's wrong, Shade? Feel something?" Ewan also stopped, listening carefully and signaling a full stop with his hand. Everyone crouched by the trees and looked around, studying the woods as they stilled. Not one sound, not even the birds chirping, could be heard. The silence felt deafening, heavy, and forlorn.

Shade still felt a twinge of fear. Her head shook, and the sweat began to bead on her forehead. *What's going on?* It felt as if something hot was being poured over her, sticky as it clung like thick syrup. Her panic boiled up inside, tumbling out of control. *What is this? What's happening?*

Ewan called out to the trees, "That's enough of that now. The girl is harmless. She's with us. We're Guildrin Clan, en route to Teleen. Bring down your guard. We're invited."

Shade looked about, seeing nothing but tree bark and dirt. The wind gusts picked up and swooshed around her, bringing her hair to float about her like an aura. Shade's breath failed her, and her heart jumped. The group unsheathed their swords, bows, arrows, and daggers. They were readied and pointed.

Pointed at what? Shade felt something was near but couldn't see anyone or anything.

"Back down, or we will fight."

"You dare defy me, *the* Mistress of these woods? You should have asked *me*, not the Teleen, to pass. You insult my authority. Queen Zinara grows careless of her lands, and she forgets me. Forgotten, I shall never be." The wind swirled around the group, sending everyone to their knees. "Beg forgiveness of your Queen, Lady Blythe, Dryad Queen of the Haunted Forest!"

Ewan slowly bowed his head, kneeled on the ground and signaled to the others to do the same. "Forgive us, dear Lady Blythe, Queen of the Dryads of the Haunted Forest. We meant no disrespect. We ask to pass through your territory to the Teleen Caves. We had no knowledge of your return to these parts, afraid we were, as was your sister, that you had abandoned the Guildrin clan. We beg mercy of Your Majesty." Shade looked up through her lashes to see if anything appeared. The wind made her blink continuously, and her eyes watered from the whipping air.

Suddenly, the wind stopped. The change in the air felt

even denser than it had before. Everyone looked up and gazed at the Queen of the Dryads. She was perched on a large branch just above them. Her skin was pale and glossy white as if she was made of porcelain. Her dark green eyes were large, so large, in fact, that the whites of her eyes disappeared, and yet somehow they had a slit-like appearance. Her long dark blond hair draped around her carelessly in soft wisps down to her legs. It was like a cape, flying in some self-contained breeze. A crown of twisted twigs and angel's breath lay on her head, spilling down like entrails in her hair. The sheer dress she wore was more like torn worn silk, swaying around her in the breeze and tied together with a belt of roped vines.

She looked just as a faery would, ethereal and almost unreal. Her skin glowed like moonlight reflecting on the surface of a pool of water. Shade gasped with amazement. She thought, at first, that it was glamour the dryad wore, but, she felt no such magic floating around Lady Blythe. Her magic was the woods, the trees, earth, plants, and creatures. All were flowing with energy that was tumbling toward her.

The faery snickered. She tilted her head, studying the group and narrowing her large insect-like eyes. They filled Shade with dread. Her face morphed from angelic to a morbid malice. "You are pathetic. Forget me not. I won't soon forget you, either. Give me the Halfling girl, and the rest of you can go."

Shade's eyes widened as she stood up and stepped back. She froze mid-step, as she couldn't move and could barely breathe. A sticky, thick magic clung to her again, paralyzing her into place. Lady Blythe cackled wickedly at her and shook her head. "Yes, Shade, that means you. Either you stay or they die."

"But why? What did I do? I don't even know you. What do you want from me? I have no magic." Shade felt frozen. Her legs didn't work; nothing worked. She felt as if she were in suspended animation, trapped in the stillness, as one would be in ice.

"Your Majesty, Shade can't stay here. She was sent by Queen Zinara herself on a quest." Ewan spoke, not raising his head to the faery queen, as though doing so might offend her.

"Silence, giant. I don't need your blubbering statements. I know quite well what Queen Zinara means to do. I don't agree with her strange decisions, but I know this Halfling serves more than just one purpose." She gazed at Shade, her lips thin and tense. Shade felt light headed from the intensity of it.

Trick her. Trick her into thinking you are only a mortal without powers. Trick her at her own game, Shade. Quickly! One inner voice yelled with urgency.

Shade came back to herself, still frozen but more clear-headed. The warmth of her guides and their voices swam in her head, helping her breathe in her frozen body.

How do I trick her? She'd know if I'm lying. Don't they all? How?

Offer her yourself entirely, they suggested. *But trick her into giving you a riddle. We can answer any question. If you answer right, she must let you go.*

Shade swallowed hard and peered up at the Dryad Queen, feeling her evil swirling around in the air.

"Lady Blythe, Your Majesty. Please, I'll come to you freely, but I was thinking. Don't you like riddles? You look like you might like them. How about a deal? If I answer it right, we *all* go free with safe passage through your land. If not, I'm yours with no fight. At least we can make it fun, you know?" Shade chuckled nervously and gasped while the air felt tight and thinner as if she were drowning.

Lady Blythe glared at her, contemplating her words. She drilled her sharp eyes into Shade. Shade's offer had evidently caught her fancy. A moment later, a creepy, growing smile spread across her face.

"Why, how quaint. How did you know about my love of riddles? How delightful! Very well then, I accept." Lady Blythe paused for a moment, looking pensive and scratching her chin. Her eyes danced with excitement as she cleared her throat. "I have one for you." She jumped up and down as she filled with anticipation. "What can walk the earth at dawn, dances in the noon sun and then never again at dusk." Her wicked smile snarled at Shade.

What sort of riddle is that?

A vampire, the voices offered.

What? Shade hissed back in her mind at the voices. *A vampire? Really? This is ridiculous, I….*

Trust us, Shade, please.

"Okay. Uh, I know that one. It's a…uh…vampire. The answer is a vampire." Shade's breath whispered from her lips as the thick magic surrounding her squeezed the last bit out. The queen would have to let up on the air prison if she were to inhale once more. Nothing but silence came from the Dryad Queen. She'd fallen into anger, and her eyes flashed a luminous green fire. She was steaming and furious.

"How dare you trick me? You defiant fool! You're pathetic to think you've seen the last of me. I have to let you pass now, but make sure you stay out of my way. I cannot be tricked twice. We *shall* meet again. I promise you that!"

Shade was hurled to the ground, coughing and gulping down precious air. Lady Blythe was gone as quickly as she had appeared. Nothing else was around. Nothing but the dark woods.

"Is she gone?" Shade whispered. Her breath still hadn't caught up. "What did she want with me? And what the hell is she?" She brought her knees to her chest and sat rocking back and forth, willing her heart to stop racing and slowing her breath.

Jack knelt down, his hand giving her shoulder a firm squeeze. "Lady Blythe is who she said, Queen of the Dryads of the Haunted Forest. I really don't know what she wanted from you." He glanced up to where the Dryad sat not a moment before. "It's quite strange. She disappeared decades ago and has not been seen until now. Queen Zinara assumed she was dead." He looked up at the surrounding warriors. No one seemed to have a clue as to what was going on.

"Unless the Unseelie have been working overtime and attempting to sabotage or stop us in our tracks. This feels like Unseelie treachery. How did you know, Shade?" He stood up, offering Shade his hand. She looked up at the handsome Teleen warrior, taking his hand as she pulled herself onto her shaky legs. Tears streaked down her face. The Dryad Queen scared her more than she'd realized.

"Know what?"

Jack looked at her intently, searching her face for something not known to Shade.

"That she liked riddles. You saved yourself—and us— with such a quick wit."

"It wasn't me," Shade said, shaking her head. "My spirit guides are speaking to me, helping me. They gave me the idea and then told me the answer." She coughed again and breathed in deeply.

"Well, quite a handy trick there. I hope they come in handy more often than not. Shall we continue?" Shade nodded. "Everyone, make sure wards are up. We will not be caught so unaware again. Count us lucky she didn't have an appetite for meat today."

Shade's mouth dropped open at Jack. He glanced at her and smiled. "Just kidding. She's vegan."

Shade groaned and straightened up. Shaking her head, she fell in line with the warriors, eager to leave these woods behind her.

Chapter Six

THE TELEEN HILLS were like large swells of waves, flowing with the greenest of emerald grasses. The blades of grass rolled and swayed lightly, caressed by the wind. The air flew in constant rushes, whipping everyone's long tresses about them like tangled dancing ribbons. Shade's own wavy brown hair looked to be the shortest of the entourage's, except for Ewan's. All the women's hair seemed to be almost waist length, many with ornate braids, ties, or thin ropes wrapped through like extensions. Most of the colors were unnatural; nothing a human man or woman would ever possess naturally. Waves of golden brown, reds deep as rubies, blacks as dark as midnight, and browns like tiger's eyes flowed in the breezes. It was quite a dance of flashing colors.

Shade felt a twinge of jealousy. Nothing but human light brown hair danced on her head, nothing fey-like about it. It made her wonder what she had that resembled the fey at all. Maybe she had turned out to be more human than fey. Maybe they had the wrong girl after all. It could be she had no magic besides her spirit guides. She couldn't perform glamour or heal anything, let alone fight or enchant like the Dryad Queen.

Shade shivered, recalling the queen's cold stare and the ice-cold prison of air which kept her tightly within its grasp. It made her want to faint from a lack of oxygen. It was not something she cared to remember.

Her legs burned with the constant strain of hiking up and down the hills. The hills appeared smooth with grass but were rocky and uneven. Her tennis shoes weren't made for such rigorous hiking. She paused, leaned over, and placed her hands on her knees. Her lungs ached with the effort, and breathing felt like a burning torture. A faint metallic taste clung to her mouth as she coughed up spit. She was not a fan of the physically gifted. Her idea of a good time was curling up on her bed with a thick book. There was no way she would've voluntarily done anything that resembled hiking before this. Her idea of camping was a campsite where you could walk to your car and a public restroom. It was as close as she got to be outdoorsy.

This sucks.

"You all right?" Soap paused just ahead of her, craning his neck to see her face.

Shade's cheeks were pink with heat from the strain. She swallowed her blood-tainted saliva and nodded. *I can do this, no problem. Just breathe, Shade, breathe.* The problem was that she didn't quite believe herself. Turning toward Braelynn, who also had come to a stop by her, she attempted a weak smile for the Sorceress when she gave Shade a gentle pat on the back.

"The trail will be hard, not just for you, but for all of us. In time, you'll grow accustomed to the rigorous terrain. Are you having trouble catching your breath? I have a potion you can take for that. It's kind of like asthma medicine. Most faeries don't have that kind of trouble, but I prepare treatments for all kinds of people." Shade grinned, feeling at ease with the kind warrior. "I knew it was a possibility with a human coming along. Let me know if you need it," Braelynn offered. She grinned back and moved to continue to trek in the direction of the others.

Shade sighed and closed her eyes. She knew Braelynn was kind, but her words made her feel a twinge of inferiority, being human and all. She wondered how all of the fey felt about humans in general. Stereotyping was probably not just a human trait, and she wondered if the group thought she was weak. She hoped not.

She straightened up, took a deep breath in, and attempted the hill again. The afternoon sun burned down on her, and her hair felt afire. Peeking into her backpack, she remembered her baseball cap, which she'd stuffed into it earlier. It came to her fingers as quickly as she thought it. She was never going to get used to how cool that was. Shade zipped up her backpack and pulled the cap over the wavy strands that now fell away from her ponytail. She was glad she'd remembered to bring it; her head was thanking her for it.

Shade was about to ask someone if they were getting any closer to the mountain caves of the Teleen when she heard Ewan's booming voice echoing back to her.

"The mountains are about a mile away, not too far. We'll be eating dinner in no time." He chuckled back toward the group and patted his belly.

Ewan wasn't the only one thinking about food. Shade's stomach was protesting for the last hour. She had snacked on a granola bar, but it'd gone straight through her. She'd worked up an appetite for something a bit more substantial before her body began to turn on itself for dinner.

The last mile seemed to drag on more than the last five. Shade's back and shoulders ached from carrying the backpack. Although it wasn't too heavy, any kind of weight seemed to get old after carrying it for a while. She was not cut out for this hiking crap. Being sweaty, thirsty and, worst of all, having a thin layer of dirt that clung to everything and her skin made her cranky and exhausted. There were streaks across her face from the mixture of sweat and dirt. Her hair frizzed out from under her cap, and some of it was stuck to her moist neck, which was itching up a storm. She suspected she had a blister or two forming on her feet, and her knees felt like they were going to fall apart.

Gritting her teeth, she rounded one of the last hills and gasped. The mouth of a cave roared above them. It was pitch black and very broad. The dirt and grass continued into the cave until the blackness swallowed it up. The wind howled over the hole, wailing eerily. To Shade, it did not seem like anyone lived there. *This can't be it.*

The rest of the gang gathered around the entrance as Ewan held up his hands to the air and mumbled some words. Shade looked about, not seeing anyone else around them. The feeling of being watched returned with a vengeance. Her eyes moved up the cliffs that gave way to a jagged overhang. The rock formation was shaped like a half moon, and it wasn't just a simple hole or opening in the wall. The rocks were expansive, and they looked as if they may crumble onto anyone who dared to walk into the cave underneath it.

A shiver of glamour swept over her and all around the cave, like ripples in a pool of water. *Of course!* The looming stones were a deterrent, like a spell of reluctance to whoever passed by, making them fear the large hanging rocks and stay clear of them. As Ewan spoke softly, the glamour melted away, revealing an enormous double door. The door had intricate carvings and was made of dense wood that appeared old and weathered. Shade drew in her breath, amazed at how beautiful it was.

The wood blended into the shades of rock around it and seemed to fade into the background if she did not stare right at it. *Wow, what kind of people live here to make such a fascinating place?* She watched as the group gathered around the great doorway while Ewan gave the enormous doors a good shove. They creaked loudly as they opened. The groan they emitted made it clear they were rarely used. He motioned for the group to follow him.

As they entered the archway, the darkness swallowed them. Soon after, flickering lights ignited from the torches that lined the walls. The doors slammed behind them with a thunderous clap. Everyone jumped, and some had even drawn their weapons while staring at the giant doors. It seemed they had closed by themselves because no one in the group had closed them. There was no one else in the room. *This is unsettling.* Shade turned back toward the darkness ahead. *Where is everyone?* She followed her group while thinking this, wondering when the people who lived there would greet them.

They walked deeper into the dismal cave to where it led into a massive room. There were tall stone columns that reached high above them, made of the same grey-streaked white rock as the rest of cave. There appeared to be no one there, but to Shade's surprise, the torches around the room began to light up by themselves to brighten the space. Soon after, figures appeared out of the shadows, also holding torches. They materialized from the darkness in the blink of an eye. Each one of them was dressed in guard's uniforms, and they were engulfed in white and blue flames while electricity crackled along their skin. Shade thought of Jack and his powers. Surely, they must be Teleen.

The guards came to a stop in the middle of the room, completely surrounding them. Their eyes shone luminously, and their bodies rippled with the heat of their fire. They scared Shade, and she struggled to contain her shock. They were much more frightening than Jack had been, maybe because there were so many of them. She hoped they were not going to harm them. They made her hair stand on end as their magic and power buzzed across the room. It was like a swarm of bees or static tingling on her skin.

"Um, Ewan, are we in danger here?" Sary shouted to the giant, one hand on her bow and the other with an arrow ready to fly if needed.

He waved back at her, shaking his head but not responding. His other hand flew up, palm facing the guards as he spoke. "Guard of the Teleen, we're here under the invitation of your queen. Our Queen, Zinara, has sent word of our arrival. Please stand down. I demand to speak with the Captain of the Guard."

The group tightened together as the guards' proximity grew closer. Everyone backed into each other as sword after sword were drawn and arrows nocked. Knives were also unsheathed and glinting. Everyone was ready, except Shade.

She was sweating and feeling her stomach knot into a tight cramp. She pulled one of her own knives out of her pack, shaking profusely as she gripped it. Once again, she realized her lack of training for a fight. She felt naked and exposed as she shrank into the circle of bodies around her and let them shield her from the guards.

The Captain of the Guard stepped up and pointed his sword at the ground. He glowed a brilliant white-blue all over his exposed skin. The fire burned so brightly, it hurt Shade's eyes to look at him. He seemed to realize this and immediately weaved glamour over his lighted body, assuming a more human appearance. The tan skin over his large muscles still seemed to glow slightly as the fire receded. His eyes were a blue-green fire that slowly turned to steel gray and gleamed in the torchlight. He was extremely handsome and had his long, black hair pulled taut into a low ponytail. In awe of him, Shade sucked in her breath. His charm ended as he spoke and narrowed his eyes at them, smirking.

"So, this is Queen Zinara's last hope? Don't really look like much, do you?" He laughed, but it sounded full of spite more than anything.

"Dylan," Jack responded. "Good to see you again. It's been a long time."

The captain briefly scrutinized Jack but barely acknowledged him. "You were so easy to surround and entrap. I thought for sure that she'd have known better than to send such a weak force to do the job of soldiers. I'll never understand her ways." He walked around the group, eyeing them with disdain. Their weapons were drawn, but no one seemed to be holding them in readiness. Everyone was waiting. *Waiting for what*? Shade wished she knew.

Dylan came around to stand by Shade, having passed through the ring of warriors in the group as if they were not even there. He inspected Shade with an intensity that dug into her skin. He reached out to her to touch her cheek, but she stepped back, remembering what Jack had told her about touching a Teleen. He could electrocute her if he wanted to. She was not going take the chance to find out.

"Are you afraid of me?" Dylan sneered as his hand returned to his side. He seemed to be pondering a thought as his eyes pierced back at her. Shade made no further movements but avoided his glare. Leaning forward, he tilted his head slightly, whispering just loud enough for her to hear him, "You rightfully should be."

He gave his head the slightest of shakes and spun back around toward his guards. Signaling them to back off, he turned back to the travelers and addressed them all.

"I have announced you to our queen. She'll be most pleased to meet all of you, especially your precious halfling." He chuckled, sending a tingle across Shade's skin. He wasn't just Teleen. She was willing to bet he was something else, too. She was almost sure of it. Even so, she wasn't quite sure that he knew it. Jack couldn't do magic with his voice like this one could. Shade shivered from the after effects of his rippling laughter and close proximity. She ran her hands up and down her arms, trying to rub the feeling away with the warmth of

81

friction. Shade wondered why she could sense that he was different. Maybe a power of hers was finally waking up.

After the captain had signaled for them to leave, the guards departed, falling into step with each other. No one was quite relaxed yet, remaining on alert. The group fell in behind the soldiers and followed. The hall seemed to stretch on forever, and Shade's stomach grumbled again, making her glad that all the noise of the footsteps absorbed the sound of it. She hoped they would find a nice banquet waiting for them. She could only hope for such a thing from what she'd seen so far.

The ground was also made of stone, smoothed down and worn from years of use. It was a darker gray, sandy in color with bits of red and yellow speckled throughout it. The entire hall was the same color. There were no decorations, and nothing but the burning torches to indicate that anyone even lived there. They reached the end of the great hall as it funneled into a smaller tunnel.

The torches continued along each side of the cave. The stone did not change much, and Shade could not find any doors, much less, windows. Claustrophobia seemed to creep in as she tried to slow her breathing to remain calm. The air was cold and never seemed to change in temperature. The smell of earth, mold, and humid dirt grew stronger the deeper they went. Shade swore she could hear water echoing far away and vibrating against the walls. These tunnels probably ran so deep that you could pop out on the other side of the world. *Not really a comforting thought.*

The hallway finally opened up once again. To Shade's surprise, it wasn't to a lair or anything she expected. A huge underground crevice loomed beneath them, opening up into a dark void. They were standing on a ledge that led to a creaky old bridge. The roof of the cave loomed high above them with small streams of sunlight spiking through and piercing the rocks above.

A bridge, Shade thought nervously. No way would she cross that. It was made of rope and wood, and it didn't look very sturdy. She sighed as she looked down over the ledge into a shadowy abyss. She could hear some water echoing and splashing down the sides of the ridge just to her right. There was probably an underground river down there, but it wasn't visible from this far up. The air was cooler and filled with light misty water sprays that she didn't find comforting. Shade was so engrossed in staring at the rickety bridge that she didn't realize the captain was now standing by her. He was watching her reaction intently with a slight smile playing on his lips. He seemed to be enjoying her horror at having to cross the creaky bridge.

"So what's so special about you? You look less than ordinary." Dylan regarded her, his breath pressing on her ear from his closeness. She turned and almost bumped noses with the captain. He didn't budge but seemed to lean closer, invading her space so much, Shade actually had to take a step back. He was still glamoured, and before she could complete her step, he gripped her arms to pull her back toward him. His fingers dug in with just enough pressure to hurt her skin. Shade's breath caught in her throat, and she was half relieved he hadn't shed his glamour to shoot her up with electricity. She knew darn well he could at any time.

"Let go of me! What do you want?" She pulled, but his grip was firm. His breath was hot and sent shivers down her neck as he pulled her to him. His arms embraced her like a lover sweeping up his mistress. Her skin prickled as he let some static electricity seep around her, making her gasp with fear. She heard clinks of swords drawn behind her. He ignored it.

"You almost slipped off the edge." He gave her an amused grin. "Is this how you say 'Thank you,' *human*? I was just watching out for you. You don't have me fooled. I don't know what Queen Zinara actually has planned, but the Teleen will not fall for her jests. She can fight her own fight. You are

83

not true fey. You barely reek of fey blood. I have more magic in my finger than you possess in your entire body. I intend to find out what trick is behind this so-called quest that will supposedly save us all." With that, he let her go abruptly, making her lose her step as she stumbled to regain her balance. Soap caught her mid-stumble as Jack stood before the captain.

"That's enough, *Dylan*," Jack stated firmly as he put himself between the captain and Shade. "We have no quarrel. We are here under Teleen protection, and you act hostile toward your own guests. The Queen will not be pleased, knowing your hospitality was so lacking." His chest puffed out, and his head tilted down, apparently challenging Dylan.

Relieved that someone had come to her aid, she turned toward Soap, who was holding her tightly. Her nerves were shredded, and she was afraid her knees would crumble beneath her.

Dylan snickered and turned back to the bridge. Walking forward to the edge of the landing, he turned around and gave her a smirk. He was enjoying the growing terror on her face as he continued walking backward over the ledge.

Shade screamed but stopped suddenly, not believing her eyes. The captain kept walking backward as he floated on air and started laughing loudly while shaking his head. He then turned and continued while the rest of the guard also laughed, following behind him. They obviously got a kick out of watching their visitors panic when they learned about the invisible bridge. The entire guard walked across and did not fall into the ravine.

They have an invisible bridge? Shade and the group followed, slowly sheathing their weapons. They stepped tentatively onto the bridge, which was seemingly made of air, still not convinced it was solid. Shade cautiously walked forward. It was like standing on glass, and she was surprised her legs didn't go through. Peering down, she could see the looming darkness below, swallowing up the rocks.

Shade took a deep breath and continued following the rest of the warriors, trying not to look down and through the glass bridge. The cold air wasn't comforting, for she didn't know where the sides of the glass bridge were or how narrow it could very well be. She made sure she didn't step anywhere the guards hadn't stepped already.

On the other side, they re-entered a cave, but this one branched into three tunnels. Everyone stayed to the left and continued down the dark corridor until they reached another large room. It was so brightly illuminated as if the daylight sun was shining in, but Shade couldn't find any windows. However, she did see other Teleen, scores of them.

The guard had split up around the room and lined the walls in a single file. High stone columns with veins of multi-colored cracks laced with gold were at the room's edges. Large drapes of fabric spilled down the walls in colors of crimson and jade, bringing warmth to the cold, stone-lined walls. Everyone inside the room wore brightly colored clothing, the women with long flowing dresses. The men were more conservative with crisp tunics and pants made of either linen or leather.

The Teleen were all staring, as though they'd never been taught that it could be considered rude. Maybe it wasn't. It could be commonplace among the fey to stare. Whispers floated in the air as people commented on the new arrivals. Some reached out to touch them, pulling at their clothes in soft tugs of curiosity. Some of the women even blushed and giggled as Jack walked by them.

Some of the Teleen wore glamour, covering their electrifying blue-fire skins, looking ethereal with their translucent skin and large eyes. Some were glamoured to appear human but were far too beautiful to pass for them. Their noses were thin and straight, and they had large almond shaped eyes with perfect, luscious rose-colored lips. She wondered how much time they actually spent with humans outside this morbid place. Jack and Soap did an excellent job on their own glamours. At least they could blend in. They had studied well.

There was a throne in the center of the far wall, and large gray, sleek and worn stone steps led to the massive dais. The queen's throne sat upon the great platform. It was also stone, but was lighter, harder and more intricately carved. It looked to be made out of marble, but Shade was no expert. Different colored veins ran through the stone, but they did not break up the smoothness of the carvings.

The Queen observed Shade with large obsidian eyes. They were very similar to Lady Blythe's luminous insect eyes, and she didn't glamour herself either. Her fiery blue skin glowed brightly and seemed to hum with the crackle of electricity or lightning. There were constant flames flowing over her body. Her hair also looked afire but didn't burn. It was dark with a highlight of blue crackling through it.

So that is what a full Teleen woman looks like unshielded? Shade thought. She'd noticed some of the guard and attendees were in full Teleen glow as well.

They reached the throne when Ewan knelt down before the blue lightning queen with his head bowed. Everyone followed suit as he spoke. "Your Majesty, Queen Gretel of the Teleen, we've come from the Guildrin clan in the city of Aturine and greet you with open arms and love from our Queen Zinara. We were told of your great hospitality and ask of you permission to rest the night and continue our journey tomorrow."

The Queen glanced around at them, taking in what she saw. She nodded the slightest of nods and spoke with a voice that echoed off the walls and rippled through the air like a cool mountain breeze. "Please stand. I am aware of your coming from my sister Zinara. She has spoken well of all of you, and I find you most deserving of her praise.

"Please also forgive my Royal Guards. They find

tormenting any visitors to be quite amusing. We don't get too many visitors here, as you can see. We're an isolated clan and the last of the Teleen bloodlines. I find it a great pleasure that I'm able to aid you on your quest to the Santiran fountains. Please, make yourselves comfortable and accept our great hospitality."

She waved her arm to the crowd as they stood and found that tables were set up in two rows, one on either side of them. One by one, tiny flying demi-fey servants came out and placed candelabras, bowls, goblets, and overflowing platters of food on the tables. They were dressed in great long robes of flowing linen that rustled around them in smooth waves. Fruits, meat, and rolls of soft bread filled the middle of the great tables. Shade felt her stomach rumble with hunger, and all of them were looking at each other with glee dancing on their faces.

They filed around a table and eagerly sat down at the end nearest the Queen. The Queen had a table set up right in front of her with anything she asked for. There were stone plates and wooden forks and knives already set up in front of each of them. The small faeries, which laid out the table and food, were now darting back and forth. They were so quick and efficient at their job; all that could be seen of them was a blur of wings and hands.

Shade watched them, fascinated by how tiny they were with their wings as thin as tissue. Still, they held the little stick-thin figures effectively in the air. The ones she was able to gaze upon longer showed her their tiny faces with perfect small lips and straight noses. Most had jet-black, body-length hair. Some tied their hair back, and some left it hovering around them like capes. Their large almond, insect-like eyes were black as night and blinked at her curiously. None of them smiled but just flitted by her, leaving a gust of cool air as they raced by.

Shade could feel the exhaustion seeping from her bones. The food was working on her already and helped fill the void in her stomach. Sleep was pulling at her eyes, and her body ached with every stretch and movement. She looked around at her friends, who also seemed tired as they quietly munched on the great feast. She had stuffed her belly full and felt a twinge of regret with the pain of her swollen stomach, making it hard to breathe.

Shade sat back in her chair and looked across the table. On the parallel stone table straight across from her was Captain Dylan. He stared at her and smiled. His face took on a softer look as he nodded to her with his cup held up in the air. He set it down and was interrupted by a guard to his left. Shade glanced at the man who was now leering at her as he spoke softly to the captain. He had a similar facial structure but looked a bit younger than the captain.

Shade was betting they were related. She barely noticed they were both looking back at her now. The other guard's dark stare was just that much colder than Dylan's. She probably had stared too long and felt her cheeks flush, turning quickly away to hide behind her goblet of sweet punch. She pushed away her plate and glimpsed at her friends, praying they'd be heading to their rooms soon to sleep.

"Shade, are you done? We're headed to our chambers soon. Ready to go?" Braelynn asked as she gave her a flashing smile. Relieved, Shade nodded and stood, following them as they began to file out.

A dark-haired and pale-skinned Teleen woman stood in front and waited for them to gather around. She smiled broadly at someone and held her arms out. Shade craned her neck to see whom she was grinning at. Jack melted into the embrace, hugging the woman tightly. As he began pulling back, the woman hung on a little longer. It was just long enough to whisper something into Jack's ear. He then pulled back abruptly, frowned at her, shook his head, and answered her sternly but softly enough that no one else was privy to the conversation. Shade wondered who the woman was and how she knew Jack.

Jack turned back to the group, now composed, with a face of serenity. He cleared his throat and spoke loudly for all of them to hear. "Okay, guys, Sylphi here is going to join us and show us to our rooms. We'll be spread out some, for these are natural caves and are quite large. Don't go wandering either. These tunnels travel far, and it's easy to get lost. If you absolutely must, please only leave your room accompanied by someone else." He waved for them to come forward, and they all filed in by twos behind him and Sylphi. Sylphi kept trying to inch up near him, but he avoided her advances by stepping back and cramming in beside Shade and Braelynn.

"Shade, how are you finding the trek? Getting too tired?" He smiled down at her and completely ignored Sylphi's raging glare. The woman turned back toward a large tunnel they were all following. Joining her were Captain Dylan and his near-relative looking guard from the table.

"Um, it's ok. My muscles are killing me. I've never felt so sore in my life. I think I might have some blisters on my feet that are hurting something awful. I'm really not an outdoors type, so this is really a big push for me."

"Ah, you will need Sari's famous foot soak. That'll take care of anything on your feet for sure. I am sure she will have something for your muscle aches as well. This journey will take a toll on us all. I'll have her stop by your room after she gets settled," Jack said.

Sylphi was giggling and turned back toward them. "Shade, you might like Darren's famous massage. He'll definitely make you forget any pain you ever have felt. And more…." Her voice had a singsong way, but with a definite malicious tone to it. She playfully patted Darren's back.

"Thank you, Sylphi. I'll try to make myself useful for anyone who wishes." Darren, Captain Dylan's sidekick, snickered. Shade swallowed, thinking the massage somehow did not sound like something she'd need at all.

"That's enough from both of you. I'm sure they're much too tired from the long journey and just want to get some shuteye. Just show them their rooms already," Captain Dylan snapped. He grumbled under his breath and gave Shade a dark look. She wondered why he didn't like her. *He doesn't even know me. Why would he be so mean?*

It's because the unknown is a thing to fear, Shade. Never forget that, the voices chimed in.

Shade sighed. She had to agree with them. She just wasn't so sure about the company here tonight. It was Darren, in particular, who gave her the heebie-jeebies. He just seemed to radiate some kind of evil. She wasn't sure why he was chosen to be one of their escorts; it didn't seem very appropriate somehow. Shade glanced at Sylphi. *She's no better.*

The dark-haired Sylphi was hanging off of Jack's arm now, whispering something into his ear. Shade wondered if those two had a thing for each other, or if it was one-sided. From the look on Jack's face, he did not seem to mind her hanging on him, but frowned every now and then at some of her comments and giggling.

She reminded Shade of the mean girls back at school, always finding a victim to torture amongst the high school kids. Sylphi was the kind of girl who would make snide comments to a good girl and send her to the bathroom with tears of humiliation streaming down her face. Shade narrowed her eyes and shook her head. Those kinds of girls thrive on others' suffering. *It'd probably be best to straight out avoid her,* Shade thought. At least they were only here for a night and would not have to endure the Teleen's 'hospitality' too much longer.

"What are you thinking about, dear Shade? Have we offended you in some way? You're shaking your head with such disdain. Has your stay been so unpleasant so far?" Sylphi asked, suddenly at Shade's side. She slipped her hand around Shade's arms and bent closer to her. Her pale skin shone like moonlight, only with a slightly bluer tinge to the glamour she wore. The smell of roses and another fragrant scent surrounded her as she invaded Shade's personal space.

"Jack's mine, you know. I do hope you understand. That's if, of course, you were getting any ideas about him," Sylphi whispered to her. "We're to be married soon. I know that, being a woman, you understand how rare it is to find such a wonderful, strong, and handsome man like Jack. Just letting you know how very much he has missed me. I feel so overjoyed to have him back. He stays away far too long. Oh, here we are now!"

She paused, smiling intensely for Shade. It was a smile that seemed to cut into Shade like a knife, full of things wickedly unsaid. "Your room, my dear. Do have a good rest. You'll need it!"

Shade scurried into the room and turned to see Darren leaning by the open door with arms crossed, smiling at her.

"Do let me know if you change your mind about the massage. I find you most fascinating, Shade. I've never met a human before. It's been quite a delight." He snickered, bowing as he left. Darren shut the door for her, and when it clicked, Shade ran to it and turned the lock as quickly as she could.

Leaning against the smooth wood, she finally let her breath out. Somehow, she did not feel right. Something about this place was setting alarms off in her head like crazy. She pulled her pack off and rubbed her shoulders, looking around the room for the first time.

The room was gorgeous. It was a cave, and it didn't have any windows. The air was cold with an undertone of dampness that left a bit of a chill. There was a nice large bed at the far wall, just opposite the door. It was piled with fluffy pillows and soft blankets and was neatly arranged to not seem messy, but comfy. There was a wooden table to one side of the room, long and polished smooth from use, that she placed her pack on. Above it was a silver mirror with a vine design frame that had crystals embedded all around the edges. It was breathtaking but seemed out of place in that room.

Shade stood there, staring at her reflection. She looked tired. A thin layer of dust seemed to stick to her skin and hair. That wasn't what stopped her though. The mirror looked like it had a tiny ripple in it. It was as though she was gazing at her reflection in a still pool of water. It looked smooth and almost see-through. She reached out her hand, letting her fingers almost caress the surface.

Suddenly, almost as if something had turned it off, the mirror was once again solid. Shade's fingers clinked against the hard glassy surface. It was nothing more than a plain mirror. Shade stared at it for a moment longer, shaking her head again. *Nothing is as it seems here.* She felt like Alice, deep down in the rabbit hole.

She let out a breath and turned toward a door in the wall of the cave that was next to the table. She turned the crystal and wood knob slowly, praying that nothing awful would jump out at her. It turned easily and opened into a well-lit bathroom. She laughed, relieved by the normalcy of it. *A bathroom…* It was both modern and well-equipped, with a massive claw-foot tub on one side and a large shower. The shower itself had several showerheads installed, but no door, and a drain on the floor. She reached in, turned the curved silver knob on the wall, and watched with amazement as water fell like rain pouring out of the spouts. She beamed; the water was the perfect temperature. Soaps and a sponge were on a ledge near the end of the shower, wrapped in twine and topped with a bow. Shrugging off her clothes, she stepped into the pouring water. It felt fantastic. The hot water ran down her skin and rinsed the day's soil away, swirling dirt down the drain.

Shade hadn't checked for towels before entering the shower, but a glance around the room revealed a neat stack of them set out on the counter. Turning the shower off, she stepped out and pulled one out of the stack, wrapping it snugly around her body. She didn't feel any cold since the steam and warmth of the water seemed to remain with her. She pulled another towel out to rub her hair, twisting it around her head to absorb the water. She'd left her bag with her clothes in the bedroom. Groaning, she hoped it wasn't too cold when she exited the warm cocoon of the misty bathroom.

The room was as she'd left it. Glancing toward the door, she listened for any movement or voices. The stone walls seemed to insulate the rooms very well, and she didn't hear anyone. *Natural soundproofing*, she pondered, rummaging through her pack. She managed to find and pull out a deep blue nightgown with a pair of underwear. After quickly dressing, she noticed the cold air from the bedroom was starting to penetrate her skin.

Shade shivered and rubbed her arms. Her hair was still wet from the shower and felt cool on her shoulders. There was something else though, making her stop what she was doing as she felt goose bumps flare across her skin. She looked around the room and couldn't figure out why she was suddenly so cold. She heard what sounded like a whisper, but saw nothing. *Where had that voice come from*? She held her breath, listening hard for anything else.

Her eyes darted around as she waited. None of her spirit guides responded to her inner pleas as if a mute button had been pushed. She didn't like it one bit. Something was very wrong. Shade grabbed one of her daggers from her pack and listened once more. Nothing jumped out at her, and there were no more whispers. Her heart raced and pounded in her ears. She held her breath, listening and frowning. It was probably nothing. Shaking off the crazy feelings, she tossed the dagger on the vanity table and walked to the bed. She slipped under the soft sheets and pulled one of the thick quilts on top of her. Looking around once more, she stared at the mirror one more time.

Is it rippling again? She shivered and felt uneasy. *I need to rest. I'm just exhausted and drained. That's why I'm starting to see things. Tomorrow will be here before I know it.* She then decided to reach for her pack and pulled out her cell phone. It still had a charge on it, but she doubted there would be an outlet here to top it off. It read 10:45pm. *Ugh, it's getting super late!*

They planned to regroup for breakfast at six am and after that, continue on their journey. She pulled out her charger and glanced down the wall near the floor. The lamp plugged into the wall, so there had to be an open outlet just next to it. She couldn't believe her luck as she plugged her cell phone in. *Faeries with modern technology, who knew?* She wondered if all the rooms were like this or was she the only one with modern comforts in her room. For certain, there'd be iron in the conduits running through the stone walls.

Shade shrugged. She'd have to ask Jack about it later. The Teleen wouldn't be bothered by it, but what about her friends? It was something to ask about. The palace at Guildrin didn't have such amenities. The light came from torch and candle, and from some weird magical spell that illuminated the place as brightly as natural sunlight.

Shade lay back, sinking into the bed and sheets. She let the blankets envelope around her, embracing the body heat trapped in the soft sheets, which made the bed feel like heaven. Reaching over, she clicked the lamp back off, trying to avoid looking at the creepy mirror again and instead closed her eyes, letting herself slip away into sleep.

Chapter Seven

"**S**HADE."

The blue fire was glowing all around her, crackling and popping on all sides. The walls seemed too near, enveloping her like a cocoon. She stood up from the ground where she'd woken. Is this real? A dream? She didn't know. Feeling the walls with her hands, they felt hard and rough with cold stones. The sound of her own breath echoed around her, but nothing seemed out of the ordinary, besides the fact that she had no idea what was going on. The fire came from the other side of the room. It stood like a pillar the size of a man. In fact, as she stared longer into the glowing flames, the image of a man surfaced in the fire. She gasped. The man's eyes remained closed, and his hands laid crossed over each other on the hilt of a gleaming sword. The blade also glowed with wisps of blue fire. Its hilt was made of dark red rubies, and the red flames spread from his hands onto the edge of his sword.

Shade walked toward him, asking him who he was. He didn't respond to her inquiries, no matter how much she pleaded. She kept going, and although her feet were bare, she did not feel cold as she thought she would. Her heart pounded in her chest as she reached out to the man.

"Help me," Shade whispered to him, her voice faint and weak. Her fingers were almost touching the blue flame engulfing his body, even though she felt afraid. She didn't know if the flames would burn or scald her hands. Somehow, she needed to wake him and make him help her out of this place, this tomb. Taking in his face, she realized he looked a lot like Dylan, the way he'd look if he'd been resting and peaceful.

Suddenly, his eyes and mouth flew open, and a bright, white light poured out of them in piercing rays. A sound like loud ethereal music filled her ears to the point that it sent her to the floor, covering them. The music seemed to scream into her, filling her with prickling pain.

Then the words came, and they were excruciating:
"WAKE UP AND RUN, SHADE!"

***

SHADE'S EYES FLEW open as she gasped, thrashing in her bed. It was still very dark, and it took a moment or two for her eyes to focus and readjust.

Am I alive or dead? Where am I? She felt panicked and couldn't breathe, her chest arrested with a searing pain.

She reached over to the lamp, but without any light, she fumbled and sent the lamp smashing to the floor. The nightmare had left her with a dull, disorientating ache in her head. Just then, the room lit up around her like a blinding floodlight, making her pupils contract painfully.

She stopped fumbling and stared at the changed silver and crystal mirror. It was on fire, with blue flames dripping out like liquid molten rock. It crackled with white electricity and poured out of the rippling surface, down the table, and into the middle of the room. The pillar it formed shifted and morphed into a man.

Darren.

Run! Run now!

She screamed as the voices returned, panicked and jumbled in her mind. However, she soon realized no one could hear her through the solid rock walls. She pulled the blankets off but never made it out of the bed before he jumped on her. He pushed her down and smacked her face. His cold laugh rang in her ears as he snarled down at her, watching her squirm and kick helplessly.

His eyes were facets of blue, white light, blinding her even more as he pinned her under his legs and squeezed her arms so hard she felt them aching and burning in protest. There were surely bruises forming on her skin. He smacked her again so hard that stars flared in a sea of darkness. She almost blacked out, fighting to stay awake and tasting the iron flavor of blood in her mouth. The left side of her face felt on fire.

When her vision cleared, she took in the horror of Darren completely engulfed in fire. His blue flames roared around them, but nothing burned, as though his fire was cool to the touch. To Shade's surprise, she wasn't burning under his grip, giving her a renewed urge to struggle. His grip kept her in place while the room spun. She wondered briefly if he'd given her a concussion or something. Her stomach lurched with nausea, threatening to spill her dinner.

Blinking, she tried to focus. "Darren, let me go!" She coughed up a mouthful of blood and spit at the faery.

He snarled at her. "You pathetic mortal, I forgot how much you bleed and injure so easily. No true Fey would be so fragile. My apologies, of course. I do wonder, though, why you aren't burning up into crumbly ash. I always did like to watch mortals turn into dust while I burnt them. I'm just a little bit sick like that." He snickered and hopped off the bed, never letting his glare slip from her. "Show me what you've got, Shade. I want to know why you're so special. What's your secret? What is it that Jack won't tell me?" His face morphed from mocking to angry as his fire was flickered in and out. The fire flashed rapidly, making the room pulse like a bright strobe, serving to disorientate her even more.

Shade tried to stand by grabbing the nightstand and pulling herself upright. She could barely balance on her shaky legs, which didn't want to work at the moment. "There's nothing special about me, Darren. I'm just a halfling. I'd think you'd have heard that by now. Really, there's nothing else. I don't really have any magic. I'm still learning. I swear I don't know anything else!"

She stood and stepped toward Darren, but fumbled, tripping on her sluggish limbs. He caught her as she slipped and spun her around to where they faced the fiery mirror, still aglow. She stared at their reflections as her mind scrambled to find a way out of his embrace.

Darren smiled coldly as he yanked on her hair with one of his hands. His other arm encircled her chest, holding her arms tightly to her sides. Squeezing her even more, he nuzzled her neck and whispered into her ear. "What do you see, Shade? Don't you like my fire? You see how insignificant you are? No human should be so special. I really don't get why they chose you. You're so fragile, weak, and pathetic. Why not choose a great faery warrior, like myself, for instance? You're a tarnish to our race, and I think I will be doing us a great favor by getting rid of you." His flames began to burn higher and licked the air around them, making it so his face no longer could be seen in the mirror.

Shade stared at her reflection. Her cheek had an angry red welt from his blows, and as the flames grew around her, she felt her panic rage. Soon, she began to see his face again as it grew more serious. He appeared deep in thought, pondering her reflection.

"Maybe we can have some fun first. You're not so ugly. What do you think about that, love? Don't you find me appealing?" He pulled her head back, making her gasp, her scalp stinging with pain. His nose grazed her cheek and earlobe, making her cringe at his touch. "This'll be fun, no?"

He will never touch me, never.

Shade attempted to pull her head away from his hot breath. He laughed again and let up on his hold so she could see their reflections again. "Do you like my mirror? I placed it here just for you. Just so I could watch your every move. That's my magic. It's a special talent not a lot of Teleen possess, the gift of traveling through mirrors. I have the matching one in my room, so wherever I place this one, I can go, even into your locked chamber. What good did the locks do you now, Shade? No lock can keep me out. No door could close on me. It'll be our little secret." He laughed hard, his chest shaking behind her back.

He abruptly loosened his grip on her head for a moment, and Shade took advantage of his careless release. She shoved him back with her entire body weight, making him lose his balance for a moment, throwing him to the bed. She ran to the mirror and looked around for something to smash it. The dagger she'd left on the table gleamed as brightly as Darren's fire. She laced her fingers around the hilt, squeezing it hard until her knuckles turned white. She swung her arm and shoved her strength into it, ramming the metal into the mirror. The crash echoed in the cave as it smashed into a thousand glittering shards.

"No! How did you know...what have you done?" Darren had just reached her and grabbed her free arm, yanking at Shade. His momentum came to a sudden stop as he was instantly pulled into the glass, along with a flash of lightning. The last glint of it blinded her and plunged the room into darkness.

Her eyes focused on the dim glow of the dagger as its light grew a bit stronger in the black room. She stared at the mirror shards, scattered and shimmering all over the room. They didn't look unusual in any way; just plain mirror pieces glittering across the floor like diamonds. She limped toward the lamp on the floor, where it'd fallen earlier, jabbing her bare feet on the glass. Blood trailed her steps in smudges and drips from cuts stinging her flesh. Her legs, weak and shaky, began to drag under her. She fell to the floor by the bed and slipped into the developing darkness. The glow of her dagger faded into the dark, and the whole world with it.

Chapter Eight

"SHADE, CAN YOU hear me? Shade? Braelynn! She's rousing, not quite awake yet though. It's ok, Shade. You're going to be ok. You're safe now. No one will hurt you. Can you hear me, Shade?"

The voice sounded familiar, safe, and gentle. Shade wondered if her mother had come. Maybe this was the hospital. Maybe she was dreaming, or worse, dead. She couldn't open her eyes yet, but she could hear the commotion all around her. She tried to move, but her body did not respond.

"It's all right. You're still hurt, so don't try to move too much. We've healed most of your wounds, but you should still move slowly. Your head is still healing."

Shade opened her eyes a sliver. The room's light was blinding, and it stung her eyes. Blinking, she quickly reached up to cover them. A thousand prickling, sharp pains shot through her arm and down her side. She flinched and stopped moving, groaning as she sank back down onto the bed. Every movement resulted in pain screaming down her body. She felt like she'd been hit by a freight train.

"Shade, are you still feeling some pain?"

She managed a slight nod as she gasped for air.

"Take this liquid. It will make you feel better," Braelynn's soft voice echoed in her head. She felt the warm liquid touch her lips and slide into her mouth. It tasted sweet across her dry, parched tongue, like honey-sweetened tea. Letting it coat her mouth, she sighed with relief. A moment later, the sharp aches faded even more, making it easier to open her eyes to the dimly lit room. Somehow, it didn't seem so bright anymore. They must have dimmed the lights when they realized she couldn't see.

"What happened?" Her voice was a harsh whisper, for her throat felt rough and dry like sandpaper. The room came into focus, and she noticed not only Braelynn but also Sary standing near her. She slowly sat up as Braelynn slipped a few pillows behind her, propping her up. She glanced down at her arms, studying a scatter of healing, scabby slash wounds. Her left hand also had stitches across the palm and was in an excellent state of healing. Holding it up to her face, she studied it more closely. Most of the wounds were in the mid-stage of healing as if she'd been hurt days ago and not hours.

"How long was I out of it?" Shade dreaded to hear the answer.

"You were attacked in your room about five days ago, Shade. You've been unconscious since then. You'll be fine. Your wounds are healing well. Braelynn was able to stop the bleeding inside your head, but it drained her so much, she was unable to heal all of your cuts completely. She was unable to wake you up, too, even though your head is fine now. It's almost like you were under some sort of spell."

Sary sat on the bed next to her. A sweet, concerned smile lit her face, crinkling her sparkling eyes as she patted Shade's arm. Her hair lay draped around her neck in soft waves of crimson fire.

"It was Darren. He attacked me. He came out of the mirror in the room!" Shade swallowed back her panic, feeling the events of that night rushing back. "Where is he? He was really going to hurt me. He wants me dead!" Tears stung her eyes, and for a moment, she wished to be back home with her mother. Her room seemed like a distant sanctuary in a forgotten dream. Sary hugged Shade tightly as her sobs overcame her.

"It's all right, Shade. I don't know how you did it, but somehow you trapped him in the mirror when you smashed it. He was incredibly angry and rendered entirely harmless. He was released from the mirror prison by the Teleen warlock and placed into one of the cavern's confinement cells, where he has been ever since. We've waited for you to awaken. The Queen is most upset and anxious to seal his fate," Sary said with her eyes shining. They were lovely and burned like jewels on fire. She stood up, retrieved a cup from beside the bed, and handed it to Shade, encouraging her to drink it. "Drink, Shade. You must be very thirsty. We gave you fluids similar to those in an IV in the human world, but nothing refreshes like a real liquid drunk into your body."

Shade nodded and gripped the cup. The cool water felt amazing going down her throat. She immediately felt better, not as upset and instantly more awake. She finished the drink and handed the cup back. She was really starting to like faery food and drinks.

Glancing around the room, she was relieved it wasn't the same place she'd been attacked in. It was similar, but lighter in color and had no mirrors. She didn't think she could handle any more mirrors quite yet. Her backpack lay on a table by the door, and the sheets and blankets were all crisp and white. This was probably their version of a hospital room.

"What are they going to do to him?" Shade's voice seemed small, her eyes staring down at the floor while she thought about her attacker. Shivers crept across her body as the memory resurfaced. He'd stolen something with his brutality. She felt more vulnerable than ever and weak. How could anyone be cut out for this magical place? She'd have to start training right away if she were going to survive the rest of this journey. Two threats on her life in one day had been two she could have lived without. She had no idea what she'd gotten herself into and didn't like how it made her feel. Darren had taught her a harsh and vicious lesson.

"That will be up to Queen Gretel. I hear they take offenses quite seriously among the Teleen. He'll probably be expected to pay an equal price for your attack. Most attempted murders are punished harshly," Braelynn explained. "Even death is considered an adequate punishment if he was planning to kill you. This, I expect, is what he was out to do from the state of things in your room and the amount of injuries he caused you. He must pay for what he did to you, Shade." She looked earnestly at Shade from the wicker chair near the end of the bed. Shade suspected that she'd sat there a great deal during Shade's period of unconsciousness.

"He said that he could travel through a matching pair of mirrors. He placed that mirror in my room to get to me. I even locked my door, but it didn't matter." Shade's voice quivered as she recalled his dark words. "He said he was going to kill me, and that I tarnished the faery races. I didn't do anything to him, and he hates me. Why?"

"That is the question, is it not, Shade?" Jack interrupted from the doorway. He took up most of the entrance with the bulk of his muscle-bound body. "During interrogations, he refused to speak of his reasons. He won't even say if he had any accomplices." He walked closer to the bed, his face weary and tired. "I have come to summon all of you—that is if Shade can walk—to Darren's trial. The Queen has gotten word that you have awoken and is anxious to proceed. We need you there for Queen Gretel to issue his sentence. How well are you, Shade?

Can you come?" He exhaled, rubbing his eyes as if he hadn't been sleeping well.

Shade looked at him, feeling almost petrified at the thought that more fey may be out to get her. Trying to shake off the feeling, she nodded. She was feeling a lot better now with the potion they'd given her. She shifted her legs out to the side of the bed and felt the cool stone under her scabbed feet. She paused, wondering if her legs would hold. She stood up slowly and found her legs sturdy and strong. Her smile stretched across her face. *That medicine is good stuff. I'm going to have to stock up on some for my whole clumsy family!*

She straightened, flattened the mess of her hair as best she could and accepted Sary's support as the warrior princess jumped to offer a hand. Shade smiled at her, grateful for her encouragement. Sary returned it tentatively and nodded in understanding as she slipped her arm under Shade. Braelynn placed two soft leather slippers in front of Shade's feet. The leather was so smooth it was almost like silk against her skin. She shuffled forward and headed for the door.

Jack took her free side, letting her hold his arm for support. They ambled down the hall to the great chamber, which glowed brightly as daylight once more. For the first time, Shade peeked up at the roof and noticed how much it looked like a bluish-white sky at mid-noon. They were deep underground, and the sky stood there as natural as it was outside. She still couldn't make out the source.

Looking around them, she saw that everyone, including all of the Teleen clan, were there waiting for them. The room was crammed full of faery people, like on the night of their welcome feast. She wondered what had been going on the days she'd been unconscious. How much wasted time has passed all because of what happened to her due to Darren's treachery?

Her friends ushered her up some steps, and Queen Gretel stood up from her throne as they approached. She glided toward Shade, stepping down slowly and bowing her head at her. Shade followed along, noticing how Sary and the others reciprocated the bow. Queen Gretel, who now wore human glamour that shielded her fire, reached out and held Shade's hands. Her pale, blue-tinged skin looked odd for a human but sufficed enough to glamour her. She smiled warmly but spoke quickly and seriously. "Dear Shade, I am most pleased with your quick recovery. I apologize for my guard's indiscretion and most unfortunate actions. Please, come with me." She pulled Shade further up the steps to sit in a chair placed next to the massive stone throne. Shade complied, sitting down and turning toward the queen as she addressed the crowd standing before them.

"My people, Shade was attacked here in our own great cavernous dwelling. Our home has been the scene of bloodshed and pain. This is not allowed among the Teleen, and such brutality will come with a dear price. Accused of such crimes against our guest is Darren, one of our own Teleen guards. He stands now for his punishment."

Shade sat up straighter and sucked her breath in at the mention of the perpetrator. She'd been feeling much better. That is until she spied Darren approaching. The crowd opened for a double line of guards who were escorting Darren into the room and toward the throne. His head was hanging down with his long, dark hair disheveled and riddled with tangles. He looked like he hadn't rested in days, and his wrists were bound with strips of thick leather. A guard held each of his arms firmly. Captain Dylan stood in front of them and bowed before the queen.

"My queen, Darren has confessed to his crime. What price shall our queen make him pay for his violations?" Dylan appeared strong and commanding, in full Teleen guard attire but without his helmet. He remained bowed and awaited her answer. Darren and his escorts mimicked his movements though Darren appeared to be shoved into submission.

"Please stand, Captain Dylan, guards." Queen Gretel motioned. "I have come to the conclusion that only one punishment will suffice for such a deliberate and violent attack." She looked up and scanned the crowd. The silence was heavy and hung in the room like a thick smog. Shade was sweating, and her heart raced with nauseating anxiety as she waited. She just wanted to have Darren gone, away from her sight, or to run from him as fast as she could. His presence was like a bad nightmare come to life, a suffocating presence.

"Darren must now pay tribute to Shade. A blood debt created demands payment. Only blood from death will be appropriate for such a crime." Gasps rippled through the mass, and whispers ignited like flames through the shocked crowd. There were even heads shaking while others began to holler out protests.

"My decision stands. As your Queen, my judgment is final. Silence!" The crowd hushed as quickly as it had erupted.

"My Queen," a voice interjected. The Teleen queen turned to look at Captain Dylan, now kneeling before her, head bowed and stiff. "May I speak, Your Majesty?"

"Rise and speak, Captain Dylan. Your Queen has acknowledged you. Darren being your only brother, I am sure you have much to say." She held her hand out as if to summon him to rise. Dylan rose slowly and stared back at the petite woman. His face was a well of stillness, eyes empty and blank with no feelings escaping from their pits.

"I beg thee to please reconsider. I ask you, my dear Queen, to spare the life of my only brother, Darren. I carry an oath to our long-deceased mother to care for him in her absence. Please, consider an alternative price." Dylan bowed his head again and did not look back up. He seemed to be acknowledging the Queen's dominance over him and over all the people that called the caverns their home.

Shade blinked as she glanced at him, the Queen, and Darren. *Brother? So that's why there's such a resemblance. Darren is*

Dylan's brother! Of course, she thought, putting it all together.

Dylan seemed genuinely concerned, but his face remained hard. He did not seem like the snickering captain of the guard she'd met her first day at the Teleen caverns. He stood still and humbled before the Queen. She wondered if he was holding his breath while he waited for her answer. Why he would defend such a rotten man, even if he were his own flesh and blood, was beyond her.

"Dylan, my faithful captain, you have served me well for so many years. I'm afraid only a fair blood trade would suffice. Knowing your mother's wishes for you and your brother, I will consider this in my decision." She tilted her head and watched him, studying his stoic demeanor as if reading his innermost desires. "What if I amend my judgment, let's say, for an equal payment? Would you trade your life in your brother's place, then? I will only alter the death price if you trade your blood and services for your brother's life."

Captain Dylan looked up at that remark. His eyes widened in surprise and seemed utterly tortured. He studied the Queen in confusion. "I'm sorry, Your Majesty, but what sort of blood price trade do you mean?"

The Queen smiled, glancing at Shade before speaking again. "I require that you say yes before I explain. Will you trade your life for your brother's? I promise this will not mean a death sentence on your part if you do so. Your brother will be freed, but only if you agree to the terms in full."

Dylan stared intensely at the Queen for what seemed like an eternity. Letting his eyes drop to the floor, he let out a defeated sigh. Shade watched him gulp and think hard on the Queen's words. He nodded to himself, blinking back up toward her. He visibly straightened, regaining composure once more. "Yes, My Queen. In place of my brother, I will assume punishment for crimes he has incurred, short of death." He dropped his gaze again, hiding his face as it flushed with a scarlet heat. He was probably not too happy about having to learn his fate after he swore to trade places with Darren.

In eager anticipation, Shade glanced between him and the Queen.

"Well then, Dylan, I am glad to hear that an honorable man such as yourself would assume a lesser man's punishment. He's undeserving of such a thing, even if he is your brother. So, in consideration of your own innocence, I hereby proclaim that your blood payment will be a blood bind to Shade. You are to protect, follow and serve her until the blood price is paid in full. Release from it will only come when the land of Faerie deems it fulfilled. Any failure to do these things will revoke the trade, and the original judgment on Darren of death will stand."

Shade shook her head, shocked at what the Queen had just done. "No, please, Your Majesty. I don't need a servant or a guard. I have an entourage already. My friends will guard me. He didn't do anything! I can't do this. Please release him! It was Darren who did it." She looked up at the Queen and knew immediately that protesting wasn't going to do any good.

"Shade, he cannot reject this punishment. To do so is to bestow death upon his brother. You must accept this, or you condemn Darren to death. Only time will tell when Dylan will be deemed worthy to be released from the blood bond. For now, please come here and give me your hand." The Queen's still face gave nothing away. Defeat hung on Shade's shoulders as she complied, giving her left hand to the petite woman. "I must bind you to make this trade complete. It is the way of the Teleen. Dylan will serve you faithfully, protect you, and keep you safe. He cannot betray you or cause you any harm, for if he does, he will break his oath, and death will consume his brother immediately. Don't be afraid. Come." She slipped her hand into Shade's, giving it a reassuring squeeze.

Shade held her breath. She was trembling so hard that it shook her entire body, leaving her unsure if she could stay standing for much longer. Fainting would be a very bad thing right now.

"Dylan, come here and give me your hand, too."

The captain stepped up to stand across from Shade, holding out his hand without further argument. The Queen held out a small, sharp knife, its hilt gleaming with blood red rubies. Shade felt its magic rush over her in a ripple of warm energy. It was an oath maker, the Queen explained, made especially for blood bonds.

She took Shade's hand, palm up and pressed the knife softly into it, dragging the blade across her palm. Soon, deep red blood seeped from the wound and trickled down her wrist. The Queen repeated the process again on Shade's other palm. Amazingly, the cuts didn't hurt at all. For all she knew, the knife's magic took the pain away. The Queen turned and did the same to Dylan. She then took both their hands and clasped them together.

Shade looked up at Dylan as their warm, thick blood mingled. She could feel his fiery aura spilling onto hers, but it did not burn. It made her feel powerful as Dylan's aura licked the edges of her own, revealing sides of him he'd kept hidden, making Dylan's grip tighten. She felt his strength and magic but did not feel threatened. Looking into his gray steel orbs, she noticed how they'd somehow gone dull and blank. A touch of contempt seeped from them as he bore his eyes into her. If he felt anything more, he did not show it.

His features hardened, like a statue. None of his feelings bled through as his magic slipped away from her once more as he regained his full control over it. His aura turned solid and hard as a shield once he'd accepted his fate coldly, and she could no longer feel his emotions.

"It is done then. You may let go. Captain Dylan of the Teleen, you will forfeit your position and assume your place in Shade's entourage until the land of Faerie decides that you have fulfilled your oath."

Their hands dropped down to their sides. Dylan turned and walked back down toward Darren, stopping about a foot away. He turned his head and glared at his younger brother, who looked a lot like him. Dylan's cold eyes narrowed and burned with a tinge of hate. He reached out and cut the binds on his brother's wrists with a rough, uncaring jerk.

"Darren, this is the last time I ever save you. You're on your own now, for we're no longer brothers." He turned once more and disappeared into the thick murmuring crowd. Many gasps sounded out at his declaration. The ultimatum was unexpected and stunned Darren. He stood still, tilting his head down to avoid the looks from the crowd. His eyes squeezed shut as some tears formed in his lids. He whirled around suddenly and pushed his way through the crowd, shoving anyone who got in his way. Both men were gone in a matter of seconds, leaving Shade frozen beside the Queen.

Shade glanced down at her bloody palm. The cut had knitted itself closed and was now healed, leaving a light, pink-colored scar that was thin and tight. Finding her group awaiting her, Shade found Soap holding out a hand for her. Taking it, she felt relieved to see his smiling face as he helped her down from the dais. She joined her entourage and shuffled out of the grand room. She could finally breathe, even if it were just for a moment.

Chapter Nine

THE GROUP HUDDLED together near the glass bridge, silent and solemn. Their backpacks laid strewn about, reminding Shade of a summer camp she'd visited in the thick forests of California. People were still skittering about, stuffing packs with rations and supplies.

Shade sat on the ground with her own backpack already stuffed, since she'd never really had a chance to unpack before the attack. It sat balanced between her crisscrossed legs, ready to go. She held onto it as a child would a precious stuffed animal or blanket for comfort. It felt like the only thing in the world that actually did belong to her. They'd risen early the day after the trial to reassemble and continue with the rest of the journey. Shade felt almost entirely healed, but her spirits remained dampened. Her head ached with everything that had happened to her. Taking comfort in her solitary spot, she watched the others frantically rushing around. At least Sary retrieved her clothes, cell phone, and charger from her old room. Shade had refused to enter it ever again. Her phone sat fully charged and put away, for there was no signal penetrating the dark stone cavern.

Her chestnut brown hair was pulled back into two thick, tight braids, making her look even younger than her seventeen years. She'd let Braelynn fuss over her this morning, even though she'd already pulled it back into a sloppy ponytail. The tight braids Braelynn had woven her hair into were intricate but restrictive. However, she could deal with it since it made Braelynn feel so useful and motherly.

Soap came by and lingered before her. His tall figure seemed gigantic while she sat scrunched on the ground. His hair was also tied back but lay in a simple half braid, with leather and beads streaming through it and shimmering under the torchlight. He was looking at her with his bright eyes, so deep in color in the dim light that they seemed to glow with their own light. "Hiya there, kid. You feelin' all right?" His voice twanged with a made-up southern drawl. He winked and tipped an imaginary hat to her.

She smiled up at him and nodded, not feeling quite as gloomy as before. He was definitely in a joking mood. "I'm okay, maybe just a bit tired. I'm not sleeping so well since…." She laid her chin on her pack as she pulled it tighter against herself and closed her eyes.

Soap sat beside her on the ground and sighed as he watched the rest of the group tidying up. He turned toward her with his smile gone and his eyes immensely serious. "Are you having nightmares?"

She nodded and breathed in slowly. She closed her eyes, still leaning her head on her pack and arms. Sleep was definitely lacking, severely affected by her anxiety and paranoia throughout the night. Every creak, every rustle made her eyes fling open and her heart jump from her chest. She resorted to sitting up in bed with a dagger in hand, just in case.

Shade wondered if she'd ever feel safe going to bed

again.

"Well, let Braelynn and Sary know. I'm sure one of them can whip you up a dreamless sleep potion. It might help for the first few weeks. We're leaving in five minutes. Did you eat anything this morning?"

"Yes, I ate some toast and fruit. I wasn't too hungry, though." Opening her eyes, she sat up as she saw Dylan enter the area. His captain's uniform was gone, replaced with different leather and metal armor. It was probably his traveling armor. His helmet was also gone, but his sword was still strapped to his back. His brown tunic was soft under the leather and lacked any kind of ornamentation at all. Wrist sheaths were strapped securely on his upper arms, and as he moved, they flashed slightly, revealing silver knives. He also had a sheath strapped to each thigh, and his belt had pouches with more weapons laced throughout. He was well armed and carried a small pack strapped to his back. The long locks of hair he'd previously possessed were now cut to a standard length for a human male. Shade wondered why he was sporting the short style, especially when he was the only faery man she'd met so far who didn't have long hair.

"I guess this means he's joining us now," Shade said with her voice lowered. "Soap, why did he chop his hair off? It was so long. Did he have to cut it for the journey?"

Soap shook his head and leaned in toward her, his voice just above a whisper.

"No, Shade. The fey do it as a sign of mourning. He's probably in mourning for his brother, treating it as a death. It may also be because it's a sort of enslavement that he has to be with us. He might just be mourning his freedom and former life. Your guess is as good as mine." He jumped up to stand so fast, he appeared to have just floated up. He held out a hand to Shade again, smiling. "May I have this dance, oh ye fair maiden?"

"You know what? You're such a dork." She took his

hand but gave him a playful whack when he started to dance, swinging her around in a circle. "Stop it already!" Shade smiled again, feeling him radiate calming warmth, too. Somehow, she just knew it was for her benefit that the Fey did that. What they gave off in their magic was like happy juice to a moody teenager. It made her feel safe at least, and that's what she wanted most of all right now.

Dylan was watching them from across the way. His empty, blank stare made Shade shiver as her happy mood faded with his icy look. She couldn't blame him for being mad, but it really wasn't her fault he was stuck guarding her. He was going to have to just deal with it.

He started walking toward her and Soap. Holding her breath, Shade hoped he wasn't going to be a pain. Dylan stopped right in front of her, causing her to take a step back as he invaded her space. He seemed to know that it made her nervous to stand near any of the Teleen, even if they were shielded with glamour.

"Dylan of the Teleen clan reporting for duty, Miss Shade. What will you have of me today?" He stood still, so close to her she could feel his warm breath across her cheek. His steel eyes were smoldering. She was not sure if it was just his eyes or if she saw a twinge of hatred swimming in them.

"Nothing, Dylan, I...." She let her words trail off and shook her head. It took a moment or two for what she wanted to say to come out right. Straightening, she decided to go ahead and glare right back at him. "I'm not your master, boss or whatever. I didn't want this, so go do what you want, okay? I really don't care." Shade took another step back to dodge around him but stopped herself. "If it's any consolation, this was not my idea. Darren should've manned up and taken his punishment though I do think death is an easy way out. If there's anything I can do to help you unbind us, you just go right ahead and let me know." He remained glaring at the ground with his jaw set hard. She sighed when he gave her nothing but silence as she swung her pack onto her back and walked away.

Jack motioned her over, as well as all the others. Everyone quickly finished their packing and circled around him. "Okay, everyone, we are way behind schedule. Today we anticipate to at least make it to the river lands. We will be near a large iron city, so once we approach, we must be very careful. We should stay near the rivers and be out of sight. If we are spotted, we might have to do memory charms on any humans that may be nearby. I would like to avoid that. You know how much fun that is," he said sarcastically.

"Oh, and we have two newcomers on our quest. Everyone welcome Dylan, former captain of the Teleen." His arm swung out toward Dylan, who stood just outside the circle, his arms crossed and his gaze at the ground. "Also, Miss Sylphi of the Teleen has so graciously volunteered to serve as a tracker. When our supply runs low, she can help us track down food around the Santiran fountains, where there are no cities for miles. Please welcome them both with open arms."

He held his arm out to Sylphi, who came over and gave him an aggressive hug, apparently invading his space. He stumbled back a bit as he shifted his weight, but he did avoid losing his balance. She laughed and smiled, as though it was nothing to volunteer on a treacherous mission.

Shade glared at her. She hadn't forgotten how friendly she'd been with Darren the night of the attack. Sylphi caught her glare and smiled sweetly at her, ignoring the look on Shade's face. *I wouldn't trust her as far as I could throw her boney, pointy body*, she thought.

"Everyone should be ready by now. Let's go!" Ewan's voice boomed in the cavern, echoing down the ravine. The group all swung packs onto their backs and sheathed the weapons they'd been cleaning. In about a minute, they were all crossing the great glass bridge. Shade held her breath as she walked across. Unfortunately, looking down made her stomach ache, so she avoided it at all costs. She'd be happy never to cross this blasted bridge again.

They journeyed through the same tunnels and large rooms they first passed on the way in. Shade felt relief wash over her as she caught sight of the great doors. They creaked open, and a stream of early morning sun beamed in and grew wider to meet them. Shade increased her pace and laughed when she felt the rush of the cool spring morning air. The sun was warm on her face, and the tension she'd been feeling seemed to be easing. Somehow, she knew she was not going to miss the Teleen Caverns.

Chapter Ten

T HEY TRAVELED UP and around the base of one of the mountains, which were at the top of the caverns they called home for a few days. The trail winded around lazily through a canyon made from a dry, dead river. The path was packed with flakey clay that crunched underfoot as they traversed through it. Rocks smoothed over by centuries of water littered the ground in different sizes. There were signs of drought as they walked along the riverbed. They spied dead bushes and wilted desert sage still holding on though barely. The occasional scent of sage bushes and wildflowers permeated the air, but so did the slight odor of old, rotted vegetation mixed with dirt.

The sand got into everything, clinging to Shade's pants, shoes and gritting against her skin inside her sneakers and socks. She stopped to empty the dust and gravel out of her shoes quite often. Most times, she'd sit on the smooth boulders that were scattered along the path. The advantage of the canyon was that there were many shady areas blocking off the blaring sun and heat that intensified as the day wore on. The occasional desert lizard or jackrabbit darted across their paths. They shimmied their bodies into the cracks of earth beneath the stones or bushes. How could anything survive out there? It was mind-boggling. Water was scarce, and Shade was grateful she had some to enjoy.

The group stopped for a rest under a large overhang of striped red, white, and orange stone. It hovered over them like a massive giant, threatening to fall at any moment. Ewan assured her it would not fall because it was well-anchored and more under the ground than above. Shade sat at the edge of its shadow. She wanted to be ready in case she had to bolt to avoid being crushed alive.

She opened her pack and pulled out her canteen. She drank quickly, and the cool water felt refreshing as it tumbled down her throat. She'd have to thank Jack for the canteen. It refilled itself with the magical water and never ran dry.

Pulling out a bag of rations, she began munching on the nuts, dried jerky, and flat bread. She immediately felt more alert and less tired. Glancing around, she noticed how the desert seemed to be transitioning into a more grassy and bushy area. Off in the distance, greenery weaved itself into the barren desert. It grew thicker and thicker the farther her eyes scanned. Great pines and coniferous trees shone small but bright in color, speckling the mountainsides. She wondered if they would be heading into that forest before nightfall.

Dylan parked himself at the edge of the shadows, too, but not close enough to be considered sitting with her. He had his head down, also stuffing bits of food into his mouth. He never spoke with anyone in the group. If he was angry or sad, it did not show. His antisocial behavior made her wonder what he was thinking.

It was tempting to inch closer to him and try to pry some

information out of him. He didn't seem hostile, but he wasn't exactly welcoming either.

Sary, Braelynn, and Stephen were sitting together and chatting loudly. They were in good spirits and enjoying the outdoors. It seemed as if they felt suffocated underground, too. They told Shade that they drew their powers from the Earth and the elements. Outdoors, the sun, nature, and life replenished their strength, what stone could not do alone. The other men were sitting near each other, remaining somewhat quiet as they chomped on their rations. They chatted amongst themselves occasionally, laughing and nodding with full mouths. Their manners were a bit atrocious, and it made Shade giggle to herself. She was enjoying their company, and they were beginning to feel like a surrogate family.

Speaking of family, Shade's thoughts wandered to her mother and siblings. What were they doing right now? Had they forgotten her? She wondered how strong the memory charm was Ilarial used on her family. A sinking feeling in her stomach made tears sting her eyes. *It's going to be okay,* she told herself. Remembering the times they had all gone camping when she was younger and her father was still alive made her smile and savor the memories.

Camping was a constant distraction from the everyday problems her family faced. She would share her tent with her younger sister, Anna, who was three years younger and, most of the time, quite a pest. She enjoyed following Shade around like a puppy, which annoyed Shade to no end. Anna would butt into Shade's stuff or activities all the time, messing with her Barbie dolls, kicking her arrangements over, or even resorting to just stealing her toys or accessories. Shade hated it at the time, but now she'd give anything to have Anna bugging the crap out of her. Maybe she'd be sitting with her, sharing food and drawing in the fine sand with a twig. Anna did have a great big imagination. She'd tell Shade the longest stories about her day at school or simply made some up. It always took hours to tell it just right. She'd love to hear an Anna story right now.

Taking a bite of jerky, she tried to distract her thoughts by concentrating on chewing the tough meat. It was suddenly lonely though she knew her new friends would not let anything happen to her. She still longed to hear from her best friend Brisa, who could be counted on for a quick joke when things were bad. She pulled her cell phone out of her pack and stared at the reception bars. For one reason or another, they were nonexistent, even out here, above ground.

Tears broke through the tension on her lids and slid warmly down her cheeks as she stuffed the phone back into the pack. Pulling her knees up to her chin, she nuzzled into them, hiding her face.

This will not last forever, and soon I'll be home. She sniffled and pulled a soft washcloth from her pack, wiping her face and clearing her drippy nose, exhaling as she stuffed the cloth back into the pack. Jumping with a start, she realized Dylan now crouched down next to her and was staring with his intense, steel-grey eyes. His face was alert and observing as if waiting for some sort of word from her.

"What?" Her voice came out sharper than she'd meant it to, but she did not like him interrupting her melancholy memories.

"You're in distress."

She fought the urge to be a smart ass. "Really, you think so?" Shade snapped.

He smirked, settling down next to her, not waiting for an invitation. "Don't get angry. I only meant to help. I am bound by blood to serve you, aren't I? Well, if you're in distress, I can feel it now, and I have to try to fix it. I'm compelled to. It's part of the magic." Avoiding her glare, he studied the dirt with increased interest.

Shade gawked at him. His face froze as he retreated into his own memories while his hand sifted through the fine sand.

Then he became so still, she could not see him even breathing. She waved her hand in front of his face, and he jerked out of his trance, shifting his eyes back to her. "Are *you* all right?" She asked.

"What do you care?" He asked coldly.

Shade pulled her gaze away first and back to the ground, smearing her tears away with the back of her hand. His words stung and put an ache in her chest. "I just thought that maybe, um, well I...oh, never mind." She pressed her lips together, shaking her head. It was useless to talk to Dylan; the walls he built around himself were too thick. She could almost feel them pressing up against her, palpable and frigid.

"Why don't you just go away?" Shade hissed at him, irritated. She began scooting away when he grabbed the sleeve of her hoodie. Looking up, she expected an angry glare but found an ocean of pain floating behind his eyes.

His mouth tensed with unexpected emotions, making her consider the seriousness of the situation. "I would, but I can't. Like a cord between us, it binds me to you. Where you go, I must then follow. If you go too far, I am compelled to search for you until I find you. If I try to run, I would freeze in my own steps and be made to turn back. I'm anything but free. I'm your slave. I intend to see this to its finality and end it." He snickered then and let her go. "'til death do us part, Shade." He ripped off a bite of his jerky and chewed without looking back at her.

Shade didn't try to leave again. A tight knot formed in her stomach, making her want to throw up what little she'd eaten. Nothing about this seemed right. She could feel the ties pressing down on Dylan. She didn't even like him and didn't believe he liked her either, for that matter. It was like having to choose the kid that no one ever picks for your team in gym class. You didn't want to do it, but you had to and it sucked.

"Alright, everyone, let's get going again. We have to make it to the Emerald Forest of the River Lands before nightfall. That's where we will stop for the night." Ewan motioned the group to follow as everyone jumped to their feet. Packs were slung back on and weapons were put away.

Shade followed suit, watching as Dylan re-strapped his sword sheath over his thin armor. He stretched his arms and legs as he stood, displaying well-defined muscles that rippled in his arms. His golden-brown tan meant he'd seen some sun, unlike the pale Teleen in the caverns. She wondered if the Teleen guards were the only ones that spent any time outside the caverns. Their Queen was so chalky-pale, Shade doubted she ever ventured out.

She had unanswered questions about the Teleen and wondered whom she could ask for answers. Glancing at Dylan, she pondered asking him but quickly decided against it. Dylan would be her last resort.

She jogged up to Sary, falling into step beside her. Stephen moved to the side when he spotted her, giving her a curt nod as she passed. He and Sary were always glued to each other's side. Shade flushed at the thought of them as lovers. Of the entire group, these two were the most inseparable.

"Hi, Shade! Everything all right?" Sary's sweet voice flowed from her cherry red lips. She was quite lovely, beautiful actually. It was no wonder she was royalty. Why she'd be out here in the middle of who knew where, getting all dirty, grimy, and really sweaty, Shade would never know.

"Um, I was wondering about something."

"What are you wondering about?"

"Why I didn't get burned when Darren touched me. I wasn't electrocuted or burned. Jack told me I would be. Darren wasn't in glamour at all, and Jack and Soap said that if you touch a Teleen when they're not glamoured, you could get electrocuted or burned. Darren did seem surprised that I hadn't. He became frustrated when he realized that, but then I think he found it fascinating and intriguing." She heard her voice quiver as a lump began forming in her throat. She could see everything so clearly in her mind as if it was happening all over again.

Sary's eyebrows furrowed as she thought about Shade's question. "Oh, Shade, I know it's hard for you to talk about that night. Honestly, I don't know the answer. You might want to ask Jack about it. He might know of some instances or possible reasons why Darren could not harm you. Somehow, I think one of your powers is some sort of protection from the fire and lightning of the Teleen fey. I find it quite interesting."

Shade nodded and thanked Sary for her thoughts. Jack would be the one to ask about this. She'd meant to chat with him about the effects of Teleen powers on her for some time.

"Jack! Wait up!" They were on a hill, and the rocks stood jagged on the trail. She slowed her pace to maneuver around the razor edges of stone until she was right behind him.

"Hey there, what can I do for you?" Jack's cheerful mood was infectious.

She matched his pace but could not walk beside him with the trail narrowing and twisting around the large, rough boulders. Keeping an eye on the shifting dirt underneath, she continued, "I've meant to ask you some things."

"Go for it." He pulled himself up a steep part of the trail and turned to help Shade over the hump.

"Thanks. I was wondering, when Darren attacked me, he let his glamour fall away as he touched me, so why didn't I burn or get electrocuted like you said I would?"

Jack stopped cold and turned toward her. Horror flashed across his face, his eyes growing dark with shock. "What? Are you sure he let his glamour slide? No, it would have killed you. There's no way you would've survived." He narrowed his eyes at her, studying her face for something unknown to her. "Are you sure you remember right? You don't think that when you hit your head, you might've thought he let his shields down?"

Shade shook her head. There was no way she remembered wrong. "No, I know what I saw. He let his glamour melt away as he held onto me while he was on fire. His skin burned with bright blue flames that lit the entire room, flowing over his skin, like sparking electricity. I remember it as clearly as I see you now."

"I know what you're saying, Shade. I do not doubt you, but it's just that it's not possible. I don't know what to tell you. I've never heard of anyone, especially a Halfling, surviving a full-blown Teleen touch. That's exactly why our race is dying." He grunted, half sliding down a boulder.

"What do you mean?"

"Well…" He wiped the sweat from his brow, taking a deep breath as he rested. "We…we can't breed outside our own race. It would be fatal to get close enough to anyone other than a Teleen." Jack pressed his lips into a thin, hard line as he started walking again. His face remained pensive.

"But Jack, isn't Soap a Teleen halfling? You're saying it's not possible, but he's evidence against that, isn't he?" Shade hurried to keep up with Jack, for his step quickened.

Soap, who'd been walking ahead of them, paused and followed them with great interest.

"Soap is also part changeling. Changelings can 'change' into a Teleen if they want to. I think that's one of only a few ways pairing outside our race could be possible. Changelings are all but extinct, though. We don't even know who his parents were. To find a changeling to mate with would be like hitting the lottery for a Teleen-born. It just doesn't happen. The chances are so slim. Only those with fire affinities could ever pair with one of us. Wait, maybe…." He stopped again and was really staring at her now. Shade stopped too, suddenly feeling the weight of his stare like she was under a microscope. "You're not a changeling, Shade. Are you?"

"No, well, not that I know of," Shade stammered.

"Have any fire magic?"

"No, sorry. I can't change into anything, or start any kind of fire. I'd think I would know if I could." Her voice cracked, leaving her suddenly unsure about anything. She was part faery, but she didn't know what type of faery.

Me, a changeling? That's highly doubtful, Shade thought. It was already unnerving to think she was anything more than human.

Jack shook his head before looking at her again. His friendly smile was beginning to light up his face once more. "Nah, I don't think you're a changeling, Shade. I know all this sounds really strange, and I wish I could help you more, but I've never come across something like this before. If I ever find out anything about it, you'll be the first to know, okay?"

Shade nodded as he patted her back and turned to walk down another narrow and rocky hill. Shade sighed. She wasn't sure if she knew anything more than she had before.

Chapter Eleven

SHADE SAT ON a large, smooth rock near her tent, proud that she erected it all by herself. The fresh breeze rippled the nylon violently, but it held. She staked it down well, just like her father had shown her. She had lots of practice staking down tents for herself and her sister. Every time they went camping, she was in charge of tent setup. Remembering how much she loathed it made her chuckle. She thanked her lucky stars that her father had pounded the basics of camping and surviving in the wild into her, just in case. She doubted he had ever considered how useful the knowledge would be on a perilous faery journey.

Dinner was cooking atop a blazing fire. There was a fox roasting over it, which Than had skinned, gutted, and staked to a spit. It turned round and round over the flames, giving off a pleasant but smoky aroma. It looked like he'd done this many times before. The fox was a good size, nice and plump, and would feed them all. She wished she could take a shower, but that wasn't going to happen out here. Once again, she was covered in dirt, and a film of her salty sweat stuck to her skin. She was sure it would never come off.

The air was cooling rapidly as the sun sank over the mountains. Shivering, she rubbed her arms to warm them. She'd traded her hoodie for a jacket but wished she'd brought a thicker one. She felt somewhat unprepared for the cold nights, even after layering her clothes and wearing a thicker sweater. Unfortunately, the extra clothes were not working too well at guarding her against the cold.

Dylan plopped down next to her, disturbing her thoughts before draping a large, thick, fur-lined blanket over her shoulders. She jumped up, letting the blanket spill off her into a cascading heap. Dylan grabbed it just before it hit the ground.

"What are you doing?" Shade glared at him, her face flushed with anger. It wasn't nice to intrude on her space, and she was through tolerating it.

He held his free hand up, smirking a little at the same time. "The polite thing to say is *thank you*. I'm not sure what humans are accustomed to, but when someone gives you a blanket to keep warm in the cold, our kind is grateful. But who am I to say so? I might be wrong to think that way," he added sarcastically.

"You're a prick, Dylan, you know that? I can see it's in your blood, by the way. Just stay away from me. You and your brother can just go to hell!" Shade stood there staring at him, her breath steaming in the cool air as her words came out in a huff. The night pushed hard against the remnants of the day, making her feel suddenly overexposed. Dylan remained calm while he watched her. He lifted the blanket up to her once more. His smirk smoothed out, and the former captain's face fell flat and unreadable. His eyes did give away some feeling; there seemed to be a spark in them that showed he was amused by her reaction.

"Shade, just take the blanket, okay? It's cold out," he muttered. "I'm not really affected by the cold, but, being that you're mortal...." He looked like he was working hard to suppress a smile. "Well, I packed for two. I knew you'd need help out here." His smile returned as he continued. "Really, it's a warm blanket. Think of it as a peace offering." Standing up when she did not go to him, he moved closer until he was in her face, almost touching. He swung the blanket around and draped it over her shoulders. Shade stiffened but let him place the blanket on her, and she held onto it this time, unsure of what to do. He nodded, looking satisfied before turning to walk away.

"Dylan, wait," Shade choked out. Her voice was tight in her throat. She turned to look at him as he stopped in his tracks. He didn't turn around but paused, waiting. "I... I'm sorry, Dylan. I feel like you don't like me, but you don't even know me. Maybe that reminds me of Darren a bit, and that freaks me out. You two are pretty similar, but I know you aren't like him. I know that... I can feel it. I...." She sighed, frustrated with her stumbling tongue. "Thanks for the blanket. I do appreciate it."

"You're welcome, Shade," he answered with a little more warmth than he had ever shown before.

She glanced around and noticed the others working on their own tents. Jack had one, and so did Ewan. Sary and Braelynn looked like they were sharing, and so were Stephen and Than. Shade thought that maybe some of the group were probably pairing up because they didn't have enough tents. Soap had his own tent, and unless they were sharing, it was unclear where Dylan was going to sleep.

"Don't you have a tent, Dylan?"

"I do, but I find it really confining. Besides, I have to stay by you, and there isn't enough room for another tent here. The ground is my bed tonight." He tilted his head slightly, one eye watching her intently.

"Why do you have to camp by me? Do you really have

to?"

"No," he stated simply.

"Then why are you hovering? I feel like you're suffocating me."

"No, I wouldn't ever do that. I'd never hurt you!" He whirled back around, his face now serious and his eyes wide. He'd taken her words at face value.

"Whoa, I don't mean literally! It's like an expression." Relieved as he relaxed, she sighed. "Look, you don't have to be stuck to me like glue. I'm not an invalid, and you're not my bodyguard. Get this straight: I do like my space." She'd lost her patience with him and headed off, with the blanket still wrapped around her, toward the smoking carcass that was dinner.

***

D
INNER WAS SATISFYING. The fox tasted amazing, or maybe it was just because Shade was starving. It was such a long hike that day, her muscles ached and burned intensely. She had never felt so hungry before, and now, so tired. Sitting on a fallen log by the main campfire, she watched the flames lick the twigs and branches smoldering with soot. Ashes littered the ground around the fire as it flickered and crackled. The heat felt comforting, forcing the chill of the evening away.

It felt cozy in the blanket Dylan had provided, making her feel just a tad bit guilty for snapping at him, especially since his gift had turned out to be so useful. *Okay, I'll try to be nicer to Dylan. This isn't his fault.* She hadn't meant to snap at Dylan, but everything was really overwhelming her. She'd been attacked twice in less than a week. It was hard enough for her to keep up with everyone in the group physically. Her lack of appreciation for outdoor activities didn't help. Taking a deep breath, she knew these were the least of her problems.

Dad... isn't my real dad, she thought sadly. It was difficult to accept. She wasn't glad he was dead, but she was relieved he would never have to know this. How would she deal with it? To make matters worse, she was bound to Dylan, sharing some kind of mutant blood bind connecting her to him, and to Darren in some weird sadistic way, too. *Dylan's blood is Darren's blood....* She cringed at the thought.

Her life was not turning out quite as she planned. She was supposed to be in high school, cramming for finals, and graduating in three weeks. This was not supposed to happen, and she missed Brisa so much. Who else could tell so many jokes, especially around a warm campfire on a freezing night? She wished Brisa had been pulled into this mess so Shade wouldn't be alone right now. Even with her new friends surrounding her and their happy chatter floating about the fire, she felt the loneliness creep in again.

Sary walked over and sat next to her on the log. She winked at Shade and then settled her gaze on the fire. The silence between them was thick; Shade could sense she was aching to ask her something. She wondered what it could possibly be. Sary was quiet, for the most part unless she was with Stephen. Shade saw how Sary stared dreamily into his eyes whenever they were talking. His face was a mirror of hers, and their devotion radiated around them like some protective, blissful bubble. Shade couldn't help but feel a little envious of their bond.

Shaking the thoughts away, she scolded herself. She wasn't the type to get jealous. She was actually quite happy being the responsible older sister in a single parent home with four kids. It gave her tons of freedom to do whatever she wanted to, and she felt like she was the other adult in the house. She had no time for boys. They just mucked things up, anyway.

Her thoughts wandered to her mother, Jade. She had shoulder length hair, a beautiful shade of brown with caramel highlights streaked throughout it. It was wavy and never wanted to stay where she'd like it. She was happy just running her hands through and did not fuss much with it. Her big, brown eyes were fascinating, too. They had a glint of gray and honey running through both of her irises. The hazel coloring in her eyes definitely stood out with only a touch of makeup on her olive skin. Shade was glad she took after her mother; she'd always seen her mother as a beautiful woman.

"Shade?" Sary's voice gently broke into her thoughts.

"Yes, Sary?"

Sary paused for a moment, studying Shade's face before speaking. "When this is over, will you return to Faerie at all? Or will you want to forget this all happened? I wonder because, you see... I can feel your reluctance even now about completing this task. I know it's a hard thing to ask of you, being that our world is so alien." She sighed nervously before continuing. "But we need you more than you could possibly perceive or understand. I can't even imagine what you think of all this, especially after everything that's happened so far."

Shade felt anxious and slightly guilty because she'd been so caught up in herself and hadn't thought about the rest of the group. She hoped she hadn't seemed too antisocial tonight. Maybe it had an adverse effect on them. She let her eyes linger on the fire, thinking hard about how to answer Sary. It was so difficult to predict the future. She never thought this would be happening to her. She searched for the right thing to say.

"Sary, I hope you don't feel like I could just say goodbye and be done with everyone so easily. You've helped me so much already. I have to admit that this new world is confusing to me. It scares me to death, and I don't feel like I belong here. I don't have the strength or the right training for this. Everyone has said I have magic in me, but I don't know how to use it. How could I ever survive in your world? I just feel terribly vulnerable. I would love to visit you guys when this is all done, but I don't think I could live here.

Sary was staring at Shade, an amused look dancing on her face. She started laughing so hard she almost fell off the log.

"What's so funny?" Shade asked, annoyed at her reaction. She was definitely confused. What the hell could be so funny about what she said?

Sary stopped and shook her head as she cleared her throat. "I'm so sorry, Shade. I don't mean to insult you. I just never thought of our world as that different. It's nice to get an outsider's view. You're right, though. How inconsiderate of me. Of course, you don't feel safe. Ilarial did tell us that it was our job to show you how to use your magic. You have more to you than you think you do. I'm still baffled on how you managed to trap Darren in the mirror shards. He was bloody mad about it, but I can't say he didn't deserve it though. He deserved that glass prison and more for what he did to you." She paused, looking a bit more serious. "So how would you like your first official magic lesson?" She grinned, her eyes twinkling in the firelight.

"Oh, I don't know, Sary. I'm kinda tired and was about to go to bed. Maybe tomorrow?"

"No, no, right now. I promise it'll be a short one." She watched Shade squirm uncomfortably. "How 'bout it?" she pushed.

Shade pressed her lips tight in frustration. *There's no sense in fighting it,* she admitted to herself. "Ok."

Sary jumped up and clapped her hands, and her vibrant enthusiasm cheered Shade up. "Okay then, pick up any stone—really it can be any one that you find. Come on Shade, just pick the first one that catches your eye," Sary repeated when Shade hesitated.

Shade groaned but bent down from the log to study the ground. Searching the particles around her, she looked at each possible stone, but none seemed to stand out. Sitting up, she shook her head slightly, about to complain that she couldn't find one when a glint of rock flashed in the corner of her eye.

She reached out toward the edge of the log and retrieved it. The gray and white stone looked slightly out of place among the other white ones embedded in the sand. Dusting it on her jeans, she put it in the middle of her palm. "Like this one?"

"Yes, perfect! Now, take your stone and place your other hand over it. You have enough power within you. I can feel it radiating off of you like a fire." Sary waved her hand at her to make her go faster.

Shade protested but did what she was told. Her hands felt cold in the night air, and the stone was cool in the center of her warm palms. About to give up, she stopped, feeling it get warmer on her skin. She opened her hands, her eyes widening with amazement.

The rock was glowing with a dim yellow hue. The heat was radiating to her fingers from it, feeling as if it should have burned her, but it didn't. Shocked, she dropped it and cradled her hands on her chest. The sand puffed up around it like a meteorite landing. The stone lost its glow until it sat still and dusty once more. She peered up at Sary, who appeared pleasantly surprised.

"Wow, that was faster than I thought it would be. You just made your first light stone! You can make your own light with it and keep your hands warm too. It won't burn you if that's what you are thinking. This comes in handy on a dark and cold winter's night," she said with a smile. Bending down, she plucked the rock out of the gravel, holding it out to Shade.

"It's ok, Shade. Take it. It will only glow when you want it to. Remember, to activate it again, put it in between your hands once more. It belongs to you and only you now, so keep it near." She gave her a quick hug as Shade took it and stuffed it into her jeans. It was small and did not bulge out too much. "Good job! I'll let you get to your sweet dreams now." Sary jumped up and joined Stephen, who was calling out to her. They walked away from the fire and over to their tents, chatting quietly.

Shade let out a nervous breath. She'd been taken by surprise with the light stone, but she liked the idea of it. She fished through her pocket and brought the stone out once more. Reactivating it, it burned brighter this time in her palms and warmed her chilly fingers.

Staring at it for a moment before stuffing it back in her jeans, she rose and walked back to her tent.

Maybe, just maybe... I can do this after all.

Chapter Twelve

THE MURMUR OF voices amplified in the growing light of the morning. Shade moaned and wished she'd thought of bringing earplugs. Rolling over, she stuffed her pillow over her head, hoping to muffle the noise. *It can't be morning already*! It felt like she'd just laid her head on her pillow and closed her eyes. Hiking was definitely not on her cool list right now. Her muscles ached and burned.

"Shade, get up. We have to pack and get going. I brought you breakfast. You're going to need it." She felt her pillow fly off her face. Dylan stood crouched at the entrance of her tent, his lips tight with disapproval. He looked wide-awake, making her wonder how long he'd been up. Was it possible he didn't need to sleep? He motioned to a plate of food and drink lying by her. In an instant, he was gone.

Shade blinked and rubbed her eyes. Stuffing the pillow under her neck, groaning and wanting more sleep, disappointment ran through her mind. Sleep was a pleasure of the past now, something she couldn't quite remember having enough of. She glanced at the food he brought; bacon and fresh scrambled eggs with a bread roll were still steaming. It looked amazing and smelled even better.

This coaxed her out of her warm bed as she pulled the food and drink toward her. Inhaling the savory aromas, she was amazed at how hungry she was. Slurping down the sweet, warm tea that Dylan provided made her instantly feel more alert. She wondered what was in that drink; it was always so revitalizing. She'd have to ask someone. Besides, it was curious how they managed to have bacon and eggs so fresh out here in the wild. Munching on the rich, thick slices of bacon, she enjoyed every bit.

Well, this is my one pleasure out here in this hellhole. Shade sighed, frowning at her empty plate. The food was gone much too fast. *Good things just do not last around here.* She stretched and fumbled through her bag, pulling her brush, washcloth and towel out, and hoped there was somewhere to wash up. She yanked on her shoes then wrapped the blanket around her like a cape.

Stepping out into the cold morning air was like being electrocuted. It stung her cheeks and sent a thrill down her body. *Yay, winter weather.* She wondered how it seemed to be a different season every place they went in the faery lands. It didn't seem possible it was spring back home.

Walking up toward the central fire, she looked around. She wanted to find and ask Braelynn or Sary where she could wash up, but Soap popped up in front of her instead. He grinned at her, showing off his pearly white teeth. "Where do you think you're sneaking off to, young lady?"

Shade froze in her tracks, her face flushing and feeling guilty without reason to. Tilting her head, she gazed back upon his still smiling but suspicious face.

"I'm not sneaking off anywhere. I just want to get cleaned up. You wouldn't happen to know where I could, um, go to uh, freshen up?" Her face flushed up scarlet once more under the cold air. Soap wasn't the one she'd wanted to ask.

"It's down that side of the hill a bit. It's a large red tent. Girls on the right, boys to the left." He winked, spun and trotted back to the camp. Shade gaped at him as he walked—no...skipped—away cheerfully. She shook her head. She couldn't get over how strange he was. They hadn't spoken much since they arrived at the Teleen caverns, making her wonder if he was just cautious with her since it was a Teleen who attacked her. It was something she'd have to talk to him about later.

She turned back in the direction he had pointed her to, gripping her supplies. Approaching the bathroom tent made her stop in confusion. It didn't look like anything special; the flaps were wind-worn and faded. She wondered how it was even big enough to hold two dressing rooms, let alone anything close to a washroom. She shrugged, too tired to contemplate it for long, and willed herself to get moving.

Inside, she was shocked at how warm and humid it was. The scent of flowers blooming in the springtime permeated the air, and the tent was definitely much bigger than it appeared on the outside. It even had a foyer with a table and hanging mirror. To the right of the wooden table hung a red curtain, and beside it a blue curtain. She supposed the colors were to separate the women and men.

Heading through the red drapery, assuming it was for women, she followed the hallway as it turned toward the left. In the end, it turned again to the right and opened onto a large room filled with mirrors on one side. On the other side were stalls with toilets and two showers next to them.

This reminds me of camp, only better. Shade was impressed but not curious enough to wonder for long how it was all possible. She was just grateful it was there. She laid her stuff on one of the chairs and pulled it near one of the shower stalls. She was definitely surprised to find actual flushing toilets in the stalls. *Honestly, I can't believe the faeries have all this.* She just shook her head in disbelief and undressed, stepping into a shower stall. Soap, shampoo, and conditioner were provided, and she was thankful the water was hot. The steaming spray felt exhilarating on her skin and eased her aches. All too soon, she stepped out of the stall, dried her body and hair, and pulled on her fresh clothes. Running the brush through her tangled hair, she gritted her teeth then pulled it back into a tight ponytail.

Her reflection stared back at her from the mirror. For the first time since the attack, she saw her face. It made her suck in her breath. Her face was covered with small, healing pink lines, like spider webs, all across her right cheek. She looked down at her arms where she saw more of the same thin scars. *They're all over me....* Tracing them with her fingers, she found them smooth and a soft pink, nearly invisible to anyone who wasn't actually looking.

She studied the mirror for a bit longer to make sure it didn't ripple or look magical in any way. A shudder ran through her as she did her best not to be reminded of Darren. Turning away when she was satisfied it was just an ordinary mirror, she gathered her things and grabbed the blanket Dylan gave to her the night before. She wrapped it around herself, realizing she was in dire need of a coat. *The weather here is so annoying.* She didn't want to think about the scars, at least not yet. In a way, the blanket served as armor, covering them up and hiding her skin away. For that, she was grateful. Bundling up her old clothes in the towel, she turned to leave and ran right into Sylphi. Shade gasped, stumbling back with her eyes wide, regaining her balance.

"I'm so sorry, Shade. Did I frighten you?" Sylphi sneered slightly, studying Shade with inky black eyes. Her dark hair was down and a bit tousled like she had just rolled out of bed. However, it still managed to have some shine. She also held a bundle of clothes and a towel in her arms, pressed against her chest.

Shade gave a small, nervous laugh. "Oh… hello, Sylphi. No, well, maybe just a little. How long were you standing there?" She tried to swallow her anxiety and stood a bit straighter. Nothing about Sylphi made her feel warm and fuzzy. The girl radiated iciness like an open window in the late winter.

"Not for too long, really. I was just going to freshen up." She smiled her sickly, sweet smile, batting her eyelashes innocently. Her eyes were so dark, it was like staring into a pair of black holes. She continued to stare at Shade with her intensely black eyes and didn't make a move to get out of the way.

A chill ran through Shade, but she pressed her lips tight, attempting to smile back at the faery. The sight of her was unnerving to say the least. "Well, ok, I was just leaving. See you later." She had to side step a bit to get around Sylphi, who was still not budging from her spot.

"Why don't you just go home, Shade? No one really wants you here."

Shade hung in mid-step as she listened to Sylphi's icy voice. The woman was still not moving but slyly snickering. "You're too weak for this quest. Why don't you give up before you fail miserably? No one wants to be out here in this forsaken wilderness with you anyway. Do us a favor and quit already, *half-breed*," Sylphi hissed through her teeth, a menacing twinkle lingering in her gaze.

Well, heard that one before…

Shade glared at her in disgust. Shaking her head, Shade sneered right back. "I'm not a quitter, Sylphi. I need to do this, and nothing you say will change my mind. I don't believe *you* have to be here, though. You came by choice, remember? So did I… Maybe *you* should go home." She dodged Sylphi and stepped hurriedly through the doorway, ignoring Sylphi's snide laughter.

I wonder what the hell her problem is.

143

The cold air slapped her hard once she left the facilities tent, and her hair felt instantly frozen. She didn't stop, though; she hurried as fast as she could to her own tent, or what should've been her tent. All she found was Dylan sitting on the ground, patiently waiting next to her pack.

"What the...? Where's my stuff? What'd you do with my things?" Shade felt her anger tipping the scales and tried to grab a handle on it before hollering at him. She breathed in slowly and deeply, averting her glare away from him. It wasn't his fault that Sylphi had such a strange effect on her. She felt discombobulated. Her breath steamed like clouds floating out her nose and mouth.

He rolled his eyes almost as impatiently as she jumped on him.

"Well, Dylan?"

"Ok, calm down. I so graciously put away your things for you, since you were taking so long in the bath. We're leaving in just a few minutes, by the way." He stood up and held out her pack, dangling it from his fingers.

She snatched it from him with her free hand, biting her lip as he walked off to the main camp without another word. She sighed, realizing she hadn't even bothered to thank him. Why did it seem they clashed over everything? If they were going to be forced to spend so much time together, this would definitely have to stop. Kneeling down, she opened her pack and pulled out a sack for her dirty clothes. She stuffed them in and shoved it back into the pack.

This will just have to do until we reach the river. The clothes had a slight odor, and they needed a wash badly. Shade marched down the path to the main camp, joining the rest of the group. Ewan was already waving his arm around to capture everyone's attention as she chose a large boulder to sit on and rubbed her sleepy eyes. *It's already been a long day, and it's only the butt crack of dawn.*

144

"Alright, is everybody present? Soap, Jack, Braelynn..." The brawny man glanced about, squinting his eyes at the group. "Where's Sylphi?" Heads whirled around and searched the group.

"I just saw her in the bath tent. She's probably still there," Shade muttered.

"I'm right here." Sylphi stepped out from behind a tree and smiled at the group. Her hair was dried and slicked back into an even tighter ponytail than Shade's. She looked radiant in the morning sun, all dressed in white furs with her pack strapped to her back. She waved at Shade, a sly smirk on her face. Shade frowned back, but not as confidently. She wondered how Sylphi had bathed, dried, clothed herself, packed and made it to the group so fast. *It's probably a fey thing.*

"Alright, that should be everyone. We are heading to the great rivers. We will be getting wet, by the way. Shade, see Braelynn for water repellant charms so your stuff doesn't get soaked," he added as a side note, and then continued on. "We will be camping in the middle of the river lands. It's made up of seven rivers that wind, turn, and meet together at the Pacific Ocean. The rivers are pure Faerie territory, close to human towns. There is to be no wandering across the borders because the iron cities are too close to us along the coast."

He held up a large piece of parchment with a drawing of the rivers. They were vivid blue lines that twisted and curved around the vast green areas on the map. He pointed out the boundaries and again warned of the dangers of wandering too near a human city. Shade stared at the map, utterly confused. It looked so unfamiliar. If her sense of direction was right, they had to be near the coasts of California and Oregon. She didn't recall seeing such a tangle of large rivers there before. This revelation had her waving down Ewan.

"Those rivers are not on ordinary maps. You said it is purely faery territory? Does that mean that the river lands are hidden from humans?"

Ewan nodded, smiling at her curiosity. "Why yes, Shade. Aren't you just sharp as a knife this morning? Yep, human maps look quite different from faery maps, but we have the real world maps. Mortals' maps are only splices of the actual world. They don't know it, but there are vast areas of fey lands that are protected by enchantments and wards. So in essence, the area looks a lot smaller to them than it is." Ewan continued on, letting his finger trace along the borders on the paper. He then quickly rolled up the scroll map, ordering everyone to prepare to leave.

The desert wasteland twisted and blended into the lush forest of emerald green leaves and bushes. The land was riper and more fertile here, almost an artificially vibrant green. No matter which trail they took, Shade could hear rushing water in the distance. It surrounded them like endless background noise. The river lands were strange; there were islands between some rivers where they intersected and weaved together like a tangle of noodles. Then there would be long stretches of land that didn't run into a river at all. Some of the islands sported bridges, while others had none, forcing the group to wade through each river carefully. Even with the waterproof charm, which Braelynn and Sary placed on everyone and their items, Shade couldn't help but feel the cold embrace of the water stealing the warmth from her body. It flowed around her thighs, and the icy cold still seeped through her clothes.

She was left stiff from the frigid waters. With the charms, she did not feel wet but felt quite dry, even though her teeth chattered and her body shook from the chill. It was a relief to emerge from the cold, wet trek through a river. Once out of the water, the sun warmed her immediately. Her stiff, frozen clothes stuck to her, remnants of a watery grave.

After about four of these submersions, she was ready to smack Ewan. Did they really have to walk through all that cold, muddy, and swirling water so much? Her love of the outdoors, what little she did have, was washing away with each turbulent wave of river water.

Once they stopped to rest, eat and do their best to warm up, Shade pulled the warm blanket Dylan had given her from her pack and wrapped it tightly around her body. Turning her head up to the sun, she soaked up its comforting rays. It felt incredible, like hot cocoa warming her core after playing in the snow and getting frostbite on her toes and fingers. She closed her eyes, not wanting to move. She felt frozen down to her inner marrow, and her lips were chapped and surely a sickly shade of blue after spending most of the day in the water.

"Hey, drink some hot tea. It will warm your soul." Dylan handed her a steaming cup, his own secured in his other hand.

"Thanks, Dylan." Shade happily accepted it, wrapping her fingers around the warmth of the drink, soothing her stiff joints. She drank it down in a gulp. The hot fluid felt great against her throat, warming her from the inside out. Still huddled in the blanket, she was afraid to break her cozy cocoon if she dared to move.

"Tired of the rapids, huh? They get old really fast, don't they?" Dylan asked, attempting to sound friendly. "I don't miss crossing them at all. You would think some idiot would've put a bridge or something on every river here by now, but faeries are lazy, you know. They'd rather fly right over these banks any day. Of course, we aren't all able to fly, let alone carry anyone else with us," he said with a sigh. "So we have to do it the tried and true way, on foot. I think it's because us faeries don't like to disturb nature too much, so progress is limited." He chuckled, shaking his head as he took another large sip of tea.

He was sitting next to her now, their sides slightly touching, and she could feel his body heat closing the gap between them. Shade turned to watch him more carefully. His unusual, steel-colored eyes glinted in the bright sunlight. The deeper they ventured into the wilderness, the more relaxed he appeared. His face had grown softer and younger in the light of the afternoon. She wondered if nature gave off some kind of natural Xanax to the fey. Everyone seemed more at ease, maybe just a touch tired, but no one was complaining. She guessed that it was better than having a group of grumpy, pissed-off faeries. Who knew what they were all capable of doing if pushed too far?

Dylan's hair was still short, but growing faster than a human's hair would. It was dark and shiny, with silver highlights peppered throughout. He shaved that morning, and his skin still shone smooth, with no lines to betray his age. She wondered how old he was, remembering Ilarial mentioned how they were immortal. Besides Soap, no one had volunteered to say how old he or she really was.

"Dylan? Can I ask you something?" He turned toward her, eyes wide with surprise. She should probably speak to him softly more often because it was nice to see him shocked.

"Yes, of course. Go for it." He placed his cup on the dirt in front of him and sat Indian-style, his arms relaxed on his thighs.

"How old are you? How long do faeries live?" She pulled her knees up and wrapped her arms around her legs, clinging to the blanket and keeping it shut.

"I'm two hundred and forty-six years old. My brother Darren is only one-hundred and fifteen. We're immortal, but only to a certain extent. The fey are somewhat delicate in a way, more so than humans. We can wither away if we choose. Your world is fragile too when it comes to this matter. It's almost like a curse. We are tied to mortals in more ways than one." Dylan paused. He glanced at Shade but quickly turned back to stare down at his cup as he continued.

"When we wither, we choose to leave this world. Our mother was five-hundred and three when she decided she no longer had it in her to carry on, allowing herself to wither into dust. It only took two days. Just two days and slowly, what was a strong, bold, and amazing woman turned into dust and ash," he said with a hint of emotion leaking through his cracking voice. "Life is not easy for the fey. The exiles wither faster because of the toxicity of living in or near the iron cities. Smaller faeries go faster, too. We have stronger clans, like the Guildrin Clan, and our enemies, the Unseelie, are sometimes much stronger than our group of Teleen. Faeries our size are the closest to humans in appearance. My people, the Teleen, are more fragile, dying off as time goes on, very slowly, of course. There are not many Teleen born each year, so our numbers have dwindled as some of us die. If the world was stronger, and the magic in Faerie was not so faded, we could be true immortals and live forever."

"Why is your clan dying? I would think you would be the strongest since humans have a lot of iron in their blood. It would be hard for any fey to live near us or among us, but you guys are fine with it."

Dylan was staring back at her now. His eyes narrowed, amused as he thought about what she was asking and saying. He licked his lips and looked back over the river. The constant roar seemed to fill the silence between them like an unwanted third wheel. Shade waited impatiently for his answers. She stared at the river while she waited for him to talk to her. *At least I beat the rivers,* she thought, knowing she'd bested the icy waters today and had nothing to prove.

"Well, it has a lot to do with there not being many mated pairs in our clan. Teleen females are rarely born to our clan now, and those who are, get paired off quickly and stay together for life. If you're not paired with one, as a male, you are out of luck. That is unless a free Teleen faery woman shows up out of nowhere," he said quietly as if he didn't think that was possible.

"What else is bothering you, Shade?" Dylan's deep voice was more like a harsh whisper. He was even leaning a little toward her to muffle his voice so no one else could hear.

"I don't know. It's just that, compared to all of you guys, I'm so weak. Even though you say you have vulnerabilities, you are still more powerful than me. I don't know how to do magic or any kind of fighting. Without you guys here, I would be useless… helpless." Shade took a deep breath before continuing. "It's all so intriguing, but it scares me so much. There are so many things I don't know. I'm as good as dead out here against other fey.

"Ilarial told me to learn, but how do I learn? I don't know a thing about fighting or handling a sword or knife." She sighed, closing her eyes as she cradled her head on her knees, tears prickling behind her eyelids. She thought back to about what he'd said about not being paired with a female Teleen. She wondered if he was paired or not, and if he was, where was his mate?

Dylan watched her thoughtfully. He nodded as though agreeing with her. His eyes seemed to glaze over for a moment as he was in deep thought.

Shade wondered what it could be that he was thinking.

"I must train you, then. You're right. You are weak without any kind of protection. If you were to be separated from us… well, I don't want to think about it. You have a sword, right?" She nodded, thinking about the beautiful sword in her pack Ilarial had given her. "Great. Then we train today." He stood, offering her a hand. "Grab your sword. I'll teach you a move or two."

Surprised, she took his hand, standing up and fumbling through her pack for the sword. Finding it, she waited, holding it slack in her hand.

"Alright, you need to stand ready. The easiest thing to do is to stand with your feet apart, knees bent. You can put one foot forward a bit. That's right. You need to keep your body balanced so you can move any which way during an attack." He moved to stand next to her, his body facing her side. Reaching out, he adjusted her arms to put both hands on the hilt of the sword, bringing her elbows to a bend. He tugged and pushed at her limbs, making her almost fall over as he adjusted her legs. Standing behind her, he placed his hands on her hips and back, pushing again to make her straighten up her poor posture while still bending her knees. Her thighs screamed in protest.

"You need to relax. I'm not going to bite." He snickered. Shade frowned but tried to do as he told her. "There. See? Flexed, ready to pounce."

Shade nodded, feeling nervous at his proximity but excited at learning something about using a sword.

"Now, I want you to do this exercise: step forward, then back, then side to side, holding the sword opposite the direction you head. It's like a dance; counterbalancing each other, like partners." His voice was just above a whisper near her face. It sent a thrill down her spine.

"Wh-what?"

Dylan groaned, motioning to her to give up the sword. She did and watched him as he showed her what he meant. His movements were fluid and well-practiced. She gulped, hoping she could look more like he did and less like a clumsy ogre.

"See? A dance. Practice it." He handed the sword back and stepped back to give her some room.

"That's it?" she stammered.

"That's it."

Shade felt slightly disappointed but didn't push him any further. Learning that 'dance' would be plenty for now. "Okay, I can do this. Oh, Dylan?"

"Yes?"

"Were you paired off at birth?" She risked a peek at his face as she attempted her first move to the left.

"No, I was never paired at birth, but our Oracle, who's about eight-hundred years old, did tell me a prophecy about it." He sighed and stared out across the river.

"What'd she say?"

"She said that I'd meet my mate one day, one who'd never resided among us and that my life would change forever. It'd be filled with great and challenging events, some unfortunate and some amazing."

"Really? So, did you meet her yet?" Shade watched his face, calm and handsome. She found him intriguing in a way she could not explain. And to think, just hours ago, he was getting on her last nerve.

Dylan turned toward her and studied her face, his flashing eyes amused at her questions. Giving her a smile, he reached out, pushing a strand of hair out of her face. Shade felt her heart jump, sending her skin flaring up at his touch. "I don't really know. Maybe." He continued to watch her, a sad smile playing across his lips. "Once camp is set up tonight, we will work on more sword fighting. Be ready!" He grabbed his cup from the ground while dusting off his pants. He walked away then without another word, leaving her stunned.

"Wh-what? *More* tonight? Dylan?" She stuttered and couldn't spit out the rest of her words. He was gone and nowhere near her now. Shaking her head, she laughed to herself.

He's so strange and drives me insane! Maybe that's a good thing.

***

SHADE STRETCHED HER legs out before her, massaging her calves and working out some of the knots deep under her skin. They stopped for a rest again after another horrible river crossing. She wondered if the fey ever even got sore. *Probably not.* She kept wondering what Dylan was thinking, too. Some of the things he did and said confused her. It made her frown at the thought of how nervous he made her feel.

Standing up, she took her teacup back to Stephen, who seemed to like being the group's cook and occasional dishwasher. He gave her a short nod, smiling as he continued to wash the soiled dishes. He wasn't actually physically cleaning them, he was just moving his hands over them, making them rinse themselves in the river.

I need to learn that! That'd be useful back home! Shade thought, turning back toward the group where Jack was talking seriously to Ewan. Maps sat spread out before them on a table. *Who brought the furniture?* Shade thought as she walked toward them. She still couldn't get over the bath tent and the constant use of magic here. When she reached the two men, they were pointing at several spots on the map, plotting their journey.

"I think going over Fable's Fair Bridge would be a better option. It goes closer to the cliffs of Raenin. We need to go past the cliffs and end up on Solare's Beach. There's a cave road there we can take to the inland forests, around the Santiran lands. If we go down to Maziel's Pass, it will take us longer to make it to the beach, and it goes too close to Unseelie territory." Jack's hand was darting around the map at several points on the unfamiliar land.

Shade studied it while the men stood there thinking. She could see the cities of Portland and San Diego along one side of the great fey territory. There were areas marked off that showed the highways and smaller human towns. The vast wilderness that belonged to the fey was unbelievable. She traced the river lands with her fingers and found Solare's Beach on the map. Shaped like a crescent moon, it was not very big at all. It had a small river that emptied into the ocean along one side. Next was Craven's Cave Road, which wound around the cliffs of the beach and disappeared into a cave. Shade shuddered at the thought of going into another cave again.

"How do we make it across the cliffs?" Shade asked Ewan and Jack. They turned toward her and smiled.

"You have to walk down the west side of the cliffs or

take a long rope bridge across this great river." Ewan pointed at a line crossing across the largest of the rivers that bisected the cliffs.

Shade cringed because crossing a bridge held together by rope was not much of a comfort either. *Caves and unstable bridges... it's my lucky day.* Her throat ached from nerves, and it felt as if there were a knot in it. "Really? Ah man, do we have to go on a rope bridge?" She glanced at Jack and Ewan. "And another cave?"

"You afraid of heights, Shade?" They said at once and laughed at the disgust all over her face.

"No! Of course not! It's just, they're so flimsy! It rocks a lot, and it just isn't safe!" She crossed her arms and huffed away. Jack started coughing, trying to hold back his laughter while Ewan slapped him on his back.

When they stopped snickering, Ewan cleared his throat, his face flushed and his eyes twinkling brightly. He motioned for everyone to gather their stuff and fall back into line to leave.

Shade fell in with the group, still grumbling under her breath. She followed everyone out along the bank of the rushing river. She began to wonder just how long it was going to take to get to the Santiran Fountains. It felt like they were gone forever. Her patience was wearing thin, especially with nature. Seeing the map made her feel even more sullen. The territory they were crossing was enormous and so vast that it seemed like they hadn't really gone that far. So much happened already, and they weren't even close yet.

"Hey, having fun yet?" Soap asked as he hung back from the others and fell in step with her. She gave him a nasty look and didn't like the fact that someone else from the group was making fun of her.

"Ok, ok, no need to be harsh," he said, losing his usual grin. "I was just wondering something, Shade, and I hope you would answer this for me."

She sighed and turned back toward Soap. His contagious good mood was already flowing over her and taming her gloomy demeanor. She grinned back, nodding. "What is it?" She slipped on a damp, mossy rock in the slick grasses. Soap caught her arm and cradled her with his other one. Her face was so close to his, he could have kissed her. She laughed a bit and thanked him for catching her, straightening herself up before he answered.

"The voices, the ones you said are your spirit guides, are they still bothering you? What do they say about us?"

Shade took a deep breath and thought about it for a moment. She hadn't really heard from her spirit guides since they'd left the caverns. As a matter of fact, she hadn't heard the voices at all since waking up from the attack. It was actually somewhat nice to hear just her own thoughts in her head. She stretched out her mind to find them, but no one answered her inner thoughts. Panic suddenly swirled inside her as she felt a kind of emptiness without them.

Why have they been silent? Maybe they're gone for good now.

"Honestly, I haven't heard them talk since Darren attacked me. It's funny, my whole life I wished they would just shut up, and now–now I miss them."

"Well, it's probably just the rivers. They're quite magical, you know. They say that the rivers are the roads of dreams. Once you stand by one, the magic is too strong. It can literally turn a fey into a near mortal. We can't use too much of our magic here. The river won't have it. That's the myth, anyway. It's like dead space to our kind, the in between of worlds. I think it might be affecting you, too. I literally can't change around the rivers. I can only use a simple glamour and charms. It's strange...."

Shade nodded as they continued down the slippery banks without speaking again for a while. She wondered if Soap wanted to ask her anything else. He seemed more quiet than usual. This would have bothered her more, but concentrating on

155

not slipping on another rock or mossy wet patch kept her attention for now. They reached the edge of the bank to another crossing area. She groaned as she watched the front of the group submerge themselves up to their waists in cold river water. The rush of the current wasn't as strong at the crossings points, but she loathed the cold feel of the water. She reached the edge of the bank and watched as Soap strode right on in without so much as a whimper. *Man up, already*! She sighed and dipped her feet into the icy water, sucking in a breath.

She was near the other side when she heard some shouting. She straightened up to see further up the bank where Ewan, Jack, and Than were wildly shouting at someone, someone she couldn't see from her position in the river.

"Shade, come on. I think we're being attacked. Hurry!" Sary waved at her frantically and held her other hand out to her. She took it and pulled herself up out of the rushing waters. The chill was there again, and her teeth chattered together. She was pretty sure her lips were blue with cold. Sary kept half turning and pressing her on to follow, practically dragging her along.

Soap already left his position in front of her to join Jack and the others, who were now taking shelter behind some trees and drawing weapons. Shade found a large tree trunk to hide behind as arrows started sailing by, buzzing like bees as they flew. She felt drugged and sluggish from the cold. She had the blanket on, but in the cover of the trees and with no hot tea to drink this time, she was not recovering as well as before. Huddling against the tree and pulling the blanket around tightly for warmth, she was still shivering. She peeked around the tree as there was a break in the flying arrows. Whoever was attacking them had either run out or was restocking their weapons.

Jack was yelling at someone. Everyone stood their ground, hiding in their makeshift covers. She couldn't see who

or what they were yelling at. She strained to hear anything…
and then suddenly it came—a voice. The grave laugh was in the
distance, but whoever it belonged to was not too far away.

"You can't hide forever, little half-breed. I know she's
with you. Just hand her over, and we'll be on our way," the
voice screeched through the trees.

Who is that? I've heard that voice before, Shade thought as
the cruel laugh made her cringe. She strained a little more to see
across the trees, spotting the owner of the voice. Lady Blythe
was perched on a branch not too far above Ewan and the others.
The Queen of the Dryad's skeletal, translucent wings were
fluttering so fast that Shade could barely see them. If there
hadn't been a slight breeze whirling around her, the tiny wings
would have gone unnoticed altogether. Shade's heart pounded.
She knew just what they wanted but not why.

"We will never give her to you, Blythe! You are far
beyond your borders, and you have no rights here. This is
neutral territory. Be gone already!" Jack's voice was strong and
sturdy. He did not seem afraid but was definitely on the side of
caution.

"You stupid fool! You dare insult me? I am Queen here.
The trees are *my* domain, no matter where! You give me the
Halfling, and I let you leave alive. Otherwise, you can all die,
and I will still take the girl. Choose wisely!" Her cackling voice
echoed through the air.

Shade didn't think it was possible, but she felt even
colder than before. She worked hard to keep her teeth from
chattering again, praying silently that the old hag of a faery
would leave her alone. She didn't look like a nice faery from the
'fairy' stories of Shade's childhood. She looked vicious, dark,
and ruthless flying up there in the branches. Shade's heart was
racing as she glanced around, trying to think of a way to get
away from there.

"No, Lady Blythe. We can't do that. It is our oath to
protect her, and that we will, to the death even." Jack was

holding his sword out. It glinted in the few rays that escaped the canopy of tree leaves above.

"So be it. Die then," she said without feeling. Lady Blythe laughed even harder as more arrows began to fly.

Shade ducked back behind the trunk and looked around for the others. Sary was pulling out daggers and weapons from behind a tree near her. Stephen was already returning arrows to whomever it was that was shooting them. Some screams of pain howled through the trees, but she wasn't sure who was behind it. Cracking branches and thumps in the bushes made her jump. She pulled out her own short sword and held it tightly in her hands. Taking a deep breath, she stood up and pressed herself against the tree, trying to become one with it. If only she could change into a tree, she could hide pretty well then.

The battle spilled around her as Lady Blythe's warriors pushed back against them. Jack was clanging swords against one tall but slender fighter. He had bulging muscles, pale skin much like Blythe's, and long white hair. All but his eyes were pale, and his skin was almost translucent. A pair of wings were tightly folded and pressed against his back to avoid being sliced by a sword. He wore thin metal armor that glinted in the streams of light as he fought. They all looked similar to the queen, and they worked and moved together like a hive of drones.

Shade ran for cover at the edge of the battle and hid behind some large looming trees. *The best way I can help everyone is to stay hidden and avoid getting hit,* she thought. Part of her wanted to help, but she was sure there was no way she could fight.

Suddenly, the arrows stopped altogether, and everyone was on the ground fighting. Even Blythe joined the fight with her own dual slender swords. She was holding off Than, who was fighting with his daggers, their silver sheen glinting with every movement. She kicked him hard in the stomach and laughed as he flew back to the ground. Dirt was flying up everywhere. Blythe caught Shade watching her, and a sinister smile crept across her face as she started toward Shade.

"Come here, little girlie." She started marching toward Shade but ran right into Jack and his swords, losing one of hers in the collision. She blocked him with her remaining sword and began battling his two. The metallic resonance filled the air as Shade backed away into the shadow of the forest. Her heart was pounding in her chest so hard that she could feel the beat vibrating in her throat. She felt flushed as her blood pumped rapidly throughout her body, her breaths growing short and quick.

"Shade!" Dylan was now next to her and tugging at her arm. He led her deeper into the woods, and she tried hard to not stumble or fall on the branches and dead shrubbery that scraped at her legs and sliced at her arms.

"Slow down, Dylan! I can't go that fast!" Her hand slipped from his as she fell to the ground, grinding her knees into the dirt and rock.

Dylan didn't pick her up. He was occupied, swinging his sword against another warrior dryad. As they fought around her, Shade managed to get to her feet. Mud streaked across her jeans and hands, making her wipe even more of the mess onto her pants. It was then that she noticed her sword had fallen onto the ground. She looked back over her shoulder at Dylan; he and his foe were still clanging their swords together. Dylan had a cut on his left forearm that was streaked with blood. Shade stepped forward and bent down to grab her sword, swearing as she did, for her right knee was on fire. *I must have scraped it or bruised it when I fell.* She stumbled to another tree and pressed her back to it, gripping the sword in her hands, the blade and hilt also caked in mud.

Her eyes were stinging with tears, although she didn't notice she'd been crying. Swallowing back a sob, she shook with fear. Breathing deeply, she looked around the large tree trunk and tried to see through the woods for anyone else in the group. She heard screams, yelling, and swords clanging, but she wasn't as close to the fighters as she'd first thought. She couldn't hear them clearly anymore, realizing she'd stumbled too far away. Her heart jumped as morbid thoughts crept into her head. *What if they're hurt or dead?* She couldn't even see Dylan anymore but continued to hear the clank of swords.

Shade moved slowly from her spot and crept closer to the voices, using the trees and bushes for cover. She hunched behind them, pressing herself close, wishing she could blend in and disappear. The hilt of her sword was cool but reminded her of playing pirates with fake swords as a child. She tried her best to slow her breathing, feeling slightly dizzy from her frantic panting. Shade listened intently, but it seemed like the fighting died down. The silence was even more frightening than the noise. Leaves rustled above her, like a flock of birds flapping their wings, startling her. She could hear a loud roar of rushing water behind her but nothing else.

This can't be good. What now? Where is everyone? Shade waited for an answer. Her spirit guides were silent. *What happened to you guys?* The silence made her feel utterly alone. The forest was daunting, dark, and forlorn. She let the tears flow but bit her lip to swallow her sobs. Sliding down the trunk, she curled herself in the oversized roots that veined the dirt. Her legs bent up under her as she hugged them, her sword still dangling loosely from her hands.

Time seemed to have stopped now. She still couldn't hear anyone but felt afraid to move. A fresh breeze rustled the canopy of the trees, and it felt like something or someone, had brushed against her, making her jump just a bit. It prickled along her arms like cactus spines, making her realize someone was very close. She held her breath and slowly stood up, still pressed against the trunk. Listening, she knew that whoever was around was trying to blend in too.

Shade could feel eyes burning into her, as though they were waiting for her to give herself away. She wiped the last of her tears from her face and gripped her sword more tightly. Her hair flew in her face, stringy and stuck with sweat. She could taste the salt on her lips, dirt and tears, and knew she was a disheveled mess. She thought about her family and Ilarial and didn't want to disappoint them. There was no giving up. There was more than just fear inside her, she could feel it. Straightening up, she breathed out slowly and began scanning the woods.

"I can smell your fear, little girl. Why don't you just give up? Lady Blythe won't hurt you, at first. I just want to talk for a bit, and then maybe the hurt can start after that," she sneered.

Shade was so disgusted by the old woman's cackling laugh. She could almost feel it rippling down her spine. Shade couldn't see her, but she could feel the old faery's magic dancing along her skin. The faery radiated power like an unchecked flame that touched Shade with its fingers. She estimated in her head that the faery was just on the other side of the tree. It was then that she squeezed her sword, feeling her fingers digging into each other and turning white from the pressure. She let out a primal scream, swinging the sword hard as she flung herself around the corner.

The blade sliced Blythe in her shoulder but failed to cut too deeply. She screeched and jumped back, bringing her sword up in defense. Crimson blood dripped down her arm and oozed off into the dark earth. The Queen did not seem very tall to Shade. Even standing up made her still look like a short, bony thing of a sprite. *No wonder she spent her life up in the trees. Anyone can look intimidating from up high.* Shade retreated behind the tree but readied herself for sprinting or fighting.

"You stupid girl! How dare you attack me!" There was a loud thump against the trunk of the tree.

Shade's bravery was being used up way too fast, and she was pretty sure the old woman had just tried to blast her with something. She stepped back from the tree and readied her sword once more. Blythe suddenly jumped in front of her from the side, hollering in another language, her pointy teeth flashing and her sword held high. Then she charged. Shade dodged her but tripped on a tree root. She scrambled to stand but stumbled backward, forced to crawl on her hands and feet to get away.

Lady Blythe hit the roots with her sword, making it stick. She tugged at it with her scrawny arms but failed to budge it from the earth. The tree seemed to grip it tighter the more she fought to retrieve her weapon. Shade took the moment to get back on her feet and run. She ran as fast as she could, glancing back only to find Blythe without her sword, moving just as fast and quickly gaining ground.

Shade dodged and wove her way through the trees. The roar of the river water was closer now, but the rush of wind blowing in her ears made it impossible to calculate how far away it was. She prayed that the land would not run out for her. She had the feeling the Dryad Queen could cross the river faster than she could.

Shade forced herself to make an abrupt stop as the land narrowed to an edge. Stuffing the sword away in her pack, she prepared to cross the river, but she was shocked to learn that instead, she found a drop-off. One of the rivers emptied over a cliff and formed into a waterfall.

*Oh my God….*Water clouds rose from the rocks below, and she could feel herself pale as the height of the cliff became more evident. The land stretched out beyond the drop-off with more forests, hills, rivers, and jagged mountains.

There's nowhere to go but down.

Shade turned to see Blythe slowing her run to a jog and snickering at her. Her large eyes flashed with her wicked smile. Her pale skin had a slight flush to it now, and she slowly stepped toward Shade. Shade felt her heart thudding hard in her chest and tried not to be afraid. The Dryad Queen licking her lips didn't help, but it made Shade feel like she was about to be dinner.

Blythe took out her dagger. "You have nowhere to go. You're so weak. I wonder why Zinara could even fathom that you could save them. The Unseelie will be greatly pleased to have you as their prisoner. The Unseelie Queen will owe me, and she will be sick with my victory. Come to me now… I promise it won't hurt much." She sneered, but her eyes were cold and dangerous. She stepped closer, pulling a rope from her waist belt.

Shade shook her head and turned her eyes back to the waterfall. There was nowhere to go. She strained to hear her comrades but heard only the rush of water overwhelming her ears. No one was coming to save her. She glanced back at Lady Blythe and her evil smile. No, Shade could not go with her. As Shade stepped farther back, she realized that the edge was inches from her feet. She knew with certainty that her fate was sealed.

"You don't want to fall now, do you?" Lady Blythe asked, eyeing her with words coming out like sweet, poisonous honey.

Shade wasn't fooled. She could feel her knees wobble but concentrated on not falling. She wasn't sure how long she could steady herself with a horrid witch in her face. Letting out a nervous sigh, she began to reach for her backpack. *This is crazy and it won't work!* After stuffing the warm blanket into her pack, she pulled it onto her shoulders. A moment later, she turned from Blythe and jumped.

The wind lashed at her body and howled in her ears. She could barely hear the queen's furious scream as the icy water swallowed her whole.

Chapter Thirteen

THE FRIGID WATERS shut down her senses, and Shade couldn't feel a thing. Everything was dark, but she heard a faint call of sparrows high above her over the gurgling sound of water. She attempted to move her fingers and arms, but they barely responded. Her eyes felt like weights were on them, gluing them shut. She was blinded, moaning as she rolled to her side. Her bones creaked in protest at the shift and moving her fingers sent a sharp, stinging pain up her arms.

The light was searing as she opened her eyes, blinking a few times so they could adjust. *Am I dead? Where the hell am I? God, my body is burning!* She was sure if this was heaven, she'd feel nothing but peace. Hell, on the other hand… *well, you can burn in pain there,* she thought nervously.

Lying there on the bank of the river, she could feel her feet, soaked and frozen, still in the water. The earth was cold underneath the rest of her body. Her backpack felt dry, probably due to the spells Braelynn casted. Shade's clothes were another matter; they were sopping wet and molded to her body, making her teeth chatter involuntarily. It felt like she'd never be warm again. She sat up very slowly and surveyed the muddy embankment, seeing nothing but the sand that irritated her skin.

At least the sun still shines, she thought, trying to hold on to the slightest bright spot in this situation. It occurred to her she had to at least try and move or she'd freeze to death. *If I don't get moving, heaven will be my next stop.* She groaned, feeling the sting of every scrape that marked her body, remembering the rocks on the bottom of the waterfall. She wasn't sure if anything was broken and struggled to get to a drier area on the shore. Her left arm was sore and wouldn't cooperate. Craning her neck to the side, she found her shoulder not quite in the right anatomical position.

I must have dislocated my shoulder.

She thought it was strange that it didn't hurt until she'd looked at it. Whimpers escaped her mouth, but she continued to drag herself up the embankment with her good arm and two heavy legs. A rush of nausea from the pain pressed at her, threatening to make her pass out. It hung on like sticky syrup until she leaned to one side and let whatever was left of breakfast shoot out. Her dark blue lips trembled, her hands were cyanotic and oddly lovely in the glowing daylight. The color reminded her of arctic blue ice.

When the heaving stopped, she found herself sobbing. She didn't hear anyone around her, and, fortunately, she probably lost Blythe in the froth of the falls. What was so great about getting away if she was just going to end up freezing to death, anyway, covered in filthy mud? Shade prayed that her mom would find her here, helpless and in dire need of a doctor, and whisk her away. All she wanted was to believe this was all a bad dream, and that she'd wake up and find herself in a safe and warm place. Shade lay there for what felt like an eternity before she heard the crunch of crackling leaves. Swallowing down the last sob, she blinked through the tears in her eyes. Her heart beat like a fluttering hummingbird, banging in her chest.

"Who's there?" She heard the crack in her voice, sounding faded and rough. She wondered how long she had screamed heading down the falls.

"Hush now. You're hurt. Don't move or you'll hurt yourself even more. One moment. This might, unfortunately, hurt a bit," a gentle voice warned.

She felt a hard tug on her body and screamed as an unbearable pain flared up her left arm. Her body shifted and dragged farther up the shore, over more beach sand, and onto a dry blanket before she looked up at her rescuer. It was becoming nearly impossible to keep her eyes open. Her head rolled from side to side as the pain from her damaged shoulder burned through her body. Before the darkness came, she caught sight of a pair of gleaming green eyes, dried autumn leaves, and a flash of brown linen. Trying to open her mouth to speak was futile as she slipped away into the silence of unconsciousness.

Chapter Fourteen

"SHADE, FORGIVE US. We have tried to reach you, but you've cast us out. We're here to help you heal and awaken you from your deep sleep. Now only dreams will find us._ The voices were gentle but spoke with urgency, echoing in her head.

Shade stood in an open field; the mountains and rivers were nowhere in sight. The breezes caressed the tall grasses and swirled about her hair, dancing and playing with the strands like unseen ballerinas.

Where the heck am I now?

Astrid, Duende, and Elaby stood before her. She knew them. Her spirit guides were familiar and comforting. They were flesh and bone standing in front of her now. The three sisters were carbon copies of each other. Their long black hair and gowns floated around them as if suspended in water. Their pale skin shone like moonlight glistening on the surface of a lake. She could not see their feet; it was as if they hung above

169

the grass without touching the ground. They were beautiful.

"What's going on? Where am I? Why can't I hear you guys anymore?" Shade felt the sting of tears as her voice wavered. She was through with crying. There was enough sorrow surrounding her, making her feel suddenly so tired. She brought her hand to her left shoulder and found it no longer dislocated, hanging normally in its place. It moved effortlessly, without any pain. She hoped she was dreaming and not dead.

"Shade, we know you're afraid, but we won't harm you. It could not be helped that we were away," the sisters told her all at once. *"Somehow, your magic trapped Darren in the mirror, but it also pushed us out of your head, too. We are unable to communicate with you, our ties now severed. We've worked hard to find you again. Your magic shields you, letting us in only in your dreams."*

Shade pondered their words for a moment. *Damn it... Darren!* He had scarred her far worse than she'd even imagined. The loss of her spirit guides was like having a chunk of her soul ripped away. She sighed and watched them smile at her. Each sister finished the others' sentences. It was intriguing to listen to them as they harmonized in one voice.

"So where am I? I was on some shore, freezing. My arm was probably broken and not in the right place. Am I awake? Dead? Dreaming?"

"You are still asleep. Fear not, dear Shade, we have healed you with our powers. We have been away for too long," said the women. *"Now, we are unbound."*

"What do you mean? I won't hear you in my head anymore? How could I have let this happen?" Shade felt her knees weaken but caught herself before they failed.

"We are so sorry. We had no idea this would come to pass. We can only believe that any further communication with us will be only through your dreams."

Shade nodded at the revelation. There was no point in trying to undo what was already done. Even so, the loss twisted in her chest, making it hard to breathe.

The dream shifted rapidly, and the bright, warm sunlight faded into a deep gray and cloudy day. Shade spun around, watching the swirling dark gray clouds grow above her. "What's happening?" The wind howled around her, whipping the grass across her legs.

"We must go. Your dream is breaking. It's time to wake up, Shade. Wake up." The clouds came down around in a dark, billowing fog that swallowed the spirits, landscape, and Shade alike.

"Wake up...."

***

"**W**AKE UP! IT'S just a bad dream. Wake up!" The voice sounded familiar, but Shade couldn't place it. She squeezed her eyes together before slowly opening them to a dimly lit room. Her eyes narrowed in at the shadowy figure in front of her, focusing on its blurred edges. His face was partially covered by a dark, hooded cloak. The hood only allowed lips to show through, obscuring the rest of his face in darkness.

The figure reached toward her, making her scramble in a panic, pushing away until her back hit the wall. Her left arm throbbed with a dull ache, but she found she could use it just fine. Still confused, she wrapped her arms around her legs, gripping them while she stared at the stranger. She concentrated on keeping her eyes in focus as the room tilted in a wave of dizziness. She'd sat up way too fast.

The figure stopped advancing and eyed her. Seeing her pull away, he retreated, stood straighter, and waited. When he did finally speak, his voice was soft but thick and flowing, like rich syrup.

"I apologize. I meant no harm. Please, I only want to help you. My name is Ursad, and I live here in the forest by the

171

ocean." He paused, waiting for a reaction from her. When none came, he proceeded. "Is there anything I can do? Do you need anything? Water? Are you hungry? Any pain? You look like you've been through a wringer." He spoke quickly, overly eager to help her.

Shade's face flushed, and her eyebrows furrowed in further confusion.

"Sorry, I don't mean to frighten you," he apologized.

"Where am I?" Shade relaxed a little, as he did not try to come closer again.

"You're here in my house. It's not much, but it's home. I hope you found the bed to your liking. I really don't have a lot of room, but it's comfortable enough for me, at least." He studied her closely, chewing on his smooth, plump lips.

Shade stared right back at him. He looked pretty harmless, but the hood hid too much of his face for her to read him well enough. Trying to relax, she sat cross-legged on the bed, pulling the soft, threadbare blanket around her. Her body was cozy warm, and her aches weren't as sharp as they had been. She sighed; at least she wasn't in Blythe's care. This was definitely the better half of her current situation.

"I'm sorry. My name's Shade. I just wasn't sure if it was safe here. I was being chased...." She stopped, wondering if she should trust this stranger with anything, especially with her story. Maybe he knew too much already. "I guess I lost them. How did you find me? Was I out of it for long?"

"Shade?" The way her name spilled out of his mouth made her shiver. "Well, nice to meet you. I found you on the beach. It shares the shore with a small pool of water that feeds from a small stream that breaks off from one of the great rivers. I live near it, and I happened to be walking by when I saw you. You passed out after that. I am truly sorry that I hurt you, pulling on your shoulder like that. I didn't know it was dislocated, but somehow it's not anymore. You must be full of healing magic. You've healed quite rapidly. It's amazing if you don't mind me saying so. I would love to know how you do it." He was smiling, but she definitely did not like having his face so hidden. She reached toward him to pull the hood back as he spoke since he was not too far from the bed. It was his turn to pull away and crouch by the door.

"No, please!" He shook his head and hid the rest of his face in his sleeve. He bounced nervously back and forth on his feet, as though the thought of pulling off the hood caused him great anxiety.

"Why not?" Shade demanded. "I don't feel very comfortable talking to you when I can't see your face. Let me see. Is there, um, is there something wrong with your face?" She sat back down and blushed with embarrassment, realizing just how forward she'd been, possibly even rude. She didn't mean to offend him. Her nervousness had her reacting without thinking.

Maybe he's deformed under there. She gulped, shaking the thought out of her head. *How bad can it be?*

"I'm sorry. I shouldn't have done that, but really, you need to take it off. It's okay. You'll scare me more with it on." Shade waited and watched him bring his arm down.

He seemed to be thinking about what she'd said because he let his gaze linger on her for a long time. Unexpectedly, he nodded. "You're right. I am what I am, but please don't be afraid. I tend to frighten everyone. I don't get too many visitors here at all, not even other fey. I've gotten used to solitude. It has been so long since I've been around others." He sighed and lifted his chin. Tentatively, he reached up and pulled the hood down, letting it fall away from his face.

Shade tried to keep in the gasp that fought to escape her lips. She knew, however, that her shock showed in her widening eyes. She immediately composed herself, hoping the slip would not anger him. His face was unusual, but she wouldn't say it was scary, not with such sad eyes staring back at her.

"Ursad, can I ask you something? What exactly are you?" *I've never seen anyone like him*, she thought as she observed his face. Where the facial hair ended, his skin grew like tree bark, all tan and dark with lines trailing through it. His hair was made of green, thin leaves with twigs and small delicate vines springing from his head. She could definitely tell he was faerie or human, but he'd been transformed into what appeared to be a tree man. His hands were smooth and human in appearance, but nothing above the neck resembled a typical human face.

"I didn't always look this way. I was cursed a long time ago, and my face and hair have been affected in this way ever since." His face turned sad, and he lowered his eyes to stare down at the floor as he continued. "I guess I should explain further." He looked up at her and paused, waiting for her approval.

She nodded to him, eager for an explanation.

"I was a faery prince once, a long time ago. I was very handsome, and women threw themselves at my feet, catering to my every whim. I had my choice of any fey or human woman. Well, you could say I was arrogant, knowing my effect on women. I thought myself undeniable and irresistible. That is, until one night I was in a tavern, enjoying the party and drinking a bit too much liquor. I was surrounded by beauties and laughing with the lot of them. It was quite fun.

"One woman approached me then. She wasn't the most beautiful woman I'd ever seen, but definitely not the ugliest. She was quite dull in appearance, with flat brown hair, plain brown eyes, and nothing remarkable in her smile to speak of. It was as if when she was created, no animation or personality of any kind was added. I was just not interested... but she had other ideas.

"She told me, *I am Elinia, daughter of Talik, the were-stone maker. I am here to offer marriage to you. I love you and would be honored to be your wife.* It came out cold, lacking any kind of warmth and stiff as a board.

"Of course, I didn't know who she was, or what she was for that matter. I laughed at her request and snubbed her in front of the whole tavern in my drunken stupor. Everyone laughed at my smart antics, and I gave her a quick shove to get her out of my immediate sight. I didn't know what it was I was doing. I laughed and laughed until she scrambled off the floor and ran out of the tavern crying, to my satisfaction. I was glad I didn't have to ridicule her anymore, relieved that she was gone.

"I finished out the night laughing and having a fabulous time. Not once did I give another thought to the girl. When I readied myself to leave, I walked out of the tavern and to the stables where my horse was waiting. When I was untying my horse, she approached me from behind.

"*I curse you, Ursad, Prince of the lands of Santire. Prince of nothing, you will be! Fair as the bark of a tree, I curse you for infinity! Return you to how you are freed, a gentle kiss from a queen-to-be!* I stared at her as she finished her words and started laughing again.

"*You'll regret this, Ursad. You will look back with a heart broken and filled with remorse. I promise you that.* She disappeared then, as suddenly as she'd come. I was left alone in the silence of the dark stables. I didn't feel different, but curses are not taken lightly in fey culture. I began to wonder what she meant by her words. I shrugged them off and rode away into the night, back to my kingdom.

"It was a long journey home, so I had to stop for the night. As I walked to a lodge at the side of a country road, I wiped my face because it was covered in dripping sweat. I felt sick then and wondered what was going on. I checked into the lodge and fell into a deep sleep, exhausted.

"The next morning, after I woke, I walked to the mirror hanging in the room to comb my hair. My hair and my face had changed. What I saw was what you see now. Horrified, I fled my country, for no one would recognize me looking like such a monster. I haven't returned since, and so here I am, alone." Ursad looked back up at Shade, and their eyes met.

"I'm drawn to the forest, the ocean, and the pools of water. They pull me like a magnet, so I chose this place to live. They give me solace in my pain and exile. The waters bless me with their favor, leaving bits of the world, and food is easily attainable here on the banks. Now they've brought you to me, and I can't help but wonder why. You were hurt, so I had to help. I hope you are not afraid of me. I mean no harm, really." He sucked in a deep breath, the memories wearing on him. "I guess you could say I have been humbled from the years of isolation." He was watching her so intensely, speaking rapidly, making it clear that he was lonely and excited to be with another person.

Shade fought to look away. His face was smooth and serious, but his deep green eyes were wrought with sorrow. When she found him still watching her, she spoke. "I'm sorry. I hope I didn't insult you."

"No, you didn't," said Ursad with a kind smile.

It was alarming to look at him at first, but she could see his handsome features underneath all of it, and in a peculiar way, found him striking. Time had not withered this man. He was preserved in the prison he'd made for himself. *I wonder if he really was a prince. This is so strange,* she thought to herself. A prince of the Santiran lands, of all things, the very place she needed to go.

"Ursad, I'm thirsty and hungry. I could use something to eat if you have anything to share. Oh, do you know where my things are?"

He nodded as he turned toward the door. "I will get them for you. I left your pack near the fireplace to make sure it dried out a bit though it seems impervious to water. I couldn't take anything out. It has a personalized lock charm on it and

would not open for me. I do hope your things are not ruined."
He ducked out the door, and Shade was left staring after him.

She suddenly became aware she was not wearing her own tattered, muddy clothes from before but wearing soft cotton, drawstring pajama pants, and an oversized tunic instead. They were clean and soft, but she pulled the blankets even tighter around herself. She tried not to imagine him changing her out of her soaked, dirty clothes. Squirming at the thought, she felt her cheeks flush red.

Ursad returned with a tray of fruit, a meat sandwich, and a cup of juice. Her stomach growled at the sight of the food. He set it gently in front of her, not smiling but extremely serious. She tried to smile and soon forgot her embarrassment. She settled in and started to inhale the meal. Food in Faerie seemed to taste so much better than in her world. She wondered if it was really better or if she was just ravenous having not eaten in hours, not to mention all the exertion of the journey. She chewed and ate so fast she started hiccupping. She guzzled down the juice, hoping to stave them off.

As Shade finished, she realized Ursad stayed and watched her. She was gorging herself, and now, embarrassed. She slowed her chomping to a moderate chew. Swallowing the last bite, she observed Ursad a little closer. Brilliant green eyes shone in the dim light of the room, piercing into her soul.

She raked her eyes over his hair of vines and leaves. It was so long, it tumbled down past his waist like tendrils of flowers. Would it hurt to pluck a leaf from the thin vines that draped him like a shroud and dangled over his shoulders? He was dressed in dark brown clothes that hung frayed and well worn, reminding her of peasant's clothing from fairytale stories.

Shade chuckled to herself. Maybe this was her 'fairytale' in a way. *Nothing is as it should be. Nothing is going the way it should be, for that matter.* The world was not normal here, and Shade wasn't sure she liked it that much. *And now, I'm lost.*

"Is everything all right? Was the food good, Shade?"

Ursad asked, breaking her thoughts and dragging her back to the present. She nodded and pushed the food tray away, signaling that she was done. Ursad promptly stood up, collected it, and left through the door. He was now smiling widely and humming softly with a happy skip in his step.

Shade shook her head. *Faery men are so strange!* She sighed and swung her legs over the edge of the bed. She grabbed the footboard and stood up slowly, feeling her legs wobble beneath her. Standing for a minute and relaxing her muscles, she breathed through the dull pain that resonated throughout her bones. It was a cold reminder of the chill of the river, making her shudder.

She glanced down at her fingers and flexed them. They felt slightly stiff but functional, the slight ache was not bothering her much at all. She'd been counting her blessings. Somehow, she'd healed her horrendous injuries, or maybe her spirit guides had done what they'd promised.

Thank you for this gracious gift. Shade hoped that somehow they heard her.

Ursad entered the room, holding out her pack and the folded pile of clothes that she'd worn before. He'd washed, repaired, and neatly folded her dirty clothes. Shade gave him a small grin and let him place the pile on the bed next to her. "I took the liberty of repairing your clothes. The rocks nearly ripped them to shreds. Your pack is dry. I take it you don't want to be staying very long, which is really too bad. I would like to get to know you and hear your story. As I said, I haven't had any company in such a long time." His voice drifted off, a longing clinging to his words.

When she didn't say anything, he continued. "I mean, you shouldn't hurry out. You're welcome to stay as long as you like, of course." He waited again, shifting nervously back and forth on his feet before turning to rush out of the room, closing the door behind him.

Shade laughed quietly. His nervousness seemed to calm her anxiety.

Rummaging through her pack, she pulled out a fresh set of clothes and stuffed her repaired rags into the backpack. She wondered if there was a shower or restroom in the little cabin. Slipping some house shoes on that she'd thrown into her pack, just in case, she opened the door and peeked out, calling to Ursad when she didn't find him there. "Is there a bathroom I can use? I could really use a shower."

"It's to your right," he called from an adjacent room.

Shade stepped out and looked down the darkened hallway. The walls were made of wood, twisting and curving in such a way as to create the rooms and halls. They must've been inside a large tree converted into a cottage. Still in awe, she retrieved her light stone from her pack and held it in front of her. The glowing light was bright in the dim surroundings and comforted her a bit. The hallway was not as long as it had looked in the dark. Entering the last door at the end of the hall, she found a modern-looking bathroom, nothing elaborate, but it was clean. She placed her clothes on the counter, along with the light stone, which continued to glow. She smiled and was glad it didn't need to stay in contact with her to stay lit. She whispered a soft thanks to it and turned the shower on.

I wonder how this all works? There isn't any electricity in the cabin, but it appears to have modern conveniences. It was still hard to take in the idea that magic and faeries were real, even after everything she'd been through and seen. The water ran over her skin, the heat and steam reviving her with every drop. Pure bliss.

When Shade was done, she returned down the hall to her room, slipped in, and put her things away. She put her shoes on and held her backpack in one arm as she left the room to check out the rest of the house and find Ursad. The main room was small but cozy; a blazing fire crackled on one side of the room in a simple fireplace. There was one reading chair made out of old red velvet, and it sat in front of the fire, along with a fluffy couch placed on the right side of the room. It had a warm, cotton throw blanket sprawled across it with bits of yarn loosened from its edges. On the left stood a small table and two chairs made out of wood, which appeared to be hastily nailed together. The wood was smooth and worn, showing signs of age.

Ursad sat in one of the chairs and had his hands on his face when she entered the room. He pulled his hands away and stood up suddenly when he realized she approached. He looked momentarily distressed but composed himself immediately.

"Oh, you're done already? I guess you will want to be leaving, then." Sinking back into his chair, he looked devastated. His green eyes glowed with the fire dancing in them, his face darkening.

"Yes, I have to. I wanted to thank you for your hospitality. I don't know what would've happened to me if you hadn't found me." She stopped. He looked almost agitated at her words. She bit her lip nervously and approached the chair that sat opposite of him. Dropping her pack, she sat down and looked up at him. "Ursad?"

"Yes?" His voice sounded quiet and dejected.

"What's wrong? Are you upset? Did I do something wrong?"

His green eyes drifted up to meet hers. She realized that his cheeks were wet with tears and waited uncomfortably for a response. She felt compelled to stay. *A moment or two wouldn't hurt.*

"Ursad?" she said, but he didn't respond.

"You don't have to go. You're safe here. Whatever was chasing you will not find you here. I have wards all around this area that prevent even other faeries from wandering in or knowing of your presence. You don't have to go and risk your life again, Shade. Stay here. Stay here forever, please?" His hands grasped the table while his knuckles turned white with the strain.

Shade studied them, moving her eyes carefully back to his face. She shook her head, feeling suddenly drowsy like she'd been drugged. *No, I'm just feeling exhausted, that's all.* "Ursad, I can't do that. I have people counting on me… I've been asked to do something, and I can't give up. I have to do this, or the land of Faerie faces a war between the two faerie courts. Queen Zinara needs me to get to the fountains of the Santiran lands and get the magic water to help them keep the Unseelie court from waging war against them. If I stay, the war will spill out of Faerie and into the mortal world. I live in that world, and my family does, too. I can't let that happen, Ursad. I can't." The warm spill of tears streamed down her cheeks as she spoke of her family. She missed them more than ever at that moment.

Ursad clasped his hands together on the table, his eyes no longer flaring, but once again filled with sadness. "I'm sorry. I shouldn't have ever asked you to stay here. I know you're meant for great things. I can feel it. It's selfish of me to ask such things from you." He frowned but handed her a handkerchief.

She wiped her face, blowing her nose and sniffling. Standing again, she felt her exhaustion growing. *When will I be able to go home and sleep in my own bed?* She thought sadly, frustrated beyond belief. She looked at Ursad, and an idea came to her. "You could help me, you know."

Ursad jerked his head up. He seemed to be wondering what was going through her mind but decided to ask instead. "What do you mean, Shade?"

"You're a prince of the Santiran lands. You would know the way to the fountains, wouldn't you? I don't know the way, but you could take me there, couldn't you? Please? My friends will probably be heading that way, and I could catch up." Shade found herself sitting forward in the chair, surprised at how eager she was for him to agree to the idea. She took a hold of his hands, flashing her hopeful eyes at him. "I've been feeling lonely and lost, too. It would be nice to a have friend with me."

He glanced down at their hands weaved together. Shade pulled back, her face flushed with heat and her stomach fluttering in an exhilarating way, making her wonder why this was happening. Maybe it was because she'd never had a man look at her like this before, with eyes full of hope and perhaps even desire. She glanced away, focusing on her hands now folded in her lap. *Don't make something out of nothing... he's just a friend.*

"Okay, I'll help you," he said.

Shade's face lit up as she jumped from her chair and hugged him, letting out a sigh of relief.

"Whoa, any tighter and I might not make the journey," Ursad chuckled, sounding winded. "I have to say, your enthusiasm is contagious."

"Oh, sorry about that." She loosened her grip and stepped back. "You won't regret this, Ursad. Oh, thank you, thank you, thank you! I don't know what I would've done without your help." She beamed, enjoying his quiet smile. She fought the urge to hug him again, settling for a curt nod. She wasn't feeling exhausted anymore but revived and ready to get started. "When should we go?"

"We can go now. Wait a moment, though." He opened a cabinet on the wall by the sink and rummaged through it. Tin cups and miscellaneous papers trailed out and clamored onto the floor. Shade pressed her lips together, not wanting to laugh aloud and hurt his feelings. *What a mess*, she thought. His place was cozy but cluttered.

"Here we go!" He pulled out a piece of folded parchment that looked like it'd seen too many years. He unfolded and shook it, letting dust puff out into the air. Coughing a little, he cleared his throat and laid the parchment out on the table. It was a map, another map of the faerie lands. It was extremely detailed, down to the tree stumps, and showed some rarely used paths.

Shade's eyes widened as she absorbed the incredible drawings and unusual names that were scattered throughout the parchment. She reached out and slid her finger over the area labeled "Santiran Fountains." "That's where I need to be." She glanced up and smiled at him, receiving his answering smile.

"We're here now." He traced the crescent of Solare's Beach and followed it down a crooked blue line. "This stream is the small river near where I found you." He traced the trail that led to what looked like a small town or village, past a small mountain range. Then, to a palace of stone near a much larger mountain range, which bordered all of Faerie.

"Yes, how long do you think it would take us to get there?" Shade asked, feeling the excitement flutter under her skin. They couldn't be that far from the fountains.

"It's a day and a half hike to reach the fountains. We can spend the night in the town of Genoden. The road is not what I'm afraid of, though." He paused, watching Shade's face fall. "The trail is filled with dark creatures and is probably already being watched by the Unseelie soldiers. We will have to sneak past them to reach the base of the Santiran Mountains, where the fountains are located. Staying off the road has its own dangers, too."

She pressed her lips together as she thought about what he was saying. *Can't any part of this be simple?* She thought, irritated. She was quickly learning life wasn't always easy or fun.

Chapter Fifteen

DYLAN'S FOOT SLIPPED as he climbed down the cliff of loose, muddy rock and dirt. He cursed under his breath as he grasped the jagged rocks firmly, feeling them rip into his palms. Looking down to see how much farther he was before reaching the lower banks of the falls, he eased himself carefully. He saw Shade jump and could hardly believe she'd done that. He was so enraged; stabbing Blythe had felt almost surreal. It had been only a second after she turned and faced him before he plunged his sword deep into her chest. Her deafening screech filled the air while her warm crimson blood soaked his hands. When he pulled his sword back out, he savored watching her crumble to the ground. Death engulfed her thin body, shriveling it into a pile of ashes.

Reaching the edge of the cliff, Dylan looked down into the misty cloud of river spray but saw no sign of Shade. His blood screamed in his veins as a wave of pain crawled throughout his body, making him hunch over with its intensity.

It let him know Shade was hurt, and the blood tie would drag him to her as long as it was in place. The farther he got from her, the more it would hurt.

He cursed under his breath, wishing he had reached her before she plunged into the falls. Glancing back at Blythe's withered body, or rather her pile of dust, he groaned. *At least the dryad witch queen will not get in the way again.* He knelt down, leaned over, and scanned the area for a way down the falls. He didn't like what he saw; the way was treacherous. Sheathing his sword and tightening the leather straps that held it across his chest, he strengthened his resolve. Unfortunately, this had to be done. He glanced around for the rest of the group, but the fight had pushed inland rather than toward the cliff. He could no longer hear anyone. *Damn, there's no time to be wasted.*

He left them behind, afraid to wait too long to see if anyone survived or didn't, for that matter. He had done well to protect Shade until this slip up. He mentally kicked himself for losing her. His hands burned and stung as he moved along the rocks while warm blood oozed from his cuts where the stone shredded his palms. Dylan gritted his teeth but continued. He could heal later. Right now, getting down in one piece was the top priority. When his feet were firmly planted on the slick, muddy banks, he scanned for any signs of her, but there was nothing that surfaced in the water or on the surrounding banks.

She has probably drifted away downstream, he thought. He ran as carefully as he could on the slippery rocks, splashing in small puddles and muddying up his boots to the knees. He didn't care. He had to find her, no matter where she was.

Dylan would never give up.

Chapter Sixteen

"**W**AIT!" URSAD WHISPERED urgently as he pulled Shade down behind some large boulders. She crouched next to him, reaching for her sword and quickly surveying the area.

"What? What is it? What do you see?" she asked. Her heart jumped in her chest as she waited, straining to hear a sound. The birds were singing, and the rustle of leaves swayed above them like an ocean wave. She saw and heard nothing. Irritated, she turned toward Ursad, but he had a hand up to stop her from speaking.

"Look." He pointed out in front of them. She followed his finger out into the woods and narrowed her eyes. The vegetation was thicker here, with small bushes, vines, and flowers covering the forest floor. Tall grasses shielded the dirt from the sunlight and made travel just that much more difficult. Shade scanned the area but shook her head. "I don't see anything."

Ursad placed a finger to his lips, pointing again slightly

farther to the right. "There, do you see them? Right there, in the rays of light the sun has cast near the stream."

Shade looked again, not really expecting to see anything when she did. Her eyes widened, and her mouth dropped. *Unicorns!* She watched the three creatures prance around the small stream. One was drinking the water, licking it up with its large, pink tongue. Its coat was a shiny brown, with a stark white mane and tail. The other two were all white, like the crystal snow in winter. Their coats shone almost like diamonds. Shade exhaled a breath in amazement and smiled widely.

Ursad was also smiling, admiring the creatures with awe.

"Are they actual unicorns? I thought that they didn't exist. Wow!" Shade turned back to watch them after Ursad nodded. One of the white ones nuzzled the brown one then also began lapping at the water. They neighed happily, unaware of the watchers before them. Their long legs moved gracefully through the tall grasses, and their glistening horns reminded Shade of the swirls of a candy cane stick. She felt an almost uncontrollable urge to touch one. Her fingers itched as she clenched her hands into fists and fought the compulsion to stand and walk straight toward them. She didn't want to frighten them but didn't know why she felt this way.

"Come on Shade. Unicorns like their privacy. They're a rare sight. I've seen these three many times, but that's only because I live near here. I thought you might like them. It's quite a gift that they're allowing you to see them, but we have to get going. It will be dark all too soon."

Shade shook her head. "But I… can I touch them, Ursad? They're the most beautiful things I have ever seen. Let me touch them, please!" she cried, her body trembling as she moved forward, filled with childlike excitement.

Ursad instantly had a hold of her arm and tugged, shaking his head. "Shade, look at me. Their beauty is unparalleled. It's part of their appeal, but if a human touches them, it could prove fatal. They will charm you then stab you through the heart. Only a winged unicorn would ever accept a rider, and as you can see, these are not of that breed. We must move on, Shade! You're bespelled. Let it go. Will it away." He tugged harder.

Shade felt herself needing to walk toward them but followed Ursad until they were out of sight, and the overpowering urge subsided. "What *was* that, Ursad? Why show me the unicorns in the first place, if they can kill me? Really, what was the point if you were just going to pull me away?" An overwhelming gloom stuck to her as tears glistened in her eyes. Her weakness seemed so obvious, and she hoped he wouldn't laugh.

"The unicorns are gorgeous, yes, and they might seem harmless... but like the sirens of mythology, they lure you to your death. It's best if you do not think of them anymore. I just thought that it would be good that you saw them, so you could see and feel the weight of their pull, and know just how dangerous they can be. If you were by yourself, who knows what would've happened?" Ursad cut down some of the branches around them as he spoke. The forest's greenery thickened as they progressed. It was almost as thick as a jungle now.

"Well, thank you, Ursad. It's weird to be drawn to an animal like that. I feel strange like I'm waking up from a drugged sleep, or like I'm hung-over, not that I really ever have gotten drunk or anything like that... You know, it's just an expression."

Shade yawned and pulled out her flask of water. The cool, sweet fluid met her lips and always seemed to chase the sadness away. She felt instantly better, revived. *I wonder why my energy fluctuates so much.* It made her think about feeling drugged at Ursad's cottage. A moment or so later, she shrugged off her slight concern. *I'm probably not healed completely.* She was still shocked that she'd actually jumped into a raging, rushing waterfall.

"Yes. Not everything in Faerie is what it seems. Beauty can be evil, and kindness can be a trap. Eating food from a Faerie could trap you here forever." He paused, glancing back at her for a moment before continuing. "Dancing to music in Faerie could make you dance until you die. Sprites and pixies can be quite devilish and conniving. The faerie courts may be glamorous, but everyone has their own agendas at heart. Goblins can be kind or wicked, friend or foe. It all depends. Entire dwellings could be just under your feet, and you wouldn't even know it. Just remember, Shade- trust no one and you'll be all right." He swung his machete-like sword again, slicing the underbrush out of their way.

"Does that apply to you, too?" Shade chuckled, teasing Ursad but throwing him a playful smile. He continued to clear the underbrush without saying anything. She watched him, wondering what he was thinking. "So is it true? Faeries can't lie?" Shade dodged a fallen log and turned into the slim openings of the grass that Ursad made.

"Tell a lie? Well, faeries have a funny way of stretching the truth. Most, you'll find, try to be honest. You can also frequently run into the type that gets off by messing with your mind." Ursad paused, rubbing his arm and breathing slightly hard. He apparently wasn't used to so much physical activity and most likely preferred to hang around his cottage as opposed to traveling. "We're almost to the small faery town of Genoden. It's about a half an hour away. When we get close, use the cloak that I gave you and pull your hood over your head. We don't want any unwanted attention." He continued through the brush as she pulled the cloak out.

It was dirt brown and very plain in design. The brooch clip at the neck was like the wing of a bird, the bronze shimmering in the sunlight. She draped it over her arm and hugged the bulk of it to her chest. At least this would definitely not make her stand out. Walking behind Ursad, she could hear him curse the hard labor, crunching on the fallen twigs and debris. She focused on what he told her about faeries and lies, but more on the part about unwanted attention. Her mind pushed on to the thought of Genoden and what possibilities lay ahead for her there.

"Fey have a funny way of stretching the truth," Ursad had just told her. The part about them messing with the mind alarmed her the most. As they traveled closer to the town of Genoden, she didn't think an old hooded cloak was going to protect her. Even so, Shade knew it was probable that she was going to get attention, wanted or not.

Chapter Seventeen

THE TOWN REALLY wasn't big at all. One could hardly call it a town. It was more like a small village, a one-street wonder. Its cobblestone streets and wooden houses reminded Shade of European cottages with thatch and ceramic tiles for roofs. There were people scurrying about all over the place. The market was the main street, and the second floors of the shops were apartments with living quarters. Shade pulled her cloak around her, hoping the anonymity of the crowd would make her almost invisible. She stayed glued right behind Ursad, holding a corner of his cloak as they weaved their way through the streets of vendors.

The faeries dressed in any and every color, from vibrant to drab, but it seemed the brighter, the better. Some were without cloaks, showing off their slender, pale, perfect, and muscular bodies. Ears and necks were adorned with glittering jewels and beads. They had long hair in braids, with adornments of gold and silver. Most had eyes like Blythe, large and insect-like, but there were many who used glamour to appear more human. Some lived in a nearby human city and were just used to staying in their glamoured forms. Shade nodded in acknowledgment of Ursad's quick lessons on fey culture, whispered into her ear as they treaded along.

Shade scanned the faces in the crowd for her friends, without any luck. Something about what Ursad said began to bother her. No matter how hard she thought about it, nothing would come to her so she shook it off.

They passed by stands of fresh fruit and vegetables, collecting a bag full of groceries as they went. The day was fading quickly, and the late afternoon sun burned down on them as it was setting behind the houses. Ursad whispered the need to find shelter for the night and said he would take her to one of the local inns for travelers where they could freshen up. She was quiet and nodded again, too in awe of the folks around them to say anything. The air buzzed with noise and excitement.

The inn was nestled on the town's main street. Ursad checked in, paying the innkeeper behind a bar counter without so much as a glance from her. She was plump and had her long, red hair bound into a tight bun at the base of her neck. Long strands hung from it, loosened from its tightness from the arduous workday. The rest lay draped down her shoulders and back. Her locks were a fiery red with a touch of orange. Shade never met anyone with that color hair, at least not naturally. The woman wore a work apron over her plain-jeweled blue dress. After handing Ursad a key, she waved them toward a set of stairs behind the bar area. Ursad nodded and thanked her, motioning for Shade to follow. They ascended the stairs quickly before anyone could notice the unusual pair.

Reaching the room, Shade fell against the door as it closed. She sighed, happy to be out of the crowded bar. She felt like everyone's eyes were staring right at her, even though they probably weren't. She wondered if anyone knew who she was and what she was trying to do. After being ambushed and attacked twice in such a short period of time, she was starting to feel somewhat paranoid. *I need to just relax. They probably weren't looking at me and have no idea who I am or what I'm doing.*

"You all right, Shade?" Ursad stood by the window, watching the crowds swirling below. He glanced up at her, his green eyes reflecting the last streams of sunlight.

"Yes, I'm fine, just tired, I guess. I was just wondering what happened to my friends. I thought they might have found me by now, but I don't know where they are." She stared at the single bed in the center of the room. Pressing her lips together, she felt the blood rush up to her face. She kept her eyes low and knelt down to rummage through her backpack.

Ursad watched her, a small smile playing on his lips. "You can take the bed. I'll sleep on that couch over there." He motioned to the dark green couch with threadbare upholstery.

Shade frowned and shook her head at it, almost letting a laugh escape. "Wow... that looks mighty comfy! Not gonna fight you for it. It's all yours, Ursad," she said sarcastically, failing miserably to suppress a laugh.

Ursad rolled his eyes, but his smile widened. Shaking his head, he walked over to the couch, pushed on it to test its strength, and laid out on it like a large, lazy lap dog.

Shade continued to laugh and pulled out her pajamas. She headed to the bathroom and shut the door behind her. She was tired, but the joking recharged her. Relaxing her shoulders, she turned to stare at the mirror and study her own thin and pale reflection. The journey was taking a toll. The exhaustion seemed permanently stamped on her face. She was gaunt and more fragile than before, making her avert her eyes from the mirror. She didn't like her reflection anymore. Disturbed, she made efforts to avoid it.

It seemed like a chore just to put on her soft flannel pajamas. She suddenly felt drained again. Closing her eyes, she thought about everything and everyone. Ursad turned out to be a good friend, but she worried about her other friends.

Where are they? Are they even looking for me? Maybe they think I'm dead and have retreated to the Guildrin caverns, after all, she thought, almost feeling defeated. *And what about Dylan?* Her mind pressed with urgency. She wondered if their blood tie affected him when they separated. She didn't feel anything at all but hoped he was at least okay. She sighed, feeling a slight ache in her chest for her friends. Even Dylan's annoying presence was missed, making her feel his loss even more.

Shade scratched her head and squeezed her eyes shut. *Darn that Blythe! What the hell does she want with me?* Shade's eyes flew open, remembering what the Dryad said about dragging her to the Unseelie's Queen. What did *she* want with her? They probably wanted the magic of the Santiran fountains for themselves. Why else would they even bother with her? *Maybe they just want it to have some sort of advantage over the Guildrin court.* Shade moaned, rolling her head around and massaging her neck, easing out some knots.

She looked back at the mirror and felt an odd sense of déjà vu. Reaching her hand out toward the smooth surface made her heart race before she abruptly yanked it back. The mirror did nothing; its hard surface lacked the ripples of Darren's mirror. Nothing but her careworn face stared back, but her feelings of shock and fear were evident.

I can't believe I'm afraid of mirrors now. She was scaring herself. Darren was far, far away now. No one knew where she was, especially the one with the powers of mirror travel. *He can't hurt me now.*

She clicked the door open and walked back into the large room, their sanctuary for the night, dropping her clothes into her bag before walking toward the windows. Ursad must have opened them. A soft breeze poured in, lifting the curtains up like floating ribbons. She could hear the murmur of the crowd outside with a random shout or two every now and then. Shade

196

stood just inside the window, afraid to peek outside. The sweet gusts of air caressed her cheeks, sweeping her now loose hair up into a streaming mass, tickling her neck. Closing her eyes for a moment, she relished the peace in this busy place.

"They wouldn't understand you. You and I have that in common. No one out there understands. We're different, but that makes us the same," said Ursad quietly.

She turned and studied Ursad, who was sitting on the couch watching her. They had yet to turn on the lights in the room, but his emerald eyes shone like two green beams of light. He stared intently into her face as their eyes met. Ursad then stood and walked toward her, but she didn't move from the spot, even when he came face to face with her.

Shade examined his very human hands as they reached up to cup her face. The blood rushed to her face, but she couldn't look away from his piercing eyes. She reached out and stroked the rough, bark-like skin on his face, running her fingers over the bridge of his nose and down over the softness of lips that remained. Glancing up, she took in the very human eyes that were staring back.

He was a man trapped in a shell that was not his. She could feel the deep resonating hunger and fear that ran through him as they touched. Something like sadness filled her inside like she could feel him drowning inside of himself. She pulled away, searching for air to quench her burning lungs. His intensity was suffocating. Immediately, she felt like she was waking up from a dream. Groggy and confused, she backed into the bed and sat, looking back up at him. Inquiring with her eyes for answers, her head filled with suspicion.

"Ursad, are you using magic on me?" Shade waited, looking at her new companion, hoping to hear something comforting come from his mouth. His head dropped down as his gaze fixed onto the worn floorboards. The grain of wood snarled and wove through every plank, the veins of a long-dead tree. Ursad backed away and slipped onto the couch, his face still and calm.

"I'm sorry, Shade. I couldn't help it. I thought I could make you stay with me back at my place and here, too, but I can see that my magic is not strong enough to work against you. Your power, it pushes against mine so easily. I... I'm so sorry, Shade. I didn't mean to ever harm you in any way. I hope you believe me. I just can't be alone again." His face hung down, and his hands came up to cradle it as he sank to the floor.

"Ursad, how could you? What do you mean, now and back at your house? What did you do? What have you *done?*" She glared at him, unmoving and dark. When he didn't respond, she ran over to him but managed to hold herself back. "What did you do, Ursad? Answer me!" She pulled at his arm, making him look at her once more. Green-tinted tears spilled down his rough cheeks, glinting in the dim light.

"Shade, please don't be mad. I thought you were just a human. I couldn't have known that you were part faery! I would have never tried to trap you if I knew that. That's probably the whole reason it didn't work." His fear leaked into his voice.

"What do you mean? *What*, exactly, didn't work?" Shade started to back up, afraid to know what he would say next.

"When humans enter the land of Faerie, they can be trapped here forever, especially if they eat something, food or drink, from a faery. If the faery who gives a human food or a drink wants them to stay, and the human eats what is offered, they belong to that faery forever, or until the faery lets them go. I thought if you ate my enchanted food, you would not be able to leave, and you would stay longer... and I wouldn't be alone anymore." Ursad pulled himself up and knelt on the floor before her, grabbing her hand and rubbing his cheek against it. "I swear I would never harm you! You have to believe it, Shade. Please don't go. I just wanted someone to talk to. No one ever looks at me like you do, without disgust, without judgment. I wanted it to stay like that forever."

Shade backed away out of his grasp, pressing against the footboard of the bed as she sank to the floor. Her sobs poured out as she curled up into a tight ball, hugging her legs to herself. He crawled toward her but stopped when she held her hand up and he froze.

"Don't touch me, Ursad." Shade sniffled and wiped her tears on her sleeves. She glimpsed up at him. He was sitting on his knees with his head hanging down, a beaten man. He was hard to figure out, looking small and harmless in his hunched-over defeat. She huffed, wondering what she was going to do. It seemed it wasn't going to stop, all the hell she'd gone through the past week, and it wasn't going to get any better. The tricks, treachery, and lies were everywhere. At least Ursad hadn't tried to kill her, but what of his betrayal?

What if it worked and she became his slave? She shivered at the thought and held back her last sob. She felt violated and needed time to think. "Are you done then, trying to mess with me?" Shade asked after a few moments. "Like you said, your magic doesn't work, right? You can't keep me here. You don't own me." She wiped off more drops of tears, watching him and waited for his answer.

Ursad's eyes were wide with surprise and fear. "Yes, I... I promise. I'm done. I would never try to hurt you. Please understand. It was foolish of me to try any magic on you when you have been so kind to me." He reached into his coat and brought out a soft, baby blue handkerchief. He crept toward her and held it out, trying not to get too close.

Shade snatched it from him and watched him jump back, concern and relief both flashing across his face. "You better not try it again. I can feel it every single time. I guess I am part faery after all." She paused and looked at him before letting out a laugh that made him jump. "It didn't work, so it was for nothing, and I have nothing to fear from you at all." She blew her nose and stood up, frowning as he pulled himself back up onto the couch and sat, wary of her.

"Tomorrow, we're going to the Santiran Fountains, Ursad. From there, you're on your own again. Just take me there, and then we're done. The maps you showed me, they're correct, right?"

He nodded sadly.

"Okay, then. I want to get some sleep now, so goodnight."

He nodded again and pulled a blanket from the arm of the couch before lying down and folding his arm for a pillow.

Shade slid down into the sheets and pulled the pillow over her head. She pressed her face into it, wishing she could dig her way into the fluffy feathers of it and fade away into the softness. She reached over and turned off the lamp by the bedside. Staring out into the darkness now covering the windows, she gazed at the soft moonlight, a small beacon from the outside world. The curtains danced in the gusty, warm breeze. It was spring now in Faerie, always changing with the hours. She'd never get used to the weirdness of this place.

Drifting off to sleep, she listened to the sound of Ursad's slow and rhythmic breathing. Cocooned in her warm blankets, she slipped away into dreams.

Chapter Eighteen

"SHADE."

"Who's there?"

"*Shade, it's us, your spirit guides. You must hurry! The Unseelie court moves to stop you. You must get to the fountains tomorrow and retrieve the magic waters quickly!*"

"What then? What do I do with it? Where do I go? How do I get back to the Guildrin Caves?"

They smiled at her with their ethereal faces and smooth hair infinitely suspended in midair like there was a silent, unseen wind that blew just for them.

"*You will know. Dylan is waiting for you. He needs you, Shade. You and only you can save him.*"

"Where is he?" Shade furrowed her brow at the sisters, worry permeating her thoughts.

"*Just follow your path. It will take you straight to him. Remember, when all is dark, you are your own light. Don't forget the stones Ilarial gave you. They can make a path where none can be seen.*"

Shade looked at them, her face filled with confusion. Why was it they never made sense? Their faces left no hint of what exactly they meant. She shouted out to them, but her voice was gone. They shook their heads and smiled, waving a goodbye. Shade screamed to them but felt the gray and the darkness grow around her, obscuring them from her sight.

***

SHADE WOKE WITH a start, her heart drumming in her chest. Her pillow was stuffed and wadded into a ball under her head as she lay on her stomach. She looked around the dark room. The moonlight was dim now, and dark gray misted across the room. It was probably near morning. She sat up on her elbows, looking toward Ursad, fast asleep on the small couch by the wall, gently breathing.

The short rays of dawn mixed with moonlight as the minutes ticked by. Stretching, she stood up and shuffled over to the open window. The streets were quiet; only the occasional person with baskets or a pushcart filled with fruit meandered about. The morning market was prepping itself for the needs of many. Shade breathed in and felt a sense of peace filling her with each inhalation. She turned and grabbed her bag before heading to the bathroom.

When she emerged, the soft sunlight filled the windows. She showered and brushed her long hair into a ponytail. With her fresh jeans on and a hoodie pulled over a t-shirt to keep the morning chill out, she pulled on socks and sneakers before tying the laces. Shoving everything back into her bag, she glanced at Ursad, still fast asleep on the couch. His soft snores told her that he was definitely out, making her grin and shake her head. She was ready to go, and he was out like a light. It was hard to be angry with him when he looked like that, innocent and peaceful. However, she wasn't ready to forgive what he had done.

She looked at the pile of maps on the small table next to the couch, scooping them up and placing them into her pack. Donning her cloak, she headed for the door but stopped. She turned and watched Ursad sleeping, dead to the world. Leaving her bag by the door, she approached him, staring at his rough face and soft eyelids. He seemed so calm and almost handsome, deep in sleep and dreaming.

She wondered what he saw behind his lids, in a world that was his alone. She hated to leave him like this, without a goodbye, but she had to go. His intentions weren't honest, and she couldn't tolerate that. Deep in her thoughts, she squeezed her eyes shut. Shade liked him but felt betrayed by his magic. It hurt that he'd done such things without her knowledge. He could've been so much more than just a friend. Flinging her eyelids open, she knew what she had to do. Bending down, she let her lips glide softly over his still very human-like ones. One lonely kiss for the road.

She stood back and saw that he hadn't stirred and remained oblivious. She silently wished him a goodbye as she left the room. At the door, she swung her pack onto her back and shut the door softly behind her. As it clicked, she never looked back again, but she'd forgiven him after all.

The streets filled up quickly. She pulled the hood of her long cloak over her face, hiding her hooded sweatshirt and jeans efficiently enough. She looked around and watched the people scurry by, none of them giving her a moment's glance.

Well, I'm alone again. She breathed in deeply and walked toward the edge of town, feeling her newfound determination filling her with purpose.

Shade felt no fear and embraced the anonymity of the crowd. It was a most welcome protection. As their magic swirled around her, she drew it in for comfort. She continued to weave around the people and made it to the edge of town. Walking along the road, she followed it until the town fell out of sight. Now she truly was alone. The gravel crunched under her feet, and the leaves of the trees rustled franticly in the breeze. Pulling out the maps she'd taken from Ursad, a feeling of regret washed over her as she thought about the way she left. After what he'd done to her... no, leaving was the only way she could forgive him. If this whole experience taught her one thing, it was that forgiving wasn't the same as forgetting.

It was time to get a move on. Obviously, this wasn't the kind of place where you made lifelong friends. *I've got something more important to do, anyway.* She smoothed out one of the maps on a flat boulder that was close to her height. She traced her finger along the road that she followed out of the town. According to the map, she was heading north toward the mountains. She could see the great mountain peaks just beyond the forest. They seemed to be taunting her, appearing closer than they really were.

Sighing heavily, she folded the maps up neatly and placed them into her backpack. Pulling out an apple and a roll of bread at the same time, she munched on her small breakfast as she walked briskly along the road.

The day wore on, and she frequently stopped, checking the maps and refueling on the many snacks and drinks she carried with her. She made sure to put any garbage back into her bag in a trash bag or bury it. Frequent stopping to listen out to see if anyone was following her ate up the time quickly. She would go many miles on the desolate road before she came across someone, then she'd crouch behind trees or fallen logs in the tall grasses of the forest floor until they passed. She wondered if any of them were Ursad. Shade highly doubted it since they all were on carriages or small carts that wheeled on by.

She thought about him constantly and his unfortunate curse, wondering what his real face looked like. She didn't like the fact that she'd left him alone again, especially when they agreed to travel together. She shook her head. It was unavoidable. *He screwed up.* She wasn't going to have people around her who she couldn't trust entirely. Not now, when she was in so much danger.

Glancing at the lonely road, she pulled her pack tighter to her back. It was lonelier still without him. Where was everyone? Her thoughts wandered to Sary, Braelynn, Ewan, Stephan, Than, Soap, Jack, and Dylan. Somehow, probably because of the blood bind, she knew Dylan was not returning to Teleen without her. He was out here somewhere, with or without her friends. She hoped she'd run into him soon. The forest seemed so vast and lonely without them joking beside her and chatting vibrantly, making her miss them terribly.

A sound made her pause as she listened to the woods. She heard the animals scurrying around and the birds singing high up, hidden in the canopy. Swearing she heard something, she turned, straining her ears for any little noise. The blue sky above was swallowed by the trees as the branches swayed in the soft breeze. The strong scent of pine and damp mulch swam in the air, circling around and penetrating her nostrils. Nothing showed itself, so she trekked on.

It happened slowly, but she realized she'd been changing and actually was enjoying the woods. So much happened to her, she barely noticed this subtle difference in her personality. Somehow, though, it was clear she was now different. Her life was altered and would never be the same.

She rubbed her arms in the coolness of the late morning breezes. The altitude grew with each step as she walked toward the mountain range in the distance. *I'll have to use Dylan's blanket soon.* Already it felt colder as she edged closer to the Santiran Mountains.

As the day wore on, Shade decided not to walk on the gravel road anymore as it was becoming congested with travelers. More traffic could be heard as carts and bands of people shuffled by, heading away from the mountains mostly, in the opposite direction of her. She wondered why there weren't as many people headed toward the mountains. The tension of possibly being seen and not knowing if the others were harmless or trouble was fraying her nerves. She'd hide behind trees until the road emptied and the people passed.

At one point, the road filled with soldiers, and she'd hidden behind a large fallen tree for about half an hour before she could get moving again. The soldiers wore armor similar to Blythe's army, and the sight of them made her heart jump and her breath tighten inside her chest.

The flashback of the fight in the river lands made her want to vomit. She had to breathe in slowly and close her eyes, praying she wasn't going to be found by this strange militia. Who knew where their loyalties laid? She was relieved when they'd moved on without a moment's glance in her direction. Shade was paranoid after that and dashed between the trees, pausing often to listen for any movement or snap of twigs. Every noise made her jump. It was hard to stay focused. She was starting to feel exhausted as the day wore on. She was about ready to hike farther from the road to camp for the night when she heard something that made her skin crawl.

"That little bitch killed Blythe! When I get my hands on her scrawny little neck, I'm gonna snap it like the twig she is!" a husky male voice echoed through the trees.

"Yeah, and give her a stab for my friend Mike. He died as well. Those warriors were no joke. Where did she find them? That red-haired one got me on the shoulder, and the darn stitches hurt! That's okay, though. I knocked her out before she got too much of me. Wish I could've finished her off. Whoever called retreat was a chicken shit," another harsh voice replied.

Shade's eyes widened at the description matching Sary's looks. She gripped her backpack straps until her knuckles were white and her fingers ached in protest, fighting the urge to scream. She wanted to pull out her sword and charge the two soldiers. She closed her eyes and slowed her breathing again, shifting on her legs, which were going numb from crouching too long. Shade cringed as she heard the snap of a twig under her sneaker. She held her breath and waited.

"Hey, did you hear that? What was that?"

"It's probably a squirrel stupid!" the second the soldier snapped.

"Shut up, moron. Someone's there," the first soldier responded, clearly sounding irritated.

The scratch of metal sliding out of a sheath made Shade swallow hard, her throat tight with nerves. *Oh no!*

Now they were whispering, so she couldn't hear them any longer. Their careless footsteps crunched on bits of wood and dead mulch under their boots. As their steps grew closer, her panic intensified. She heard them come to a stop, but they didn't speak. They seemed to be waiting for her to betray herself. The delay made her impatient, and she decided to risk peeking over the log to get their position.

She spotted them not too far from her. They were scanning an area to the right, but soon enough, they would be near enough to see her. She glanced behind her, into the endless forest for an escape route.

"There she is! Get her!" They grunted as they turned toward her and began sprinting, dodging other logs and debris. Shade's eyes widened, and she bolted, running as fast as she could through tangled branches, twigs, and wet leaves.

"Stop! You're in a lot of trouble! Stop and we won't kill you," one of the men called. He did not sound very convincing.

Yeah, that's gonna make me come to a halt.

She jumped over boulders and logs, occasionally slipping and sliding as the terrain became uneven and full of dips and hills. Falling to her hands and scraping them on twigs and rocks, she felt no pain but was sure it was going to leave marks. She came to a rock bed where the boulders were enormous and bobbed out all across the land. She hopped on the flattened tops, nearly losing her step as her feet slid over the smooth surfaces. Her arms waved in the air, catching her balance just in time before she fell into one of the crevices.

"Get back here, you little... Damn! Reike, my foot's caught! Get her!" One soldier was struggling to pull his foot from a crack between two boulders. He waved at his partner to follow her.

Shade glanced back but was near the end of the boulders when she missed her step and slammed against one side of a large stone. She tried to grip the rugged rock but only scraped her hands as she slipped down into the large hole between the rocks. She slid and slipped, down under the boulders, until the hole morphed into a tunnel, sending her spiraling down into darkness.

Chapter Nineteen

THERE WAS NOTHING but darkness and silence surrounding her. Shade was face down on the fine, sandy dirt floor. Sparks twinkled in her vision as she moved, causing her to slow down and breath through the wave of dizziness. She must have hit her head when she landed. Moving her arms under her body, she pushed herself into a sitting position, or what felt like it because the darkness seemed to cancel out her sense of direction. This did not help her stomach. She lurched the last bits of her afternoon snack into the black dirt around her.

Yuck! Shade spit onto the ground, trying to expel the remnants of the nasty taste in her mouth. Breathing in deeply, she sat up again, balancing herself with her hands in the dirt. Bending over to let some more blood rush to her throbbing head, she let her senses normalize. *I think need a doctor or something.* As the moments passed, the pounding lessened, and her stomach settled. She was able to sit straight and fished through all her pockets for the light stone. Finding it in the back pocket of her jeans, she wrapped her hand around it, willing it to life.

The soft glow grew with every breath she took. Her fear subsided just a bit when the light brightened and showed more strength. Holding it in the center of her palm and stretching her fingers straight, it lit the room like a small lantern. The light was dim, but she could see that the room was rounded and made out of stone. Dirt, rocks, and debris littered the floor of the underground cave. She studied the smooth walls all around her, not seeing any exits or cracks in the stone. The ceiling where she was sure she'd come from was sealed and just as smooth as the walls.

What the...? How the hell do I get out of here? How the hell did I get in?

Shade once again scanned the room to no avail. It was like being inside a very hard bubble. She placed the stone in front of her in the dirt, thinking *Please, just keep glowing.* She prayed as she watched the warm yellow light, her only solace in the dark. She smiled, proud that she'd managed to do some sort of magic. She attempted to stand up and take a better look around, but the floating stars in her vision caused her to kneel back and wait out the dizziness.

After a few moments, Shade felt well enough to stand and was glad she didn't hit her head on the ceiling. Walking along the side of the walls, she felt along the stone, finding it rougher and grainier than the boulders aboveground. The bumps scraped against her already wounded and sore hands. After inspecting every inch of the surface, she was sure there was no way out. Spinning around with her heart pounding in her chest, she felt claustrophobic and frustrated. All kicking the stone wall and punching it with her hands gained her was more pain. Her hands were burning as her closed fists irritated her excoriated palms. Shade slumped to the floor, leaning against the cold rock. She hugged her knees to her chest and rocked back. Her sighs echoed in the cool, still air. She could smell the dampness and mold intermingled within it.

The time ticked by, and she didn't know how long she rocked herself, but it was long enough for her quiet tears to dry up, staining her dirty cheeks. Even her hands stopped throbbing. She pulled off her pack and dug through it for some water, hoping that afterward, she might be able to think more clearly. Her ravenous chewing on a small snack filled the emptiness for a moment or two. She wished her spirit guides were still near and giving her much-needed advice. It made her wonder why the attack caused her to expel them along with Darren. Rubbing her arms, the chilling air ran down her entire body. Pulling out Dylan's warm blanket, she wrapped it around her until just her eyes were visible from within its folds. The warmth provided by the coverage was instant, and her eyes were drooping with drowsiness, heavy with sleep.

Feeling the solitude pressing on her, Shade breathed in the faint scent of Dylan's skin on the blanket. She sighed and watched her light stone glow softly in the dark. *What now?* She pulled out her sleeping bag from her tent and laid it on the soft dirt. Setting her pillow down, the exhaustion overwhelmed her body, and her bones ached from the events of the day. She hadn't realized how tired she'd become after being chased through the forest. Wrapping the blanket around once more, she drifted to sleep, hoping to find someone, even in her dreams.

***

SHADE'S EYES FLUTTERED open, adjusting to the blue flickering light in the room as it intermittently broke up the darkness. The rock seemed to bounce the glow around and reflect the blue coloring. She blinked again and sat up, confirming that she was still in her stone dungeon. Realizing her light stone wouldn't be as bright as the glow shining in the cave, she rubbed away the sleep from her eyes and looked around.

Did someone just call my name?

"Shade! It *is* you! I knew you were close, but I never thought that you would be here!" a male voice said, filled with relief and eagerness. She stared at the figure; electricity crackled and flames radiated from him like a torch. She stood up quickly, wavering for a moment, eyes wide in disbelief.

Dylan! It was Dylan, without glamour, aglow in the most amazing blue fire swimming along his skin. It licked the air around him.

"Dylan? How did you get here? How did you find me?" Her eyes scanned him, waiting for his still-familiar face to change into someone else. Her heart leaped with the utmost happiness at the sight of him. She smiled and tried to stand until a sway of dizziness changed her mind.

"I don't know. I came to an ancient riverbed with enormous boulders throughout it. I was compelled to be there, and I'd been tracking you for a while. I can feel when you've been in a place, almost like I'm experiencing a feeling of déjà vu. It felt so strong there, but I didn't even know where to look. Suddenly, the land opened up and sucked me down between the boulders, and here I am. That's never happened to me before, definitely a first." He paused, beaming at her. "I was meant to find you. I can't even explain it. It's the weirdest thing to fall and be right here with you. No, wait. Don't get too close. You might get burned." Shade retracted her hand, just realizing she'd been reaching out to him.

"Oh, I'm sorry. I didn't realize."

He smiled and nodded. "It's ok. You know how we look without the glamour to encase our actual bodies. If you were to touch me, I could hurt you."

Shade pressed her lips together, confusion flashing across her face. "Darren touched me when he was unglamoured

212

like you are now, and I didn't get burned. I asked Soap and Jack about it, and they had no answers for me. It makes me think that I might not be harmed if I do touch you." She admired his flames and took in his handsome face.

It was a mask of shock as he shook his head. "I don't know about that, Shade. Maybe it was a trick of his. He could do so many things with mirrors that would make you believe things were real when they were really just illusion. He was a genius at that." Dylan's face was grim at the thought of his brother.

"No, I know because he was shocked when I didn't burn. He said that much, and I saw it in his eyes." Her eyes glazed over with the memory of the malice stamped on Darren's face. He was filled with so much pleasure when he'd seen the fear wash over her. She looked at Dylan and almost expected to see Darren standing before her. They were similar in appearance, but even as brothers, they didn't exactly look alike. They certainly didn't behave the same way.

"Well, if you must, Shade, I will tone the flames down. Then you can touch my skin with just a finger. That way it won't hurt you too much. Deal?"

She nodded and watched his flames shrink back into just embers glowing across his skin. She studied it and watched how his skin looked smooth and untouched under the heat. He watched her as she walked forward, extending her arm and hand up toward him. They both held their breath as she reached her finger up to his skin and slowly ran it up his arm. Dylan was still holding his breath when her soft touch reached him, seeming to freeze time.

Nothing… is happening. He felt warm, not hot. There was no pain, flying ash, or fear. She extended the rest of her fingers out to brush his forearm. His flames spread to full glow, and she remained unscathed. She brought her hand back and studied it. Dirt and drying scrapes peppered the skin across her hand but no burns or soot. She looked at Dylan, who was as stunned as she was. He was observing her intently, making her suddenly aware of his closeness.

"Dylan, nothing happened. What am I? Why am I protected from your fire?" She stared at him, awaiting an answer.

Dylan seemed to come back into himself, shaking off whatever was holding him in his thoughts. Gazing at her, he shook his head. "I… I don't know, Shade. I wish I knew. There are so few who can do what you just did, so very few. Most are just Teleen, but you…." He kept his head shaking back and forth in disbelief. "Amazing," he whispered and then looked back at her, a smile now hiding the seriousness of his face.

"Do you know what that means, Shade? You could marry a Teleen. You could, without difficulty, find a mate within our court. Being a female, you have no idea how rare you are, and how well you shall be received."

"What? I don't want to get married. Well, at least not yet. Where did that come from? I… I'm just a kid. Why would I even think of that yet?" She huffed, flustered at his statement. "Dylan, what do you mean there are so few who can do what I did? Do you mean the not getting burned part? Who else besides a Teleen can do that?" She waited and watched his smile fade just as fast as it had come.

"Our race is dying out, Shade. We can only marry another Teleen, and very few of us are able to have children. Only another race compatible with us would help strengthen our line. Our clan dies otherwise. The only other races of faeries that would even be compatible with us, strong enough to withstand our powers, are even rarer than the Teleen."

"Who are these people?" she asked impatiently. The look on his face was definitely disapproving that she'd even asked him.

"Changelings, for one thing, or elementals of fire, such as fire-witches. Finding someone like that is so rare. I have only known of one changeling and one elemental fire-witch ever, and they were paired already." He paused, narrowing his eyes at her. "Do you know if you are either of those, Shade?"

"Me? No, no way. If I am, I wouldn't know it. I mean, what's a changeling and an elemental witch? How would I know which one I am if I am one of those?"

"Well," he offered, "a changeling is simple. They're capable of changing into anything they want to. Human, bear, squirrel, different types of fey, like Teleen, Enlors, which are sprites, or Gidals, which are trolls. Anything really. It's a rare ability like I said. An elemental fire-witch is, well, a human mortal witch, in every meaning of the word, but with an affinity to fire. They can control it, wave it around, and send it roaring through a forest. Whatever you can imagine doing with it, they can do it. They can cast spells, charms, curses, and things of that nature. There are many kinds of witches, Shade, but rare is it to find elemental witches. They're special." His face darkened as his eyes met hers.

"Shade, if my people knew that you could be one of this kind of unique individuals, especially since Darren exposed it with his attack…I have to warn you and let you know that upon returning to Teleen, all unmated, unmarried males in my race will be courting you for your attention. You'll probably be bombarded by them, pushed to choose one of them for a mate."

"What? Oh no, no, no. They can't make me do anything. I won't choose anybody. I won't be staying there at all. I wouldn't return there after what happened, and besides, I'm going home."

Dylan nodded and sighed. "Yes, Shade, of course, you will want to go back, but I must warn you. Even at home, you will not be left alone. Teleen men are relentless. Our Queen will not stop them, either, not until you choose one of them as your mate. Only then will it be ordered by our Queen to leave you alone. It is vital for the survival of our people. I'm sorry, Shade. At the very least, I had to warn you before that happens."

Shade let her face screw up in disgust. Marriage was the least of her worries. She wished he hadn't said a thing about it at all. She turned and slumped down onto her sleeping bag again. She still felt tired and was now irritated on top of it all. She stared up at the ceiling, lit up in Dylan's glow. The whole cave was flickering in the light. There was still no sign of a way out. She pulled the blanket over her head and curled up into a ball.

"Dylan, how are we getting out of this place? I looked everywhere. I don't even see where I came in! What is this place? I feel claustrophobic, and it's cold down here." She closed her eyes and waited.

"It's a place to forget oneself or forget about someone. It's either a blessing or a curse, depending how you look at it. This cave is one of the ancient prisons of Faerie. People were left here for years to forget about themselves, wither away, or to emerge fresh, with a clean slate. It's an immortal's dungeon, or oubliette, Shade. I am surprised you stumbled across one. Usually, they can trap only immortals." He paused. She listened to the silence, waiting for him to continue while pondering his words. "It does make me wonder why you are down here. You must be immortal then, to end up in such a place. You could be a powerful changeling for all we know."

"Who gets people out of these things? Who made them? Was it the Unseelie?" she muttered. She felt her eyes become heavy with sleep, rubbing them as she struggled to stay awake.

"No. As I said, this room could be used as a prison but not always. It can be a safe place, you know, like when you're being pursued and you need to seek a sanctuary. No one gets people out of these places except for the faery who put you here. In your case, it's you. You must will it so yourself–to escape, I mean. *You* must get us out of here, Shade."

She thought of his last words as she drifted off to sleep.

What a bunch of crock.

Chapter Twenty

SHADE WOKE UP in darkness yet again. She heard soft breathing across the room. Was she still in the oubliette? The cold, damp air confirmed her disappointment as she sat up, pulling the blanket down from her head. She felt around for her light stone, which lay cold and dormant in the center of the room where she'd left it. Grasping it, she reignited it. Her eyes focused in the dim light as it grew. She watched the bundle that was Dylan softly sleeping. He wasn't aglow anymore. He must have slipped his glamour back on like a robe before bed.

She set the light stone down again, wondering if she should wake him and also how long she slept. She didn't know what day or time it was anymore. It could have been hours or minutes, and she wouldn't even know it down here in the dark, dank bowels of the earth. Her cell phone was long dead since she hadn't charged it recently. She leaned against the smooth stone and thought about everything they spoke about before she'd let sleep win her over... had it been the night or day before?

Shade felt sorry for doubting Dylan, but he didn't make much sense to her half of the time. She was glad that she wasn't alone down here anymore but pondered the subject of escape. *Just will it so? What the heck was that about? Like, tell the stone to open up and let me out kind of thing?* Shade thought with frustration. She was pretty sure she hadn't asked to be placed here, at least not on purpose.

She stood up again and shook her head. *Oh, whatever, this entire situation doesn't make any sense. Changelings, witches, faeries, and whatever the hell else pops up.* She wondered how much of the world she'd grown up in was real at all. It seemed like none of it was. It was just a lie, just a façade that the Fey played on all of humankind. They probably got a good laugh out of it all the time. *Oh, what dumb humans they are. They can't figure out that more than half their land isn't even on their maps because it's ours. We can do whatever the heck we want, and they don't know any better. Idiots!*

She kicked the wall again, but not hard enough to hurt her foot. It did force her to grunt, though. She thumped her back against the wall, groaning.

"You all right there? The wall isn't going to kick you back, you know. It didn't really do anything to you, anyway." Dylan had his hands behind his head while he remained lying, head up and staring at her, grinning.

"Oh, shut up. How do we get out? We need to get out, like yesterday, Dylan! How do we do it?" She stared at him, huffing out her anger as she marched back to her sleeping bag. She shook it out violently and stuffed it into her bag. Pulling out her canteen, she gulped down the cool drops of water. She tossed her bag to the side as she sank down to the ground, feeling the tears sting her eyes. Darn it if she was going to give Dylan any more signs of her current breakdown. She just couldn't take the mortification.

Dylan sighed and stretched out. He stood up and held

his hand out to her. "Come on. We gotta go." He waited as she stared back up at him, tears still pooling in her eyes. She took his hand and stood up, swinging her pack on her back as she followed him over to the smooth walls of stone. "Now, to leave these prisons, one must believe in impossibility. Lay your hands on the stone and think. Think about the mountains you saw before you got here and the fountains. Wish your way out. Make a road in your head that will lead you to the place you want to go, and it will happen. Make a way for yourself, for us."

Shade studied his face, feeling a prick of hope mixed with disbelief as he spoke. She licked her lips and did as he told her. Closing her eyes, she wished the stone would open and let her out into the sunlight, into the wilderness she so longed to see again. She prayed and wished as hard as she could, caressing the cool rock and waiting for the stone to do something under her dirty fingers.

Nothing.

Shade opened her eyes and frowned at the rock. She looked over at Dylan and shook her head. "Nothing's happening, Dylan. What if we're stuck here forever?" She stared at the curved wall, wanting a way out where there was none. She sucked her breath in. "Wait!" She'd just remembered something and grabbed her pack, rummaging through it frantically. She pulled out the rune stones Ilarial gave her. She held them in her gritty hand and stared at the symbols. How was she supposed to know what she had to do with them? *Ilarial said they would help me find my way when there is none, but how?* She stared at them and closed her eyes, silently praying for a way out of the oubliette.

"Shade! Something's happening!" Dylan pulled her out of her thoughts. She glanced around to find the rock fading in front of them with a soft rumble. The bubble was no longer a bubble but extending into an elongated hall. It grew longer into the earth until it reached the top of the soil. Steps formed out of the smooth rock, and sunlight gradually began streaming in through dirt. Roots dangled down from the forest floor.

The walls stopped rumbling, and the ground stilled. She looked over at Dylan as they now stared down the small corridor to the stairs. She smiled and looked at him as he reached back, grabbing his cloak and her light stone from the ground. He tossed the stone to her as they walked up the stairs. "Way to go, Shade. See, you just have to believe in yourself."

"It worked! Ilarial gave me these rune stones that would help me out when I needed it. I didn't even do much but wish for there to be a way out. Wow, it's amazing Dylan!" They both shouted with glee as they scurried up each step.

The sun bore down on them like a spotlight in their faces. Shade's eyes cramped in pain as they adjusted to the bright sunlight. She blinked and shaded her eyes with her hands, looking about. They were no longer in the river of boulders but at the base of the Santiran mountain range. She pulled herself up and out of the hole in the ground, with Dylan just behind her. The ground seemed to swallow up the darkness of the prison as they watched it close. Only grass and leaves lay where the exit used to be. She bent to touch the patch of grass and dirt. It felt firm and undisturbed.

"Look, Dylan!" She pointed up the massive wall of the mountain. "It's the Santiran Mountain! We must be so close to the fountains! We're almost there!" She walked with a little skip in her step, almost bursting with anticipation. She'd find the magic waters of the Santiran fountains, and then she'd be that much closer to going home.

Home. At the thought of going back to her snotty-nosed brothers and bratty sister, she missed them so much, her heart ached in her chest. She'd be able to hug her mother again. She wanted to run up the mountain as fast as possible. She could barely contain herself.

Dylan grabbed her arm and tugged hard. She was about to curse him out when he pressed a finger to his lips and pulled again for her to follow him. Her eyes widened as she strained to hear what he heard. She followed him behind a boulder near a dip in the mountain's side, almost like someone had taken a scooper and scooped out a chunk of the rocky base. She wasn't sure she liked being inside the hollowed stone, but whatever Dylan heard tripped his alarms at full force.

"What is it, Dylan?" Shade whispered. She was about to ask him again when she heard it. Murmurs of voices seemed to dance on the rock walls and made her turn her head in all directions to discover which way they were coming from. Maybe this hiding spot was not such a good idea. The voices grew louder and echoed even more like they were hitting a concaved amplifier.

They waited quietly, barely breathing in fear of discovery. The voices continued to dance around them, as they would in a crowded arena. She knew they were coming from the side they would have to follow to get to the fountains. She gritted her teeth with impatience, willing the men to move along already.

When the murmurs faded away, Dylan peeked over his shoulder at her and nodded his head in the same direction as the voices. The strangers were going where they needed to be. Shade nodded in agreement, but the pit in her stomach flipped with anxiety. She wasn't sure how many people might be waiting for them around the bend. How many Unseelie were guarding the mountain?

They found the path deserted and were breathing out sighs of relief as they crept out silently up the gravelly path. Climbing the rocky path, they frequently slipped from the loose dirt. They eased their way up the mountain, the altitude shifting into thinner and cooler air. The view was breathtaking, with emerald green treetops where the forest spread out for miles. The mountains stood tall, like a row of kings standing around the valley and framing the forest with their embrace. Shade took it in and smiled, finding nature beautiful even in her current situation. Again, she felt as if she'd changed somehow. The woods seemed alive all around as if breathing in the air along with her.

A cool breeze caressed them as they ascended. The forest began to grow again as thick as it was in the valley below. The mountainous path turned into a narrow crevice as they slid through one by one. Inside was a plateau cove, green and partly shaded by the mountain. Trees stood in all sizes around the path that led to the other side of the cove's rock walls, where a carved opening stood in a shadow that never reached the sun's rays.

Shade followed Dylan, taking refuge in the shrubs and tree trunks that kept them hidden from the sight of the two soldiers, who were both standing casually by the entrance. The men were chatting loudly and hadn't noticed the intrusion. Shade snickered, sure the Unseelie queen would not be happy with the help around here. Dylan glared at her, warning her to be quiet.

He studied them and then sank back down to a hidden crouch. "I only see the two guards. The Santiran fountains are inside that darkened doorway. If we can get through them, we should be all right. It seems that they weren't expecting us to be here at all." He paused, furrowing his brow in deep concentration. "Unless, of course, it's a trap." He bit his lip, furrowing his brow again in thought.

"How are we going to take on two guards?" She glanced over at them. They didn't even have their helmets on. They were the same height with the same color and length of hair, blonde strands that hit their shoulders. They were tossing jokes back and forth and giving each other friendly pushes and punches. As she looked carefully, she could see that they were identical twins.

Great, double the trouble. How am I going to take on two husky guards? She squatted back down and out of sight, glancing at Dylan with worry spread across her face. "I'm not a fighter. I haven't learned enough to take on one of these guys. They're each as huge as a house! They could crush me with a finger!" She took a deep breath, attempting to calm her nerves.

"Shh, it's all right. You can distract them, and I'll take them out. They won't know what hit them." He smiled and began pulling out his weapons, unsheathing his sword and draping a rope across his chest and shoulders. She watched him prepare, her face contorted in horror.

"You mean, I'll be the bait? Wait a minute. I don't know. That doesn't sound very promising. You might as well mark me for death. What do I say? How do I distract those two big buffoons? They don't look that smart, but who needs brains with brawn like that?" Shade rambled on nervously. She wrung her hands over and over, feeling almost faint with anxiety. She grasped Dylan's tunic as he started to leave.

"Hey, don't worry. You have to trust me a little, Shade. I've done this before, many times. I was captain of the Teleen Guard, remember? One doesn't become captain by letting their wards get killed." He snickered but stopped, catching her daggered look. "Calm down. Just prance out there and act like some lost little maiden who needs their help. They will fall for it, believe me. Just act dumb. It shouldn't be too hard." He laughed quietly but stopped again when she threw another nasty glare at him. He turned and started to move, keeping cover in the trees, until Shade could no longer see him.

Shoot, shoot, shoot! She looked again around the tree she was hiding behind and watched the twins. They were still cackling at each other's jokes. *Okay, Shade, you know you have to. Sometimes we have to do what we don't want to. Just get it over with already!*

She crept closer to the twins. Peeking at the guards made her stomach twist in a bad way. Taking a deep breath, she stood up straight, fixing her hair as best as she could. She put her most convincing clueless face on, including a broad smile. She then walked straight into their line of sight.

"Um, excuse me, boys, but do you know where the nearest town is? I've done gone and got myself lost. Would either one of you gentlemen care to show me which way to go?" She batted her eyes at them in the girliest way she could think of. Flipping her hair back, she didn't think she looked irresistible, but she'd figured, *what the hell. It's worth a shot.*

"Stay put there, miss. Andre, grab her and make sure she ain't got no weapons." Draden waved at his brother. They were immediately on full alert and converted into the soldiers they were trained to be. Shade swallowed hard and stiffened but recovered almost immediately, trying to act like it was no big deal.

"Oh, come on now, boys. Why would a little lass like me be carrying around a weapon? I wouldn't touch those filthy things if you paid me. It would ruin my nails." She curled her fingers into her palm, hoping they wouldn't notice her dingy and short cuticles. She cranked up her smile and flashed her eyes at the approaching guard again, the one named Andre. He crouched by her and signaled her to hold her arms up as he did a quick sweep of her sides and yanked her pack from her back. She was about to protest but decided that silence would be the safest choice. She hoped the glamour charm Dylan waved onto her pack was good enough to hide all her stuff, especially the weapons.

"I don't see any, Draden. She's got nothing but makeup, a brush, and some clothes in this thing." He tossed it back to her, and she caught it as it whacked her chest. She frowned but slipped it back on, widening another smile across her face and twirling her hair. It dangled from her ponytail and flew about like a wispy halo around her face. She waited, observing the other guard, who squinted his suspicious eyes at her and frowning.

"What's your name, *girl*?" Draden approached her with

224

his sword drawn. Shade held her breath as he came up to her, bending his head down to meet her eye to eye. With the cold stare of ice blue eyes, he appeared more menacing than his twin. His long blond hair was pulled into a loose braid and dangled partially in his face. Up close, his face was worn with years of hard fighting. Deep lines creased his eyes and mouth, and stubble grew, sprinkled across his skin. His twin looked just as hard, but maybe not as cold. She swallowed and wondered how to answer this big man with his sword pointed right at her. She took a breath, staring back into the warrior's eyes.

"My name is Alice, Alice Coleman. I'm sorry. I must have interrupted something. I'll just leave then and go along my merry way. I really didn't want to impose or anything." Draden, pressing his sword into her clavicle, cut her off. She stepped back, but he grabbed her arm to stop her. She felt her panic rush over her.

Where the hell is Dylan?

"I don't believe you." He pressed the blade a little more, and her skin burned with the tiny cut. She held back a cry and stared back at him, anger spilling across her face as she clenched her lips together.

"I don't care what you think. I said, I'll be on my way now." She continued to stare and waited since he did not let up on his grip. He glared back and seemed to ponder her face, stamping it into his memory. She wondered if he would actually hurt her or even kill her. She didn't want to find out, but her impatience grew with every second.

She decided to chance another step backward. Slowly, she retreated but watching him dart his eyes just a moment made her pause. He continued to press the sword into her but did not push it in any further. She stared at his eyes and willed him to drop the sword. She beckoned with her eyes, like a silent prayer. She felt her magic swirl within her, inside her heart, spinning around like a mirror ball and growing with each moment. It seemed like a breath flowing out of her, up to her wound and down the sword Draden held firmly in his hands.

The moment it touched him, she saw him waver. He looked away, down at the sword and back up to her face. His face fell, eyes widening and fear creeping up into his icy stare as his eyes darted from the sword to her and back again. Finally, he stepped away, relenting, and let his sword slide down until it grazed the soil and hung slack in his hand.

"What did you do? How did you... who *are* you?" He stepped away, and his firm stare met her gaze, mixed with confusion and suspicion. "Who sent you?"

Shade licked her lips and watched him as he backed away. Andre approached with his sword in hand but halted with a wave from Draden. The dominant brother was apparent to her. She hoped that whatever had just happened would save her.

"Drop your swords, or we will not stop. She will churn your insides into pulp, and she will not hesitate." Dylan held two swords readied and crept up behind the twins, cautiously poking them in their backs simultaneously. They both froze, surprise and anger spilling across their faces. Draden glanced at Dylan and then back at Shade, seemingly contemplating the situation, probably pondering their chances against them.

Whatever magic filled him from Shade had gotten the best of him. He dropped his sword and straightened, holding his head up and puffing his chest out in some male attempt at superiority. Andre followed suit and dropped his sword, hands in the air for surrender.

"Shade, tie them up and hurry. I don't know when their replacements could show up." Shade ran over, kicking the dropped swords out of reach, and grabbed the spool of rope Dylan handed over to her. She took the slim ropes and walked over to Draden. "Ok, tell your brother to turn his back into that tree there, and you can back into it, too. Stand next to him with your arms behind you."

Draden glared at her with tense lips and hard eyes. She waited patiently, not letting his stare creep into her again or letting any fear slip out. He did what she said and waited as his brother walked over and turned around behind him. Shade snickered and hastily tied the ropes around their wrists. She silently thanked her mom for those scout campouts, where tying knots was a requirement to earn those nifty badges her mom would carefully sew onto her uniform vest. She still had that vest, hanging neatly in her closet.

Once she had them tied, she directed them to a tree. There, she wrapped the remainder of the rope around them several times, as tightly as she could get it without cutting off circulation to their bodies. She knotted the ends securely. She looked at the brothers and beamed with satisfaction.

"I know what you are. You're a changeling. Only changelings can send magic into others to make them weaker. I met one once. He's dead now. He was powerful, though. You will never be that strong." Draden sighed and looked down at the ground, pensive and serious. "You look like him, though, your father, I mean."

Shade stopped. Her face froze in surprise. "What did you say? Who are you talking about?"

Draden snapped his head up and watched her face, smirking.

"What are you smiling at?" She felt anger flush over her face, but she tried to contain it, not wanting to give him the satisfaction.

"You don't know, do you? You didn't even know you were a changeling. How'd you do it, then? Wild magic flows through you like a cancer. He had the same powers. I could help you, you know. I knew your father. He was a powerful man. I was his second in command for centuries until he died and that crazy queen took over." The husky man squirmed in the ropes, grimacing and obviously trying to loosen the ties. Shade was no longer smiling, but at least there was no way in hell he could break loose.

She turned to look at Dylan. He was standing nearby, his dual swords ready in hand. He was not as sure as she was that the rope would hold. His lips were firm, straight, and almost colorless. His eyes furrowed in concentration, contemplating what the soldier said. "Don't listen to them, Shade. He's trying to trick you and delay us. Let's go to the fountain before someone else shows up." He brought the swords down, turned, and motioned for her to follow.

Draden's eyes widened, seeing the two of them walking away. He fidgeted again and yelled after them. "I swear it's the truth, girl. I know things you need to know. I was his second in command. Your father would have wanted you to know these things. *Stop!*"

Shade turned her head, still following Dylan, and glanced back at the brawny warrior. His wild eyes watched her intently, waiting for her to turn back. She shook her head and looked away. She had a strange feeling that the soldier was telling the truth. If not, he was an excellent liar. A part of her wanted to go back and ask the warrior so many questions, but she knew it wasn't the right time.

The doorway to the fountains lay in shadows. They stepped into the darkness and waited as their eyes adjusted to the dim light. Following Dylan and activating her light stone, she grimaced at the stone walls. Another cave. *Great*, thought Shade.

Just as she thought that, a light shone through another doorway, making her realize the hall they were in was more of a semi-circle. It led to an open courtyard in the shape of a full moon. Here in the middle of the mountains, the sun streamed down above the sharp cliffs that reached up to the sky. Shade drew in her breath, amazed at the sight. Hidden from any prying eyes was a vast, fertile garden. It was large, and the sound of water trickled and gurgled all around them. The grass was a brilliant, glowing green with the most brilliantly colored flowers and vines weaving throughout it.

The air was moist and warm here. It felt akin to being in a large greenhouse, like one she'd visited in her childhood with her father. It contained an immense glass dome as a ceiling and held in butterflies and birds of all types. The warm mist felt much the same and made her want to curl up under a tree and take a nap. It was a piece of untouched land that seemed to be heaven on earth.

They stood in awe of the sights. Dylan motioned her forward again and broke her out of her thoughts. She followed but was stunned by the beauty of the place. Near the middle of the garden, they came upon what looked like a massive natural fountain, made of rock and crystals of every color. The crystals glinted and parted the light into beams of rainbow all around the fountain, making it hard to look at because the jewels shimmered so brightly.

Dylan stopped. He reached into his pack and pulled out a glass flask with a stopper. He held it out to Shade, signaling for her to take it. "Here, I can't touch the waters, but you can. Take this and fill it. Then we will be done."

Shade took the flask and smiled. Excitement hummed through her veins as she approached the fountain. She paused at the edge and stared down at the glowing crystals. The water swelled around them and trickled down the rock, spraying up a slight mist of warm water. She wondered what made it so special. It looked like water, plain water. The fountain itself was impressive, but that's where it ended.

She licked her lips and took the stopper out of the flask, dipping it into the warm embrace of the water. She let it fill as it bubbled up around her hand. She felt the magic stir. As she immersed her arm in the water, the magic seemed to intensify. She felt it crawl up her arm and deep into her core. Her eyes widened as the euphoria overwhelmed her.

Shaking her head to clear it and think better now that the

flask was full, she pulled the bottle out to examine it. Rainbows swirled in the glinting sunlight inside of the glass. She felt the cool liquid run down her arm and drip onto the moist earth below. The dirt vibrated with life as green vines and leaves sprouted at every drop and reached for the sunlight. She smiled, enjoying the euphoric feeling and peace all at once. She realized she was glowing, reflecting light off the pool of water. It felt incredible.

"Shade? Are you okay?" Dylan's eyes were wide in concern. His face appeared paralyzed in shock and disbelief. She looked up at him and smiled, nodding as she pushed the stopper into the flask.

"That was amazing, Dylan! I feel like someone just jolted me awake with a million double shot espressos. I feel great!" Shade laughed and hopped back to where Dylan stood, drying her arm on her hoodie. He approached her and smiled, watching her illuminated face and feeling the warmth spill onto him. He reached out and touched her cheek, sliding his fingers over her skin, and the vibrating magic spilled onto his skin too. His hand glowed, and the light crept over him as it did her. They stood in a cocoon of light and peace.

He laughed and smiled at her. Her smile was contagious. Her cherry red lips seemed to beckon him, and her dreamy honey eyes seemed to pull him into the deep abyss of her soul. He moved closer, cupping her face. Bending forward, his lips brushed against hers, warm and soft, sending Shade's heart sighing in bliss. A feeling of drunkenness filled him, as though he'd been empty and now was filling up to the brim. He gave into the embrace, letting it swim around them like honey dripping from the trees and leaves around them, imprisoning them in a bubble of swirling magic. He wanted to kiss and hold her forever.

"There they are! We have you surrounded! Drop your weapons!"

The shout jerked them back to the garden and the trickling water. Dylan spun and stared at the squad of soldiers pouring in through the door in the rock wall and fanning out to surround them.

"Drop your weapons, or we will be forced to kill you, warrior. We only want the girl with the flask of water. Give her to us, and we will let you live." The leader stared at Dylan's swords, now loose and unsheathed, held in a fighting stance. The captain of this band shook his head and laughed. "You can't win. We outnumber you, young man. Drop the swords."

"Sir, I can't locate the twins. It's like they've disappeared. I found pieces of their armor, but they're nowhere to be found. Maybe the little witch dispatched them before we arrived. I've heard strange things about her, sir." The captain waved the subordinate away, furiously shaking his head.

"Don't be stupid! Just as well. We'll assume they're dead. Now, secure the girl, and let's get back to the palace before dark. The Queen will be most pleased. Move in!" The circle of soldiers began to press in on them.

Shade turned to watch the soldiers closing in on them and backed into Dylan, her hands clasped around the bottle. Her eyes darted nervously at the soldiers. "What now, Dylan? There's no way out! We're trapped!" She bit her lip as the fear spilled over the fading euphoria.

"It's all right, Shade. Listen to me, and do just what I say. Hold onto me. I'm going to drop my glamour and call my powers." Shade looked up at him, eyes wide in terror.

"What are you gonna do?"

"I'm going to call my power of lightning. When I discharge it, the first ring of soldiers will drop with the shock. Hold onto me tightly. I have to control it so it doesn't go too wide and fry the garden. Come on!"

Shade shook her head as she turned to him, letting his arms embrace her tightly. "I... I don't know if this is a good idea. What if I get electrocuted, too?" She trembled in his grip.

Dylan looked down at her and smiled softly.

"Believe, Shade. I believe since you are able to touch me, you are immune to my powers. It will be alright." He whispered the last words and hugged her tightly. They closed their eyes as the blue flickers of fire crackled over his skin. The next thing she knew, she felt the bolt of energy discharge from his body, like a small earthquake vibrating through her. The bolt snapped and sent a thunderous boom around them. When it was done, just a moment later, she peeked around his chest to see that the first ring of soldiers surrounding them were down, most knocked out while others moaned in distress.

"It worked, Dylan!" She stopped as she watched the next wave of soldiers creep in, stepping over the others cautiously and staring at the pair of them in disbelief.

"Damn it! It's a blasted Teleen. Grab the lightning rods from the armory stash now! We've got to control the lightning before we can overpower him!" The captain's face was beet red, and sweat beaded on his face as he fumbled back from the fallen ones. "Hurry up!" he yelled.

The soldiers stood back as they waited for the rods to be handed out.

"Lightning rods? Dylan, what are they gonna do with the rods?" Shade turned around and watched the soldiers pass stacks of rods around the group.

Dylan breathed in and shook his head. "The rods will render me powerless. They will draw my power into the cylinders and leave me harmless. We've got to get out of here now." He spun around and watched the soldiers gear up and advance again. He then turned to Shade and looked down into her shining brown eyes.

"Shade, listen to me. There's a legend that says the holder of the water of the Santiran Fountains can use it to wish for anything they want, just once, and it will be granted by the water's magic. Now, I'm going to hold onto you, and you try to think as hard as you can of the Guildrin forest and imagine being back there once more, got it?"

"Yes, but, there's no freakin' way that will work!"

Dylan re-sheathed his swords, pulled her into his embrace, and smiled. "I guess we'll find out. Now wish us home, Shade. Do it now!"

Shade closed her eyes, feeling the soldiers' auras vibrating around them and closing in. She breathed in, thinking of Queen Zinara, Ilarial, and her newfound friends. She visualized the steps leading down to the Guildrin living quarters, the only place she'd ever felt somewhat safe in Faerie.

Dylan's arms felt warm and strong around her, and she only hoped he would continue to hold her this way. She wished him safe, herself and the others too. Unscrewing the cap of the flask, she whispered her thoughts into the bottle grasped tightly in her hands. She felt Dylan's lips on her head, warm and firm as she wished them all back home safe, as hard as she could.

A peaceful feeling washed over them like a crashing wave. In just that instant, yelling and cursing blew up around them, followed by an intense silence. The sound of tree leaves rustling and birds chirping in the slight breeze made Shade open her eyes. They stood by the great tree to the Guildrin Court, as if they'd never left. She gasped, looking up at Dylan.

"You did it! Oh man, you did it, Shade! We're home!" Dylan jumped and hopped about, hollering out his joy. Returning to her and lifting her up with his arms, he swung her around. Shade breathed in with relief. A moment later, another whoosh sounded around them. The entire gang stood there, looking startled and shocked.

"Oh, wow!" She ran and hugged the tall sorceress Braelynn, and then turned to embrace them all one by one. Hot steaming tears streamed down her cheeks. Every one of them was there. Everyone but Sylphi returned, just as she'd wished. They were all shocked and surprised but intact and safe. Shade didn't ponder very long about where Sylphi had gone. Shade wasn't missing her.

"What just happened? We're home! How the…? What the…?" Soap was spinning around, looking at the landscape, absolutely petrified. Shade ran hugged him tight and pulled back an inch to see his face. He grinned back at her and nodded. "This can only mean one thing. You did it. You actually did it, and without us to aid you, at that! You made it to the fountains, didn't you? Incredible! How did you do it? How did you get us all home? One minute we were searching for you around the base of the Santiran mountains, we'd just picked up your trail, and now here we are, home sweet home." He sighed and hugged her again even tighter.

"Okay, let go. I can't breathe!" she cried happily. He let go abruptly but caught her as she stumbled backward.

"Sorry!" He grinned and laughed. She laughed along with him, feeling elated.

"Do you have the water, then?" Shade nodded at Sary, who'd worked her way up to her. "You did it, Shade. You saved our people!" Sary hugged her and joined the laughter.

"Let's go home, everyone. It's been a long journey, and it's time to celebrate! Queen Zinara will be absolutely delighted. We will win this war against the Unseelie after all! We have new allies joining us for victory!" Jack smiled widely as he hugged everyone in the group. Everyone agreed and nodded. The stairs to the underground opened, and they each descended, laughing and chatting with each other, all the strain of the journey lifted at once.

"Who are our new allies, Jack?" Shade inquired.

"Oh, sorry. You probably haven't heard about it yet, but, on our way to the Santiran fountains, we ran into a group of villagers who proclaimed that Prince Lotinar has returned and sided with Queen Zinara. This will prove most useful to our cause." Shade pondered what he'd said, not really knowing of whom they spoke, but suddenly thought of something else.

"Wait, um, was Sylphi with you guys? Where is she?" Shade asked, not that she really cared.

"Sylphi? She ran at the battle with Lady Blythe. She probably returned to the Teleen Caverns. She most likely got too scared to fight," Ewan chuckled. Shade wasn't the only one not missing Sylphi.

Shade approached the first step to the mound but turned to see Dylan watching her.

"The blood bond is still in place. I thought it might be fulfilled at journey's end, but it's not," he whispered as his eyes stared off into the forest, glazing over. His face was serious and contemplative.

"I'm sorry, Dylan. You know I would break it if I could. What do you think has to be done to end it?" Shade placed her hand on his arm to pull him back into the present. He returned his gaze to her and smiled through the sadness.

"It's all right, Shade. I know now that this is my destiny. I'm not meant to be captain of the Teleen guard anymore. I'm glad I met you, Shade. Changes are good." His eyes sparkled in the dimming light of the dusk. The orange glow spread across the sky and dimmed the forest floor as the sun crept away to slumber.

"I'm glad we met, too. Come on. Let's get some real food and rest for once. After we give the flask to the Queen, I can go home and see my family."

Dylan's face darkened in gloom as he stared back at her. "Home? You're leaving? Well, I guess you would want to go back, wouldn't you? I won't be returning home, probably not for a long time." He pressed his lips together and stepped forward toward the stairs. "I have to warn you, Shade. I have to stay close to where you are, or my blood burns inside me."

"I know. You could come, you know. You could meet my family. I'm sure I could think of something to tell my mother. You could definitely pass for a teenager. I could say your family is moving out of town, and you need a place to stay so you can

235

graduate from our high school. What do you think? We do have a guest room. My mom rarely uses it, but I'm pretty sure she'd agree to let you stay with us." She stood before him, staring down the stairs of the faery mound.

He suddenly turned, a broad grin spreading across his face. "Yes, that would be good. I think that since our blood bond is still in place, I will have to stay near you somehow. I guess that would be best, at least until the bond's requirements are fulfilled and it lets me go home."

Shade beamed. She could feel his anxiety pulsating out toward her. Something about the fountains linked them even closer. She flushed red as she remembered the burn of his lips against hers. She hoped for Dylan's sake they wouldn't be bound for too much longer. However, as they descended into the faerie court and out of sight, she knew she wasn't ready to let him go.

Evangeline

Dark Faerie Tales...

Alexia Purdy

Evangeline

(A Dark Faerie Tale #0.5)

A Prequel

By

Alexia Purdy

For Rayven

Chapter One

T HE SLOW BURN of fire never promises an end. But the end does come. The licking flames that consume all matter until it ceases to exist, extinguishing into tendrils of smoke and soot, Evangeline never tired of watching it. It was hypnotic, calming with the crackle and snap it produced—a snake dance to pull one in and perish with one embrace. This was what she was, and she knew it. The poisonous venom of death, disguised in warmth and light.

Evangeline and her sister, Jade, were unique. She'd never met any other fire elemental witches before. Yet, Evie, as her sister had called her since toddlerhood instead of fumbling with her long name, was just that much different. Her faery blood fed her elemental fire powers and amplified them in every way.

With these powers came the effects of life in a human city. Iron poisoning. It made her bones ache and her head spin. The nauseating stench of it swirled around the buildings, cars, and the streets near her home. Every place. Even the house she'd grown up in was laced with the endless poison adrift in every breath. Jade wasn't part faery, she was all human, even with her fire elemental magic, the iron did not bother her at all.

Evie didn't really care, but she'd felt the twinge of envy

curl into her mind, at times, right before she swiftly swatted it away. She loved her sister. They were two lights in the vast dark of the world.

"Is it helping?" Jade's voice broke into her thoughts. Evie turned, gave her a weak smile before gazing back across the yard. The forest was calling her tonight. Its power whispered promises more like a lover would deep into her mind. It beckoned her from the confines of her childhood home. She wondered if Jade felt it too. Something told her, unfortunately, Jade's full human heritage didn't allow for this.

"Yes, it helps a lot. It takes the edge off, for sure." Evie sighed. The headaches were bad lately. Her glamour magic, which kept the iron from affecting her, wavered when the headaches came. Only the power of the forest in the Land of Faerie nearby and her sister's magical drinks, which were laced with whatever spells she had concocted and perfected to keep the iron sickness at bay, made it better. As she got older, it was getting harder to stave off. She rubbed her temples and pushed back her long black hair, wondering why that was.

"If mom were here, she'd know what to do about that." Jade slumped into the creaky, old rocking chair, which sighed when she let it rock under her weight. Evie swayed in the porch swing, hoping the fresh air would calm the raging pain in her head.

"She might've, but I doubt it." Grumbling the last part made her resent her faery heritage just a bit. Jade didn't worry about iron sickness, she was just a year older than her but had a different father. Though he had not stuck around after their mother found out she was pregnant, neither had Evie's supernatural father. It had made the three women thick as thieves. Their mother's death had come suddenly and left Jade, barely eighteen, Evie's guardian. Nothing could have prepared them for that. Nothing filled the void that their mother had left behind.

"Maybe we should go there then."

Evie tilted her head up towards her sister. Jade's chocolate eyes twinkled with the knowledge of a person older than their years. The color matched her own, even though they were different in many ways.

They had both excelled in fire manipulation and elemental witch magic, which their mother had made sure to mentor them in. But Jade had excelled in the fire magic and elemental powers of the world around her—far more than Evie ever could. The only thing that had saved Evie from being a miserable failure was the faery blood that amplified the elemental magic she possessed. Only by this miracle had she managed to fumble through the lessons enough to satisfy their drill sergeant of a mother. Jade was more powerful than her, even with mortal blood.

"Go where?" Evie replied. She didn't want to hear the answer. She knew what was coming next. Though Evie wanted it more than anything else, the danger Jade could face joining her in Land of Faerie made her shove the desire so deep inside her and into the crevices of her deepest thoughts. No, she couldn't take Jade into Faerie. It might eat her alive. Even though Evie was a faery, it had already taken nips and bits of her already.

Jade wrinkled her lips into a semi frown, knowing full well her sister was pretending to not know what she meant. "You know where, *into the forest*. You need it. It's like a life force for you." Jade paused as she glanced out across the expanse of trees and shrubs swaying with the push of the wind. The far-off roar of the leaves vibrating with the air rumbled in her ears as she contemplated how it would go if they did venture in. Their mother had warned them of the dangers and malice that filled the Land of Faerie. They'd heeded her until now. Yet, Evie could no longer resist the call of the land anymore, and Jade had to help her. She was, after all, her only living relative.

Evie shrugged, trying to look apathetic.

3

"I dunno. Maybe."

"You should accept it, it's part of you. You need to be where you belong. Mom said…."

"I *know* what mom said." Evie stood up abruptly and stormed into the house. She wasn't angry at Jade, she wasn't even angry at their mother anymore for dying. She didn't know what she was angry about, but it ate at her like a cancer. She knew what she had to do, but she didn't necessarily want to do it.

In the meantime, Evie would wait. Wait for the right moment to come to make a move. Then, and only then would she follow the pull to the endless lands of Faerie, where the magic was boundless and dangerous at best. She could feel the time approaching, whispering to her that the time was now. But, she'd wait until tomorrow. Tomorrow was a better choice.

Chapter Two

"OKAY, IT'S TIME," Evie gave a little tap to her sister's messed up head, which poked out from under the blanket. The early morning sun had barely risen and Jade's stubborn moan filtered from underneath her comforter.

"Okay, what?" Jade shoved the covers down and gave Evie a deadly look. "It's the butt crack of dawn. What are you babbling about?"

"I think it's time to go into Faerie." Evie plopped down onto the bed with its swirled, multicolored sheets. She played with a loose string that hung from the corner of the soft, well-used, threadbare blanket. "I think I'm ready. As long as you are too, and we stay near each other, I think we'll be fine." She sighed, hoping her doubt didn't leak into her voice.

Jade sat up, shoving her long medium-brown hair out of her puffy eyes. Rubbing them, she gave an extended yawn, stretching her arms to the sky. A moment later she gave her sister a weak smile, wondering how it was that today, Evie was ready. Yesterday her reluctance had been oh so apparent.

"Great! Let me wake up a bit and we can get going." Jade rubbed her face again, feeling more out of it than anything else.

"I need some coffee…"

"Done! I'll get it going, you get ready. I'm all set to go." Evie jumped up, her mood elevated with every passing minute as she rushed out of the room. Jade frowned, not particularly happy about anything quite yet.

Today was it. Evie knew it. She felt it vibrating through her bones like a thrill that hummed under her skin. *Today.* She didn't know what it was going to show her or bring around the corner, but something about today was calling her in every way.

The smell of honeysuckle and grass clippings swam through the cracked kitchen window as she filled the coffee maker. Along with the ozone of the dawn, the scent was incredible. She adored the way the forest's sounds and smells wafted around the place. It was the closest they could've lived without actually crossing the borders into Faerie. The invisible wards, which generally kept humans out, were but a few hundred feet away. Mom had known this. She'd loved this house for that. It served to torture Evie with the proximity of the magic that ebbed from it. She'd felt it in every cell her entire life. It was part of her in every way.

Evie had just finished dropping creamer and sugar into two mugs of coffee when Jade shuffled in. Her hair was dripping wet and hung in long snarled tangles as she pulled her brush through the mess. She was definitely more awake now as she plopped onto a chair at the kitchen table and inhaled the enticing aroma from the mug.

"Thanks! You always make it so yummy." She took a swig, not caring that it was still steaming hot. The thing about being a fire elemental witch, burns were not a problem.

"Yeah, super strong. Just like you like it." Evie took a swig of her own, loving the feel of the hot fluid coating her raspy throat.

"So, where do you want to start at? What's the agenda?" Jade muttered from her cup, reaching for a muffin that Evie had

6

laid out on a platter atop the table. She stuffed a bite into her mouth and watched her sister suspiciously. Evie couldn't hide much from her. But that was fine. Nothing to really hide, at least not today.

"I want to go into the forest together. Then, let me go in further by myself. I want to feel the magic around me, see what I can sense."

"You better scream loud then, if anything happens or you need me." Jade frowned, not liking the idea of leaving her little sister alone to roam a dangerous forest of magic. "I'll try not to lose my mind while you're gone. But don't take too long, I say, one hour, and then I'll be hunting you down." Jade waited, hoping for the answer she wanted.

"Sounds like a deal, sis," Evie flashed a smile as they finished their breakfast and headed out into the fresh early summer morning.

Chapter Three

THE SHIFT OF damp moss and dead mulch made the trek into the forest slightly unpleasant. It had sprinkled the night before, leaving a layer of moisture clinging to everything and the air hanging thick. The soil was almost muddy. The damp and sticky clumps gripped onto their shoes and shifted with their weight. Once their house had faded into the thick rows of trees behind them, they were alone, with only the calls of birds and small animals to accompany them.

Jade peered around, sniffing the air. The scent of pine and rotting foliage filled her nostrils. Not necessarily unpleasant, just stronger than it would've been without the rain.

Evie was delighted. The place reeked of magic. Life vibrated from the limbs of trees and the small saplings swayed in the slight breezes that caressed their leaves. The earth and sky harmonized, sending waves of intense calm through her. She was in her element again. The only place she didn't feel sickly or different. She let the tendrils of power seduce her, enjoying every second.

Jade could feel it too, prickling along her skin like static electricity. It wasn't as potent as Evie's senses, but she could feel it nonetheless. Her elemental magic was by no means weak–she could match Evie easily with her own spells and fire-wielding. Faery magic was more amplified than hers, though. It reeked from everything in Faerie. The land was enchanted, alive and breathing just as she was. It was both exhilarating and terrifying at the same time.

"Where do you want me to wait?" Her voice sounded quiet in the density of nature. She didn't quite feel at ease yet though her magic was also earthly bound. Hers was human-born. Evie's were supernatural.

"Here is fine," her sister's voice was smooth and filled with excitement. Evie's eyes were wide, her vision filled with the extraordinary things around her. Small demi-fey flew past and paused slightly in their flights to observe her, momentarily, before zipping away, finding nothing unusual. Just another fey girl wandering the forest. They lingered on the human a bit more though, their eyes stared hungrily for seconds longer. But Jade knew better. She gave then no attention and sent them off in their unacknowledged spite.

"Okay, remember; scream loudly. I'll be right there in a flash." Jade placed her hand on her sister's shoulder, ensuring she'd been heard. "Don't go too far, and don't *talk* to anyone." Her eyes gleamed her warning as Evie turned toward her.

"I *know*, I promise. Not too far."

Jade nodded as her hand slipped off her sister. Evie made her way deeper into the foliage and shrubs, letting the forest swallow her up in no time. The woods claimed her, happy to take one of their own. Jade felt alone in the desolation of Faerie. It was no different than a regular forest. Except for that tingle of magic that crawled across her like ants swarming. She found a fallen log with moss growing on one side of its bark situated on a small incline on the forest floor. Sitting down, she sighed.

Patience. She needs to do this. I must be patient and just sit and wait. I can sit still for a bit. One hour, that's all. What could go

10

wrong?

She swallowed down the parched knot forming in her throat. So *much* could go wrong. This was the Land of Faerie, after all, where nothing is what it seems, and nothing is impossible.

~~~~~

NOTHING COULD COMPARE to it. Nothing would ever be enough to replace the feeling this place gave her. Evie had already decided this. Only a few minutes in, she just knew. No other strip of earth would ever make her feel this way. No human city, no land anywhere, but here. This was home. She could feel it to her inner core. Smiling, she let it flow over her as she watched the creatures of Faerie slowly creep out of their places and curiously watch her. They would acknowledge her with a narrowing of eyes or a curious glance, and then be on their way. The trees would sway in her direction, almost wanting to envelope her in a welcoming hug.

Welcome home, they whispered. *Welcome home.*

A crack echoed nearby, breaking her solace with a jerk. Evie turned to study her surroundings, waiting for whomever or whatever disturbed the land to show themselves. Even the birds had quieted their songs, silenced with caution, awaiting the intrusion on their solace.

Evie wondered if she should scream. No, she would wait, she could handle it. She just knew she could, no matter what or who it could be. Listening, she attempted to narrow in further onto the noise. None came, but she felt eyes on her, studying her with an intensity so strong, she could actually feel their eyes almost burning into her.

"I know you're there," she called out. The forest didn't answer. Even the sway of branches had stilled as she waited. Slowly sucking in some air, she glanced around again and caught sight of him. A man. Dark hair and blue eyes watched

11

her with a curious interest and a slight smile hovered on his lips.

"Who're you?"

He tilted his head, amused by her words. His smile grew, curled up and flashed the ivory white teeth underneath. His magic called to her, like fire for fire. It made her breath catch as she felt it across the air. He was a faery, but his power matched hers somehow, leaving her completely enthralled.

"I'm Jack. Who're you?"

Chapter Four

JADE FELT A presence. It was unworldly and felt like a rush of earth and water tumbling around her. She stiffened. The hairs rose on her neck as she turned around, flicking her eyes about the forest but found nothing.

"Evie?" she whispered. The trees didn't reply. They danced in a sway, rippling like a tide as the wind rode the branches. Jade couldn't help but feel that someone was watching her. Shivering, she ran her hands over her arms and backed into a tree, hoping it was all in her head.

"Evie? If that's you, it's not funny!" Nothing but space and a haunting whoosh of breezes greeted her. She sighed. It was probably just her imagination. Feeling paranoid was not uncommon for her. When you're different from your peers to the point you can manipulate others and the elements, she could trust no one. No one but her own flesh and blood.

Jade settled against the tree and scolded herself for being so jumpy. The feeling ceased and the calming sounds of the woods resumed their songs. She didn't blame Evie one bit for loving it out here. Nature was an entity unto itself and its power was intoxicating. Jade was sure that whatever pleasure she derived from the earth itself was amplified a thousand fold for those bound to Faerie. It reeked of magic and power. It was like a surge tingling across her skin, vibrating and teasing.

She could never use it like her sister could. It was bound to faery blood only. But, that was okay with Jade. She had her own elemental magic to consume. And it was just as good.

A twig snapped, sending her jetting to her feet. Her breath huffed and burned in her chest as she spun around once more to find the perpetrator. This time he walked slowly into her vision. This time he wanted her to see him.

"What do you want?" her voice cracked, suddenly dry with the tingle of fear that slowly embraced her. She licked her lips, wanting the desert in her mouth to go away, but it didn't comply. Not with an ethereal looking man standing before her.

The faery stood just a bit taller than her. His waist-length thick brown hair and skin the color of pale cream shined in the sunlight. Almond eyes blinked back at her, amused with her widening eyes and opened mouth. They twinkled and were the same color brown as his hair. Jade found it interesting that he looked very near human. She'd expected wings, translucent skin, and bug-like eyes. Maybe more like the demi-fey who fluttered on their tiny, fragile wings with their sharp cornered eyes without whites. No, he was the size of an ordinary man, only more mesmerizing than anyone she'd ever met.

He was dressed head to toe in dark, rich leather, soft and worn with use. It enveloped his body, fitting snuggly against his muscles and giving him a warrior's look. She gasped as he stepped closer, an amused smile played at the corners of his lips.

"Stop!" She pressed her back against the tree, feeling trapped yet amazingly curious about the faery man. "Don't come closer, or I'll…I–"

"Or you'll do what?" he snickered. His eyes twinkled playfully, making her seethe as its effect made her fear chip away.

"You don't want to know," she gritted her teeth, hoping it was a sufficient enough warning. She readied her magic, letting it tingle on the tips of her fingers.

As if sensing it gathering, he paused, sniffed the air and glanced around. He refocused on Jade and gave her a warm smile, no longer approaching her. "Forgive me, elemental. I can be off-putting." A tilt to his head as he continued to watch her, but she held her ground, stilled and readied to slam the magic onto him if necessary.

"What are you doing in Faerie, elemental? Your kind are not native here. You risk much by treading here." He pressed his lips together, looking slightly concerned, but it faded just as quickly. He edged over to the fallen log she'd just been sitting on, sank to sit on it and patted the other side for her to join him. When she didn't move, he sighed and slid off his sword, propping it next to him and pulled out a sack, which had been strapped to his back.

"Forgive me, I'm tired and parched. Been on the move all day, and I do regret barging into your solace, but I must have some nourishment." He pulled out a flask of water, uncorking it to take huge swallows. He then clasped it shut and pulled out a small sack, grabbing some nuts and berries out of it and shoveled it into his mouth.

Yuck, Faeries have no manners apparently.

With a mouthful, he offered her some of his sticky snack, but she shook her head and waited. Hoping Evie was not nearby.

"I don't bite, elemental. I am really quite harmless. You can put that fire away you got there. You might subsequently start a forest fire if you let it flicker a little more." He nodded towards her hands. Jade pulled them up and stared in horror to see that her hands were afire, dripping slight embers to the forest floor without her realizing it. She quickly extinguished the flames and stomped the smoldering ashes with her shoes.

He gave her a haughty laugh, amused by her loss of

15

control. "You know, if you wanted to burn me, I'll be pretty vulnerable in a few minutes, being that I'm exhausted. Would you mind if I hung in your woods for a bit? It's quite quaint actually." He looked around and pulled a blanket out of the pack, laying it on the soft mulch of the ground and plopping onto it, using the fallen log to shelter one of his sides.

"Wh–what? Y–you're going to stay here?" Jade stammered. He couldn't linger around here–their house was just a few strides away. What if he discovered it?

He placed his head on his pack, one arm easing over his eyes. "No need to stutter. I'll keep to myself, don't worry your pretty little head about it, miss." He nestled into the ground, sounding truly exhausted. After a few minutes of silence, she wondered if he really was just going to rest here for a bit. What did he want?

"Who *are* you?" she asked one more time, her voice sounded suddenly small and squeaky. She cleared her throat as she slid to lean against a tree once more.

"I'm called Verenis. What's your name, elemental?" he asked without getting up. His face was still hidden under his arm, blocking the light out. His breathing slowed to rhythmic and peaceful. Jade wondered if he'd fallen asleep already.

"Jade."

"Now, Jade, what are you doing in Faerie?" Verenis rolled to his side, leaning on his arm as his eyes flashed toward her. A sea of earth drifted in them. It made her dizzy and wary of him, though his face was pleasant enough to look at and sent shivers down her skin.

"What do you care?"

"Heh, touché," he smirked at her remark with his eyes dancing. She crossed her arms and frowned, feeling somewhat childish.

"What does it matter? What are *you* doing here if I may ask."

16

"Trying to stay alive." The faery promptly shifted onto his back, covering his eyes again to cover them.

Nothing about him made sense. Jade had lost her patience and muttered her annoyance. He didn't stir, but softly snored as he drifted away into sleep. Jade watched him, unable to tear her eyes from his resting body. She wanted to ask him a thousand questions, but right now was not the time. She wondered if she would ever see him again after today. The thought of where Evangeline had run off to in the desolate woods had temporarily slipped her mind.

Chapter Five

EVANGELINE ENJOYED THE power that Faerie circled around her as it quenched her thirst. The headache was all but gone as the exhilaration of the land filled her to the brim. It was heaven. Pure and organic. Nothing in her human world compared to it. Now, nothing ever would. That, she knew was for certain.

The invasion of her private moment had jolted her out of the clouds. Jack hadn't attempted to hide himself from her, and now stood in plain sight, watching her with utmost scrutiny. Evie felt naked under his gaze, not the kind where her clothes were being stripped away, but like she was a student in a class caught daydreaming and failing miserably. She brushed the self-conscious fear away, like cobwebs that stuck to her skin and made her feel icky. He was intense and she knew she had to get to know him.

"You need to pull more of the earth's energy rather than from the air. It's sturdier, less volatile." His voice sounded out across the tiny clearing they stood in. The sun streamed down the canopy in spikes, warming her face and throwing shadows across his chiseled one. Black, wispy hair fell across the cusp of his eyebrows, partially hiding his features. Stark, blue eyes stared back at her, but a hint of a smile was nowhere to be found.

"What?" She was stunned. Not knowing what to do. The stranger approached her and held out his hand, showing how it burst into a wave of flames and cracked with electricity. It made her gasp and back away, unsure what to do. His eyes watched her calmly as his intrigue danced across his face.

"It won't hurt you, I wouldn't let that happen."

"What *are* you?" Evie's fear receded with his words and traded places with curiosity. The flames danced along his skin in a vibrant blue-white. It was entrancing, called her like a moth to a light. She'd never met another faery, ever, and this man was one. A true and real faery. She unwittingly reached out to touch him, surprised when he pulled away, extinguishing the flame.

"I'm a Teleen. A fire and lightning faery–it's what I'm made of." He smiled, flashing a set of perfect white teeth. "Well, I told you my name. So…what, can I ask, is yours?" His eyebrow lifted in questioning.

"I'm Evangeline, but my sister calls me…"

"Evie?"

She furrowed her brow at him, wondering how it was that he knew that. "Yes, have we met?"

Jack shook his head as he gave a short laugh, clearing his throat and pulling of his pack strapped diagonally across his chest. "No, but I've seen you and that fire elemental witch at the edge of the woods over there. Didn't mean to pry, just happened upon you two practicing one day, not too long ago." He winked, sending a thrill through her. She felt her heart hammering away in her chest. "Evie is excellent. I like it better than Vange or Angela."

"Oh, thanks," she stammered. Her focus was off completely, this strange being had tilted her world the moment he had walked into the clearing. She felt an odd attraction toward him, feeling her cheeks flush as she watched him pull out a flask of water and gulp down some mouthfuls. His movements were fluid and his physique was of someone who had spent many a day outside hunting or running. Not an ounce of fat on this one. A perfect man, in every way.

Evie pulled her eyes away. Held out her hands and called her flames into being, letting the fire flicker on her fingers. Hers was not blue, like his, but the orange/yellow of an ordinary fire. The colors danced across her skin, feeling warm and comforting as she maneuvered it.

She glanced at Jack, bringing her brown eyes to meet his deep, blue sea ones. The moment felt suspended, even the air seemed to calm into an odd stillness that embraced them. The overwhelming scent of pine and mulch circled around, fueling the magic of the moment. They continued to stare, lost in each other's eyes.

The feeling suspended time. Evie felt lightheaded and snuffed the flames out, breaking their connection. What was that? No man had ever held her in such a frozen shock. But, this was no regular man after all. The boys at school paled in comparison to him. The confusion he caused her made her want to run, but her feet were cemented to the ground and wouldn't budge. Jack's staring didn't help either. It was like he could see all of her soul, every last bit of it.

"Well, it's been a pleasure meeting you, Evie." He smiled, picked up his pack and headed toward the edge of the clearing.

"Wait!"

Jack came to a stop, turned his head slightly and brought her into his periphery. The sides of his mouth twitched up and his eyes betrayed his eagerness to do just what she had asked.

"What is it?"

"Will I see you again?" Evie bit her lip, praying that the request didn't make her look desperate or needy. She didn't really expect anything, but the chance to speak with the Faery was just too good to let it fleet by without a word. To never see

21

him again already made her insides ache. No, she had to see Jack again, even just to speak and ask him about Faerie. Just for a little while.

"Most likely, I'm usually out here everyday hunting around morning and late afternoon. It's nice out here. It's purely exhilarating in Faerie, you'll see." Jack closed the distance between her and held out a small blue orb, it shined in the late morning sun, swirling inside like smoke and lightning flashing within it. "Take this and just call my name into it, I'll hear you."

Evie held out her hand and he placed it gently into her palm, his other hand cupped hers underneath sending a jolt of pleasure up her arm and into her chest. Letting go, he turned and disappeared, running so fast that his body became a blurred streak as he vanished into the forest.

Evie was left breathless. Jack was fascinating in every way. She smiled to herself, knowing that his coming back was like hitting the jackpot. 'Jack' was just who she'd hoped to find, a faery with an affinity to fire, like her. A kindred spirit in a sense. How lucky could she have been? Breathing in deeply she turned her face up towards the warmth of the last rays of sun, peeking over the canopy of rustling leaves before the forest blocked it out. This was paradise at last. And it was finally hers.

Chapter Six

"I DON'T THINK that's a good idea at all." Jade protested as she paced the living room, finally tiring and flopped onto the lazy boy. The TV flashed along with the incessant laughs of some comedy show where the audience was live and their giggles permeated the soundtrack. Evie's admittance of seeing a faery man named Jack for a few months had made her stomach knot up with guilt. She had a similar secret. So why was she so upset? She wasn't the one about to go deep into Faerie on a journey to his home like Evie was.

"Oh come on Jade. I'm eighteen now. I can do it if I want to." Evie pressed her lips together, annoyed with her older sister. She was still treating her with kid gloves, trying to keep her safe when all she needed was to let her go. She was going to visit the Teleen Caverns with Jack. With, or without Jade's approval.

"What if you get hurt? What if..." Jade swallowed the lump forming in her throat, stifling back a barrage of tears. "What if you never come back?"

"But I will come back, you know that!" Evie sighed, trying to form a smile toward her overly concerned sister.

"Besides, Jack won't let anything happen to me. I already visited his home in the Guildrin Seelie Court. It was fascinating! No one hurt me there. No one will." She stood up and stared at her sister, wanting to know why she was so worried. It was would be a quick journey, he knew the way very well.

Evie's heart fluttered at the thought of Jack. He'd been nothing but kind and pleasant to her. He'd taught her more about faery magic than she could've imagined. The time they'd spent together had made them realize how much their feelings had grown. It was unbearable to be away from him. He was her light, the only one that made the days right. The only one she would ever want.

Jack had made it clear that he intended to marry her. He had told her how much he had felt compelled to be in the clearing that first day when they had met. Nothing short of fate had brought them together. For a Teleen warrior, there was never a question when matched pairs met each other, it was an instantaneous connection. That's what had happened to them, there was no fighting it. Evie felt entirely all right giving in to it. She loved him, and that was all she needed.

"Don't act so innocent either, Jade." Evie's voice came out soft but accusatory. Jade's eyes flew back up toward her, a flash of guilt slipped from them, but she quickly covered it up. It was too late. Evie had seen it and knew down right well what it meant.

"What do you mean, Evie?"

"Oh come on, that faery guy you've been seeing too, did you think I wouldn't notice that? Did you think I would never find out? Who is he, Jade?" She glared at her sister, awaiting a response.

The look on Jade's face was nothing short of shock as the color drained from her face. Jade looked away, her lips tensed as she contemplated her answer.

"Verenis, that's his name. He's a faery prince in exile."

Her eyes flicked back up in a panic. "Evie, don't tell anyone, please! He'll be killed. They're hunting him."

Evie knelt down next to her sister, a warm smile spread across her lips. Pressing her hand down onto Jade's. "I won't tell anyone, not even Jack. I promise." Jade let out a sigh of relief and grinned back at her, tears lining her eyes. "But, I have to tell you because I love you, and I'm worried about you too." Evie paused, hoping the words would come out right. "Don't see him anymore. Faeries are dangerous for humans. He'll enchant you, trick you or hurt you if he wants to. Never underestimate him, Jade. *Never.* Promise me you'll stop seeing him, please..."

Jade pulled her hand away from her sister, curling into the opposite side of the lazy boy. Her fear morphed into a slight disdain, unsure how to answer her sister when she knew what she would do anyway.

"I can't do that," she whispered, closing her eyes and let the pent up tears spill down her cheeks. They splashed onto her clothes and the chair, leaving small drops of wetness where they landed. "Please don't ask me to do that. Anything, *but* that."

Evie stood up slowly and sighed with worry. The faery already had a grip on Jade. It was probably too late to break their link. She closed her own eyes and wondered if everything would be all right. Maybe. Maybe not. There was no telling the future, not even with magic or superpowers. Not even a Faery can see such things. Some caught glimpses; the oracles she'd met could see many things. Nothing was for certain, that was the only certainty.

"Okay, just promise me to be careful, please Jade? Do that for me while I'm gone."

Jade nodded, sniffled and rubbed her tear-streaked face. "Alright, I will."

Evie leaned in for a hug, holding her older sister tightly. Evie felt as if she'd grown up these last few months. She was no longer the younger sister, the child. Faerie had changed them both in ways they'd never imagined it could. As they separated and Evie went to her room to pack some things, she knew it had already happened. Nothing would ever be the same for either of them. Nothing.

Chapter Seven

GRAY STONE OF granite and marble was everywhere. It composed the walls, the ground, and the looming roof overhead. Only the caverns that were fed by waterfalls and springs shined in blue and gold light from the faery lamps surrounding the small lakes of water which rippled softly like pools of black ink. These were her favorite spots in the deep underground city of Teleen. The only solace she could find in the vast rocks and boulders.

The fresh air that dissipated across the water felt fresher here and less claustrophobic than the windowless chambers of the stone rooms and halls. It was always cold too, much colder than she would've ever thought it could be underground. At least it was constant like the thermostat was stuck on one setting only–ice cold.

Evie had returned here many times with Jack. This last time, she had returned to stay forever. There was nothing left for her back home. Verenis had made sure of that. She wiped away a lone tear that slipped from her eye and pulled her knees closer to her chest. The cool rock beneath infiltrated her warmth like ice, making her concentrate more on radiating her inner fire toward her skin to keep the cold at bay. At least her fire elemental power had come into great use here. The Teleen never were cold. Under the glamour they wore to look more human-like, they were pure blue fire and lighting, never made to feel the cold. Never without light and warmth.

Evie wondered if this was really home now. It didn't quite have that feel yet. Only being with Jack had made her stay here even one bit comfortable. It was scary and so big, she felt lost in this entombed place. There were more men than women too. Engaged to Jack had kept her from the clutches of being courted endlessly by the single men here. She'd been relieved, but felt the desire in their eyes as she walked past some of the men. Their stares sent ripples of fear through her, but she would walk with confidence to repel any malice they might be thinking. She made sure to perfect her fighting skills whenever she could, just in case she ever would need it. She was near warrior status now, she was that good.

The thought of her sister Jade brought a slight whimper to escape from her lips. Evie couldn't believe what Verenis had done though she understood why. Erasing Jade's memory of anything to do with Faerie included her memory of Evie. She'd discovered this when she'd run into him after he had enchanted Jade. Questioning him of his intentions with Jade, he'd made her understand what he had done and why.

Verenis was a hunted man, and the Unseelie army was coming for him after, hunting his faery family, to bring his kingdom to ruin. Jade had just told him she was pregnant with his child. Even with all the happiness which had surged through him, he had felt the dread creep in. The Unseelie Queen would kill them all without a doubt. If she discovered Jade was his wife and carried the heir to the Summer Seelie Court, they were doomed. Verenis was not equipped to defend them against the evil or the power of the Unseelie army. The Queen would crush them all. She'd already taken so much from

Verenis as it was. *So much.*

Knowing there was no other way, he had erased Jade's memory. The conversation echoed in Evie's head as she choked her tears back.

"What have you done?"

"I made it safe for Jade and our child."

"Made it safe? What happened?" Evie's eyes had grown wide with fear as realization filled them. *"The Unseelie...they're coming aren't they?"* The look on Verenis' face told her everything.

"I have to warn her..." She started for the house, desperate to get to Jade.

"No!" He grabbed her arm and pulled her back. *"She won't remember anything. I erased the memories of Faerie, of our relationship..."* He had let his head hang down as his voice cracked. *"...and she won't remember you."*

"What?"

"You're a faery. I couldn't weed out the memories selectively, she won't remember you either. It'll keep her safe. They'll find no trace of me or anything of Faerie here." He let go of her and stepped away. *"I'm sorry, Evangeline, I had to. Jade and the child will be safe this way. Please understand."*

As he had told this to Evie, she knew he was right. She had let him go, turning to look into the windows of the house that had been her childhood home. She saw Jade washing dishes as her new husband came up behind her, nuzzled her neck and kissed her skin. They looked happy though it was all a farce.

Verenis had chosen him personally to take his place. A human husband, oblivious that it was all a spell—a trick. He thought he was the father of the child in her womb. He thought Jade was the woman of his dreams. Verenis had made it so and nothing Evie could do would change it.

But, she didn't want to change it, even though her heart was breaking. To save Jade and because she loved her sister, Evie turned away. She left her to her new happiness without memories of Faerie. Without memories of Evie. Never to return again.

Evie had slipped away into the dark clutches of the forest, back to the Teleen Caverns, back to her Jack. The only family she had left.

Acknowledgements

I'd like to thank Cyndi Stauff for doing some last minute editing for me, you're amazing! Thanks to all my literary family, you guys are so talented and I am so honored to be on this ride with you.

About the Author

Alexia currently lives in Las Vegas, Nevada–Sin City! She loves to spend every free moment writing or playing with her four rambunctious kids. Writing has always been her dream and she has been writing ever since she can remember. She loves writing paranormal fantasy and poetry and devours books daily. Alexia also enjoys watching movies, dancing, singing loudly in the car and Italian food.

ALSO BY ALEXIA PURDY:

Novels:
Reign of Blood
Disarming (Reign of Blood #2)
Ever Shade (A Dark Faerie Tale #1)
Ever Fire (A Dark Faerie Tale #2)
Ever Winter (A Dark Faerie Tale #3)
The Cursed (A Dark Faerie Tale #3.5)
Ever Wrath (A Dark Faerie Tale #4)
History of Fire (A Dark Faerie Tale #5)
Ever Dead (A Dark Faerie Tale #6)

Short Stories:
The Withering Palace (A Dark Faerie Tale #0.1)
Evangeline (A Dark Faerie Tale #0.5)
The Cursed (A Dark Faerie Tale #3.5
The Faery Hunt
Never Say Such Things

Poetic Collections:
Whispers of Dreams
Five Fathoms

Anthology:
Beyond the Never
Soul Games
Faery Worlds
Faery Realms
Faery Tales
The XOXO Collection
Lacing Shadows

AVAILABLE via all book retailers online

ALSO CHECK OUT THESE EXTRAORDINARY AUTHORS & BOOKS:

Alivia Anders ~ Illumine
Cambria Hebert ~ Recalled
Angela Orlowski Peart ~ Forged by Greed
Julia Crane ~ Freak of Nature
J. A. Huss ~ Clutch
Cameo Renae ~ Hidden Wings
Tabatha Vargo ~ On the Plus Side
Anna Cruise ~ It Was You
Ella James ~ Stained
Kelly Walker ~ Soulstone
A.J. Bennett ~ Unintentional Virgin
Tara West ~ Visions of the Witch
Heidi McLaughlin ~ Forever Your Girl
Melissa Andrea ~ Flutter
Komal Kant ~ Falling for Hadie
Melissa Pearl ~ Golden Blood
L.P. Dover ~ Forever Fae
Sarah M. Ross ~ Awaken
Brina Courtney ~ Reveal

40805095R00169

Made in the USA
Middletown, DE
24 February 2017